COPPER, GOLD & TREASURE

'Don't worry about being late,' he cautioned Copper and Gold magnanimously. 'Should have stopped you coming at all. Fact is . . . fact is . . .' Unsteadily he began pacing the width of the room, drawing hard on his cigarette. 'Fact is, without a miracle the Rudyard Trust is shutting shop.'

'You surely can't mean . . .' The Major— the first to react—felt Miff must be exaggerating for effect.

Benny Gold mused that the arrangement had sounded too good to be true but he felt a pang of disappointment all the same.

'I mean we've run out of money, which because of Marmaduke Rudyard's crack-pot Trust also means we have to wind ourselves up . . . or should it be down?' Miff gave a loud hiccup . . .

COPPER, GOLD & TREASURE

David Williams

Mysterious Press books (UK) are published
in association with Arrow Books Limited
62-65 Chandos Place, London WC2N 4NW

An imprint of Century Hutchinson Limited

London Melbourne Sydney Auckland
Johannesburg and agencies throughout
the world

First published in Great Britain by Collins (The Crime Club) 1982
Hamlyn Paperbacks edition 1983
Mysterious Press edition 1989

Printed and bound in Great Britain by
Courier International Ltd, Tiptree, Essex

ISBN 0 09 959310 6

This one for
Jim and Margot Garrett

COPPER, GOLD
& TREASURE

PROLOGUE

'You don't think we look conspicuous, Freddy?' enquired Mark Treasure waggishly.

It was eleven in the morning on a damp Friday in November. The two men were stepping briskly down the almost deserted broad walk of the London Zoo in Regent's Park. They were dressed for the City or for Whitehall—not for the Zoo.

'Not a bit,' replied Freddy Hinterton confidently. Freddy was an Assistant Secretary at the Foreign and Commonwealth Office: he was paid to sound confident at all times. 'This is one of the places Civil Servants use to brief Intelligence people in spy thrillers. Nobody'd come here in the ordinary way.'

The logic—and as yet the relevance—was entirely lost on the Vice-Chairman and Chief Executive of Grenwood, Phipps & Co., merchant bankers. Freddy's logic had been defeating Treasure since Oxford days though it had impressed Freddy's examiners well enough: he had got a First in Classics. That had been twenty years ago.

The two saw each other from time to time: they had never been particularly close. For Freddy to telephone from the office about meeting some time ahead would have been the normal thing. That he should have called Treasure at home the evening before, pressing the need for urgent and confidential discussion at a bizarre rendezvous was out of character.

'I'm not in Intelligence.'

'Quite,' Freddy agreed as though Treasure had made *the* fundamental point. He glanced about him warily. The only potential eavesdropper was a lonely rhinoceros, some distance away. 'You know François Cruba's living in this country now?'

'President Cruba of Ngonga. Yes, I did. Too hot for the French to shelter, of course.'

'*Ex*-President Cruba,' emphasized Freddy, 'and he wasn't exactly welcome in London either, but he is . . .'

'An anti-Communist West African ruler — sorry, ex-ruler — with a sporting chance of re-instatement.'

'Something like that . . .'

'Exactly like that. The French backed Cruba as the coming chap from the time they gave Ngonga independence. They had a lot invested in him. Still have, come to that.'

'President Agabu ran the show pretty well for fifteen years . . .'

'And died in harness. Dear old Papa Agabu. Yes, but when it was Cruba's turn he blew it. He'd still be there if he hadn't been greedy. The army never liked him but with the French behind him he should have been sitting pretty.'

'He was till the Afro-Communist coup this year.'

Treasure shook his head. 'Tribal, wasn't it — not Communist? Those corporals turned colonels who ousted Cruba are no more Commie than he is. Not yet anyway.'

'Which is why the French recognized the revolutionary government with almost indecent haste.'

'The day after us and the Americans, as I remember. Yes, Freddy, *positively* indecent on our part, wouldn't you say?'

'Want to see the lions?' asked Freddy, avoiding the question.

'No thank you. I want to know what I'm doing here.'

They turned about. Freddy slowed the pace. 'There are powerful influences working to topple the present Ngonga regime,' he announced portentously.

'With more to play for now they think they've found oil.'

'Right. Ngonga isn't just a little Gulf of Guinea

corridor state any more . . .'

'It never was,' the banker interrupted. 'Small, yes, but relatively much richer than the others, surely? Grenwood's were interested from the start. I was last there three years ago. Latterly we didn't care for Cruba's style. Of course, most of the outside capital was French.'

'Still is. Don't know how long it'll be before they start nationalizing, of course.'

'When it suits,' Treasure offered reflectively. 'Cocoa, palm-oil and livestock well husbanded. Small, literate population — less than a million, I suppose. Strong Catholic influence still. Was a model French colony. Equally model republic under Agabu. Very little corruption in high places till Cruba mucked it.'

'Cruba wasn't corrupt. I mean, not covertly dishonest.'

'You mean taking a commodity levy in London while you're Head of State is a form of overt dishonesty acceptable . . .'

'It was brokerage actually. The gutter press made far too much of it. And the payments were taken in Ngonga through his family connection with the Ngonga Trading Company.'

'Very cosy. D'you think we could go inside somewhere for a coffee or something?' Treasure was tiring of light drizzle.

'Better not. Won't take long.' They passed on through the tunnel towards the mid-nineteenth-century Giraffe House. 'The colonels are giving the French a hard time. The French want Cruba back in. So do the ordinary Ngongans — and the Americans . . .'

'I suppose he's the only sensible alternative but . . .' The banker indicated reservation with a shrug.

'The French can't afford to be seen siding with a deposed President while they're still trying to make a go of it with the new government. At least on the face of it.'

'Which is why we've taken Cruba in . . .'

'With strings,' said Freddy firmly.

'What sort of strings?'

'That he doesn't use his large fortune . . .'

'Accumulated in Ngonga. Is it still there?' Treasure asked with mock ingenuousness.

'Actually,' Freddy began, while attempting to outstare an unblinking Bactrian camel, 'actually it's mostly in London now.'

'Ah, the blessings of unfettered international exchange.'

'Yes.' Freddy paused. 'Well, we, that is, the French . . .'

'And certainly the Americans don't want Cruba financing a private army. Is that it?' The other nodded. 'I see. Of course he hasn't the temperament or experience to cope, and inevitably anything of that kind would be branded as CIA.'

'Quite. Anyway he should wait to be called back officially. We can't risk his trying to barge in.'

'Can you fix for him to be reinstated by what passes for a democratic process?'

Freddy stiffened. 'We can't *fix* anything, but the elections promised in a year *will* take place. Meantime Cruba has to be patient.'

'And he can stay here provided he is?'

'Getting the not inconsiderable benefits of acceptance by the British Establishment.'

Treasure felt this was putting it a bit high. 'You mean he gets dining-out privileges with the Party in Government, private welcomes at sympathetic embassies, a bit of fuss made of him in the City, and a few prestigious appearances on the BBC. Mmm, I suppose that should keep his reputation adequately burnished pending positive developments. But how are you going to lock up his money-box? The Treasury can hardly sequester . . .'

'The Treasury can't, but you can, Mark.'

'Whoa-up Dobbin!' Treasure came to an abrupt halt

and turned to face Freddy. 'If you or the Government think Grenwood's are in the business of taking over embarrassing chores . . .'

'Hear me out, Mark. You're right, of course. We can't risk anyone proving we control Cruba financially—even though it's his own money.'

'How much money?'

Freddy hesitated, then gave a short cough. 'Actually, in the region of twelve million pounds.'

'Good God, that was some brokerage operation.'

'A good deal of it's in gold.'

'It would be.'

'But there's a lot of paper, liquid funds and earnings that need to be properly managed.'

'We are in the business, Freddy. I know what would have to be done.' Conscious that they were debating over the sodden contents of a trash bin they had stopped beside, Treasure moved off the way they had come, leaving his companion to follow. 'And Cruba's agreed . . .'

'That instead of having his assets frozen they can be actively managed by a merchant bank of his own choosing. All disbursements to be approved in advance by my Department until he decides to live in some other country.'

'Or until you agree to blow the whistle on the deal. I mean if he chooses to give up the unequal struggle and settle for ever in Budleigh Salterton.'

Freddy nodded gravely. 'That's allowed for, but at our discretion. By the way, he's living in South Kensington. Rather swell mansion near The Boltons.'

'So Cruba has his estate looked after, generous living expenses and funds for approved activities along with his being respected—oh, and presumably protected—in exile. You'll know he can't be buying an armoury, at least without your consent.' He glanced quickly at the other's face. 'And that he'll be a safe and grateful guest . . .'

'Against the day when we may . . . er . . .'

'May be queuing up to recognize his reinstatement. And he's picked Grenwood, Phipps? We don't have a Paris branch, you know.'

'An advantage in the circumstances. By the way, Cruba wants to deal only with you personally. He trusts you implicitly.'

Treasure's eyebrows lifted. 'Suppose I should be flattered. Only met the chap twice. Liked his second wife, the English one. Very lively. Name was . . . Beatrice. Had been a secretary at the UN. Would now be early forties.

'That's about right. The first wife died while Cruba was Ngonga Ambassador to the UN. He married Beatrice before going back to Ngonga as Foreign Secretary. She was the daughter of a prominent Rationalist. Bit of a fuss at the time.'

'I remember. I read they broke up about two years ago.'

'The marriage was annulled under the Pauline Privilege.'

'Which means? Oh, I know. Since she'd never been baptized the marriage could be declared invalid.' Treasure dispassionately considered the subtleties of Catholic casuistry.

'Cruba then married Yvonne Tshube, a twenty-year-old Catholic. She was considered a more suitable escort for a Chief Minister.'

'And a prop to his survival when he became President. Didn't work. Serve him right.' Treasure now gave an un-dispassionate sniff. 'I think I met the girl's father. Wasn't he manager of the Ngonga Trading Company?' Freddy nodded. 'Hmm. Another cordial arrangement. Didn't Beatrice have a son?'

'Pierre. He's fifteen. Cruba's only progeny. He adores the boy. Having him educated here. Been boarding at one of the international schools. Totally bilingual. Now they're cramming him for Eton next year. Cruba's suddenly gone a bundle on the English Public School system.'

'So Miss Tshube hasn't come up to scratch in the maternity department?'

'No. At least, not yet. Oh, I should have mentioned the second Mrs Cruba is a non-subject, if you follow — and definitely not a charge on the Cruba fortune.'

'He makes her an allowance surely? He probably has to.'

'Legally, yes. In fact, I understand she won't take a bean. Proud and independent. Works in London. He got custody of Pierre at the start . . .'

'Naturally, through a Ngongan Court.'

'Right. Now they're all in England she could probably get that reversed but she doesn't make trouble. She has plenty of access — always did have. Before the coup she used to have Pierre for the Christmas and Easter holidays. Used to make things easier all round. The boy doesn't care for his stepmother.'

'What size of staff does Cruba keep here?' Treasure asked, changing the subject. 'I don't mean domestics. Professional aides.' He began steering them towards the Decimus Burton Clock Tower. He hadn't admired it for years.

'Very small. Only one Ngongan national. Gerard Opac. He's virtually a complete government in exile. Very bright. Was the Trade Minister. Stayed openly loyal to Cruba and fled with him. Heaven knows why. A good many of the old guard just crossed a border, lay doggo for a bit, and filtered back when things returned to normal.'

'There's been surprisingly little recrimination.'

Freddy nodded in agreement. 'Opac's the best of the bunch, and he's obviously playing a long shot. He's young still — just twenty-eight. Educated at the Sorbonne and MIT.'

'Married?'

'No. No ties of any kind so far as I know. Probably the

biggest reason for his opting to take a flyer on Cruba.'

'Or one of them,' Treasure observed thoughtfully. 'Cruba's now fifty-five or fifty-six?'

'Six. Relies completely on Opac to handle official business . . .'

'Including contact with the French, the Americans and sympathizers inside Ngonga. And there's no one else of any consequence on the payroll?'

'A couple of English secretaries and that's it.' Freddy noticed Treasure glance at his watch. 'Mark, can I say you'll take it on?'

'Yes, subject to the way the FO lawyers have arranged to protect the Government in case of leaks. You have the documents with you?'

Freddy was beaming. 'No. There won't be anything from us. Just a letter from Cruba to you . . .'

'Giving us absolute control of his oxes and his asses and everything that is his until further notice. There'll be another letter from you to Cruba saying he can stay here at the Home Secretary's discretion.'

'That's all.' Freddy's head had been nodding like a mechanical toy.

'If our mandate is cancelled Cruba knows you'll send him packing. Very neat. Meantime what won't go down in history as the London Zoo Agreement remains verbal . . .'

'In the circumstances . . .'

'It'll do. Cruba will need to understand I'm not going to be dancing attendance day and night. Our Investment Department will treat his account with the same care and flair we apply to all our activities. I'll arrange regular review meetings with him. Oh, and I'll let you know if he asks me to buy him any war surplus.' A baboon caged nearby had just lost interest in the pair. Treasure watched it retreat indoors. He sighed. 'I just wish I found the fellow more attractive.'

CHAPTER 1

Major Roderick Henry Copper saluted himself in the looking glass above the H & C wash basin in his tiny attic bedroom. It was a daft thing to do, and he knew it. It was not as though he had ever cared a rap for military ritual. You did a lot of daft things when you were sixty-seven and living alone in what must be the seediest hotel in Earls Court or—as he used to think—possibly in the whole of West London. In fairness he had seen several worse in the weeks of searching for a new place. He sighed: April was nearly over.

He knew it would be 08.31 hours without looking again. He had been up, as usual, since six. He preferred to be sure of first go in the bathroom: it was on the floor below—next to the thunderbox. He liked to be first with both of them. You could never be too careful as his dear mother would have said—and she might have said it again if she'd been alive to see the other tenants.

Invariably he made his tea before going down to bath. It got the old bowels on the move. Breakfast was served at seven, or more like ten past. It made for a long day. Still, this day would be different.

'Resigned my commission in '49, actually,' he advised his reflection. 'Didn't wait to be passed over and then axed.' There was no point in telling them he had suffered both indignities. It was far too long ago for anyone to bother checking. 'Yes, felt I'd done my bit as a Regular since well before the War. Infantry, actually.' He gave the County Regimental tie a touch which brought in view the turned cuff of the red and white checked Viyella shirt. He'd turned the collar too: did all his own mending and repairs.

'Then it was prep-schoolmastering for donkey's years.'
He practised the unequivocal gaze that would go with this
bit — the tightened, out-thrust jaw, the extra wrinkling of
the strong forehead under the thinned, steel-grey hair.
The twitch of the lip under the clipped moustache was
involuntary. He did it again and decided to make it
standard for the occasion.

'No, never married. One dear lady — old lady now, I
expect — pledged me her hand, but came the war with its
uncertainties. Well, we lost touch . . .' Thank God, he
thought, then, remembering this was a rehearsal, he
shrugged, lifted his head and squared the shoulders of the
tall spare figure in worn but decently cut West of England
tweed. He let the eyes complete the sorry tale of war-lost
love. It was, as it happened, largely invented.

'The children at my last school were mixed. I mean
girls as well as boys — and if you must know, after twenty-
five years of schoolmastering my distaste for both sorts
was as cordial as it was mutual.'

Of course, he would never say the last bit; nor was it
strictly true. He quite liked children, but not in *that*
way — the way they would mean when vetting a bachelor
ex-regular army officer turned prep-schoolmaster.
Perhaps he was just over-sensitive. It was easy to mistake
disdain for suspicion. He had been a failure — nothing
worse.

'Room ready, Major?' The voice came from the
corridor. It was the Filipino chambermaid aiming to
please. She knew he was usually out for his constitutional
by this time and liked to have his room cleaned early. It
saved embarrassment if he wanted to slip back later with
something for lunch. The hotel terms stipulated no
cooking in rooms, but there was a gas-ring for the kettle
so one could heat soup as well as make toast before the
popping, coin-metered gas fire. It was just that the staff
had to report irregularities — not that such things

mattered much any more.

Three months from now the Paragon Private Hotel and the whole crumbling stuccoed terrace was coming down. The developer had already put up a hoarding illustrating the ten storey 'apartotel' to be erected on the site.

He had thought about quitting London often enough: now there was no option. There were no sub-standard rooms in newly built 'apartotels' for permanent residents on reduced rates.

The Rudyard Trust for Retired Officers and Gentlemen—the people he was going to see—had three residential clubs all outside Central London. He'd miss Kensington Gardens, the occasional concert at the Albert Hall, St Stephen's Church in Gloucester Road, the museums and his libraries.

They said you could be lonely in London. He never had been. He enjoyed his own company. Perhaps he had acquired a few eccentricities, but people didn't bother you. He had his own television set—second-hand, with a black and white picture, but it was all he needed for the evenings. Thank God for TV. As always, he glanced at the set last thing before he left the room. He could hear the maid busy next door.

'I've locked my door,' he called pointedly as he went to the top of the stairs: there was no lift. That was to remind her to lock up again when she had done the cleaning.

'OK, Major,' she answered, betting he'd be back soon for whatever it was he'd forgotten.

Perhaps he should have worn his British-warm overcoat after all. It was cold for late April, even on the Paragon stairs. The raincoat he had on was newer-looking—it was washable and had a sort of lining. He should be all right if he kept the pace brisk. He had allowed more than an hour for the walk to the oddly named Strutton Ground which, according to his twelve-year-old copy of the *London A-Z*, was a turning to the right off Victoria

Street, just over half way between the railway station and Westminster Abbey.

Out of London, of course, there would be less opportunity to supplement income with private tutorial fees. In Town he had the connections, and he was pretty good at cramming teenage slow starters through the Common Entrance and 'O' levels. There would be compensations, though.

The Rudyard Trust let you keep what was left of any income after taking 'a reasonable and equitable sum, depending on circumstances' to cover your keep. You had to deposit some capital too for bequeathing to the Trust, up to a figure which in his case meant there would be nothing left to leave to anyone else. Since he had no family nor any close, deserving friend the arrangement suited well enough—in return for peace of mind.

Mark you, there was an awful finality about the whole thing. What if he did not like it at the 'residential club' which, in plain language, would be an old men's home? Well, if that was the case, again, as his mother might have said, he'd have to lump it.

'Good morning, Major.' Mr Chauder, a dispossessed Asian from Kenya, beamed proprietorially from behind the small reception desk and in a reflex action straightened the plastic notice announcing the acceptance of American Express Credit Cards.

Few of the Paragon's clients were rated credit-worthy by their closest friends, let alone the American Express Company or Mr Chauder, but the notice promoted general confidence. Major Copper at least looked solvent. Mr Chauder had more than once considered offering him a room in his next establishment on special terms but had always managed to overcome the impulse. It was doubtful, in any case, that the Major would have felt at ease in a Birmingham Commercial hotel.

' 'Morning, Mr Chauder.' The Major used the hook of

his walking-stick to touch the brim of the bowler now normally reserved for church, special events like the Armistice Day Service in Whitehall, and the funerals of army contemporaries: most had outranked him but fewer were outliving him.

'It is very cold outside, Major sir. I hope you are well wrapped up enough. We don't want you catching the pneumonia' — and thus causing no end of extra trouble for the staff, not to mention, in the event of anything serious like death, the difficulty of letting the worst room in the place for the next twelve weeks.

Mr Chauder remonstrated with himself for harbouring such uncharitable misgivings. He even thought again about offering the room in Birmingham — but not until the Major was through the street door.

As Roderick Copper turned the corner and made for the Cromwell Road an east wind was biting hard. For the moment he was too preoccupied to notice. His total capital stood at £5,862 on last night's count. It was permanently beseiged by inflation and occasionally raided through absolute necessity. So the future was scarcely bristling with options.

A good deal of his service pension he had foolishly commuted at the time of his discharge for what now seemed a ludicrously small lump sum. He had thought of buying an annuity often enough but had never done anything about it. Now he'd had to accept that his income would nowhere near cover his staying on in a London hotel.

He stopped to buy a copy of *The Times* from a corner vendor — an exceptional expense these days since he could perfectly well see the paper in the library reading-room, but today was special. *The Times*, like the bowler, was a necessary prop.

Over the years he had twice tried existing in digs. He had been smothered by unsolicited attentions from a motherly landlady in Fulham and almost starved to death by a more genteel but savagely parsimonious member of the same sorority in Swiss Cottage.

In both places he had missed the independence—the relative freedom one enjoyed even in an hotel as small and limited as the Paragon. Surely a residential club inhabited by, as it were, one's own kind would be better than paying-guest status and restrictions?

It was not the thought of death that hung in the back of his mind but the period that came before death: there, he was facing the real issue. He was fit for his age and made sure he kept himself that way. But he had to die of something and he was ready to give up a good deal—a very great deal—to ensure there would be people about he could depend on if required.

Having come to terms with his need for the Rudyard Trust, the Major gave his mind over to the state of the weather. A moment later he turned back for his overcoat.

While the Major was setting out for the second time, Benjamin Gold was putting the finishing touches to making his bed. It was not a job he did well. It saved work for his daughter Denise, though he sometimes thought she did it again after he went out. He tried to get out in the mornings, rain or shine and whatever the season: it stopped him being under foot.

It was during his walks he did his best to commit to memory whatever new knowledge he had gleaned from the Open University Radio broadcast he listened to in his bedroom early. He wasn't studying for anything in particular.

Denise and her husband George Potts lived with their two children in a neat semi-detached 'executive type' house in Putney which they were in process of buying. For the past year Benny Gold have been living there too.

It was three years since the death of his wife Rachel.

For a while he had tried living alone. Then he had sold
the house in Golders Green and gone on an extended visit
to his other daughter Rebecca who, with her husband,
had emigrated to Australia.

The vague plan that Benny might stay on in Melbourne
had not come to anything. Although Rebecca had
married a nice Jewish boy, her father had never felt
comfortable with them. He blamed himself, arguing he
was anyway too old at seventy to settle in a new country.
So that had been that. He had come back to England,
moving in temporarily with Denise and George until he
found a suitable place. There had never been any
question of his staying with them permanently—not
really.

'Dad, I'm back. It's five past nine,' his daughter called
from downstairs. She had been taking the children to
school. 'If you want to catch that train . . .'

Did he want to catch the train? Did he want to keep his
ten o'clock appointment with the Director of the Rudyard
Trust? Was he ready for an old men's home?

Well, you had to remember it would be a residential
club for retired officers and gentlemen: that was
important. He had pressed the point when they discussed
the whole idea again after supper last night. George had
been against his going from the start. Benny wished
Denise had pressed a little harder for him to stay at least
for a while longer.

Of the two girls, Denise had always been his secret
favourite from the time they were little. Her marrying
out—marrying a Gentile—hadn't bothered Benny. His
wife, God rest her, had been upset at the time but such
things heal. George had always been a fine son-in-law and
a good provider for his wife and the children. He was
doing well with the office equipment company. There
had been another promotion only last month.

It was after her marriage ten years ago that Denise had

begun to grow away from her father. So, there was the increasing social gap. So, a London Area Sales Supervisor kept different company from a retired London cab-driver—except this retired London cab-driver qualified as 'an officer and a gentleman': just.

Denise did not look particularly Jewish. Her father did, and anyway with a name like Benjamin Gold, what else?

Benny absently shrugged his shoulders as he came down the stairs. Maybe it *was* all to do with their being Jewish. Maybe he felt out of place because . . .

'Dad, you're arguing with yourself again.' She smiled affectionately as she stood waiting to help him on with his muffler and the double-breasted, dark blue overcoat. Now, when they were alone, she was the old Denise: more like her mother.

'You think I look all right?' He gave her his happy cherub grin as he turned around slowly like a marionette.

'You look smashing.' She paused. 'Bit short . . .'

'Bit short . . .' he echoed gleefully before they chimed in unison—'Bit short, but look at the quality?' That had been a family catch-phrase long before boy-friends and weddings and births . . . and deaths.

'You don't think the pinstripe is too formal? I could wear the light grey. You pressed it last week.'

'Dad, you'll knock 'em over with the pinstripe.' She thought he looked healthier than he had done all winter—put on a little weight again, and that was no bad thing. His asthma had been so bad last year, after Australia.

She felt torn over his going to a retirement home but it had been his idea, and they'd have nursing staff if he was ill again, and it was difficult to get into the good places if you left it too late . . . besides which there was the new baby to think about.

They hadn't told him yet there was another child on the way. It meant they would need the room—or else they would have to move to a larger house. George was for moving, but they could scarcely afford that and the baby—not even with the £7,500 her father had given them. The money made her feel guilty. But he had given the same to Rebecca.

He waved to her again from the gateway, then set off towards the station. She had offered to drive him. She was a good girl. He settled his narrow-brimmed pork-pie hat firmly on his almost bald head, looking about him as he walked. It was a pretty little avenue. Tiny leaf-buds were showing already on the silver birch planted along the pavement. He stopped a moment to wiggle his gloved fingers at a baby in its pram on the lawn of a small front garden: he adored babies. This one must be six months now: time flew.

Yes, it was a good class neighbourhood: nice houses—not big, but modern with garages and central heating. They were expensive, though—so what was cheap these days?

He was glad he was able to give Denise and George enough to pay off half the mortgage after he sold his place. He had never wanted them thinking they owed him for that. It was only money. He hadn't needed it so what else except share it between the girls: pray God they would want to do the same some day for their kids.

He still had more than enough to get into a Rudyard Club. And if they wouldn't take him, so there were other places. It was just that he enjoyed feeling his wartime commission in the Royal Army Service Corps still counted—like it did at the time. Then they had been living in Stepney. He had just done his 'knowledge', qualifying to drive a cab, when the war started. To have been promoted through the ranks after Dunkirk had been quite an achievement. He got no higher than lieutenant—but he'd been an officer; that's what rated with a background like his.

After the war Rachel had wanted him to do something better than cab-driving, but he had stuck at it—bought his own cab with a loan and his army gratuity so he had been his own boss all his working life. They had done well enough, he and Rachel—not as well as the girls would do, but well enough. If it was written he wasn't to end his days with his dear wife—nor to be in the way of his daughters—then ending up with other retired officers and gentlemen sounded good. Maybe he was no gentleman in the old sense—but always he had behaved like one.

He crossed the road to the station, giving a thumbs up sign to a cab-driver who had halted for him at the crossing.

So, as the song went, he'd be far better off in a home—and if there was time to kill before that he still had his licence so he could do relief cab-driving. He had thought about it earlier: now that he felt pretty fit again and with spring on the way . . . He turned into the station, getting out the money for his ticket.

Thus, on the morning of Friday, April 19th, Major Copper and Mr Gold made their separate ways to ten o'clock appointments at the offices of the Rudyard Trust. Not in his wildest flight of fancy would either have believed he was walking into a murder plot involving the sovereign state of Ngonga: nor, of course, until much later, was anyone else going to believe it either.

CHAPTER 2

Strutton Ground was a short, narrow and unusually busy thoroughfare with buildings of mingled heights and styles. There were small shops at pavement level, while the roadway itself was lined on one side with the colourful stalls of a regular street market.

Major Copper had threaded his way through the heavy human traffic wondering how the motorized variety fared. He found the street number he needed above an open doorway between two shops. He passed through to a long, badly lit corridor. Half way on the left was a worn wooden staircase. Opposite, a hand-painted board indicated that the four floors above were occupied by organizations none of which sounded important—the more so the higher you went. The Rudyard Trust for Retired Officers and Gentlemen was at the top.

Ignoring the staircase, the Major made for what he took to be a lift at the end of the corridor. The door opened inwards just as he was reading the inscription 'Happy Public Relations Ltd'.

A tall, late twenties and startlingly glamorous brunette was emerging with difficulty. She was wearing a well-cut yellow trouser suit and a rich brown sun-tan. Grasping the strap of an over-stuffed handbag in one hand, she had an unwieldy wooden table-lectern in the other. Clutches of large bulging envelopes were wedged under both arms. She was using her feet to dribble a medium-sized cardboard packing-case into the corridor. She flashed a helpless smile at the Major just before the door—activated by some powerful spring—punched her firmly in the back.

'Knickers!' she cried as the lock clicked shut. 'Sorry. Not my day.' The smile was still there. 'Christine's out, Linda's sick, Soo'll be back in a minute. You'll have to fish the key out of my bag. It's . . .' She had begun a contortion that would have brought the bag to a fishable position except the movement allowed several fat, open envelopes to cascade to the floor. The contents scattered at the Major's feet.

'Shoot!—that's the place-cards wrecked. Should have

made two journeys. Thanks awfully.' The girl and the Major were now crouched together pushing pieces of lettered paste-board back into the largest envelope. 'By the way, I'm Happy Brown.' She stood up. 'You *are* looking for Happy Public Relations?'

The Major resisted an inclination to answer in the affirmative. 'The lift, actually,' he offered lamely. 'But I suppose everyone's looking for happy public relations' came as an afterthought. 'My name's Roderick Copper. How d'you do.'

'Mr Copper, you've made my day.' Miss Brown's pleased expression gave way to one of sympathy. 'No lift, I'm afraid. Which floor?'

'The fourth.'

'Poor you. There's a loo on the third. You can stop there for a breather. Did you have a taxi?'

The question seemed hardly relevant when one's destination lay up four flights. 'No, I . . .'

'Pity. He'd still be hacking his way to Victoria Street.' She was already half way to the door, the packing-case moving well. 'Thanks again. Nice to know you, Mr Copper. *Ciao.*'

'Actually it's Major . . .' But she was gone, and anyway who cared? He should have helped with the case but people were so quick these days—or he was so slow—and it could have been heavy. He had avoided a rupture so far—and false teeth. He contemplated the stairs without enthusiasm. They seemed steeper than those at the Paragon.

Some time later Major Copper gratefully opened the door on the third-floor landing. The oval enamel sign had stated 'WC'—and a short Jewish gentleman was sitting inside.

Mr Gold stood up quickly. 'Please, I was only resting.' This was evident from his appearance. He still had his gloves on. 'There's no lock on the door.' This intelligence he delivered *sotto voce* and with a touch of outrage. 'Wouldn't try . . .'

'Quite,' replied the Major. 'I stopped for the same reason as you.' This was not strictly true. Miss Brown's suggestion had prompted a reflex need.

'Guard the door for you if you like.' Mr Gold was unconvinced. Men of their age tended . . . 'Then you can do the same for me.' He shrugged his shoulders and smiled disarmingly.

'Done,' said the other without dissembling— completing a first exchange of some significance.

It was obvious from the beginning that Copper and Gold would be especially compatible.

The final flight of stairs had seemed to be nearly vertical. The attic storey did not run to a corridor, only the door to the offices of the Rudyard Trust which stood abruptly close to the top step.

The two visitors had entered a large outer office with three dormer windows in the long south-facing wall and a Spartan collection of no-nonsense furniture—sturdy if aged filing cabinets, big wooden cupboards, a token square of worn, dark red carpet in the centre emphasizing the lurid green, wall-to-wall linoleum around it.

There were two desks. One, near the entrance, was empty and bare of fittings, its chair firmly tucked into the kneehole, giving the impression its occupant was not so much out as gone for ever. The other, at the far end of the room, was beside the open door to a second office which, from what could be seen of it, was smaller but better furnished than the first.

The woman behind the desk was middle-aged, well-built and commanding. She was dressed in a coat and skirt of serviceable grey flannel and a starched white blouse. Her straight black hair was cut short like a man's and parted on the left. Her name was Miss E. R. McSlope and she was secretary to the Director. The monocle she wore in her right eye fascinated Benny Gold. He and the Major were seated on armless wooden chairs in front of the desk.

Monocles neither enthralled nor intimidated the Major. He was preoccupied in tracing the source and nature of the foul smell that permeated the room. He was sensitive to odours, always had been. It occurred to him that this was one you might appropriately associate with *decaying* officers and gentlemen. He was also being drawn to the uncomfortable conclusion that the smell seemed to stem from around the person of Miss McSlope.

'I'm really very sorry about the error,' she was saying. There was a marked lack of penance in the tone and a good deal of lowland Scots in the accent. 'But if Mr Miff makes appointments on the telephone without telling me, then of course someone is bound to be . . .'

'Miffed?' Mr Gold blurted, immediately regretting his rashness and grateful for the Major's supportive grunt of amusement.

'. . . inconvenienced.' Miss McSlope spun out the word slowly, glancing at, or—as it seemed to him—through Benny Gold before continuing in the Major's direction. 'You're here by written appointment at ten o'clock, Major Copper.' She studied the face of a Mickey Mouse alarm clock on her desk: they all three did, with unnecessary gravity. There was a pause. Unless anyone was extremely short-sighted, or unless the clock was wrong, they had all confirmed it was twenty minutes past the hour. 'I'm sorry the Director is late. A very rare occurrence. An urgent meeting outside the office . . .'

'No matter, I can easily . . .' the Major began.

'. . . but I'm sure he'll be here directly.' Miss McSlope was not to be deterred in her excuse-making. 'As for you, Mr Gold . . .' The monocle fell from the eye to swing hypnotically from side to side across an ample and well supported bosom.

'I can come some other day.' Benny Gold half rose, as much to observe the whole arc of the monocle as to demonstrate his instant readiness to leave.

'The Director will no doubt see you as soon as he's finished with Major Copper. These interviews rarely last more than half an hour.' She refitted the monocle. 'Sometimes a good deal less.'

Benny tried to ignore the possible implication of the last comment. 'Mr Miff did say on the telephone he'd be writing to confirm . . .' he began defensively.

'Ah, but here he is,' the secretary interrupted.

Suddenly the smell had become almost unendurably worse. Did Miff suffer some terrible bodily disorder so that his scent, as it were, went before him? The Major gagged at the thought.

While they could all hear the slowly approaching footsteps on the stairs outside, it was Mr Gold who noticed the stout old liver-and-white Springer Spaniel which had moved out from behind the desk, working slowly but determinedly towards the door.

A minimum turn of the head allowed the dog to appraise the visitors through one very bloodshot eye, and without interrupting its peculiar progress across the room. Maintaining momentum appeared to be critical, the animal gave the impression that if it stopped it would probably fall over.

The legs on each side of the overweight, sagging trunk functioned more in unison than in sequence, so that forward movement was matched, pace on pace, by an arthritic, seagoing sort of roll. The head hung so low that had the dog been standing still it might have been difficult to tell one end from the other. This wasn't a problem now, due to the more or less advancing motion, the earlier rheumy glance and the just perceptible erratic wagging of the undoctored tail. It did not go undetected either, at least by the Major, that this pathetic creature was passing wind with every other step.

'There's a good Hercules. Run to meet Daddy, then.'

It passed human understanding—or at least the understanding of Roderick Copper—that otherwise mentally efficient people like Miss McSlope should descend to mouthing imbecilities when addressing canine familiars.

'Is that his name? Good old Hercules. Keep going, old chap.'

And now Gold was doing it.

The door was thrown open in a theatrical kind of way. Its leading edge missed Hercules by a well-judged hair's breadth—well judged, that is, on the part of the dog which had allowed its rear end to collapse into a sitting position.

The animal's tail began polishing the lino with a fairly regular action, like a hairy windscreen wiper. Its head and neck stretched ceilingwards as the taut throat emitted what began as a low moan but soon built up to a sustained high wail. The Major was thankful this fresh obscenity emerged from an acceptable orifice: it was presumably intended as a greeting.

'Clever Hercules'—Miss McSlope and Benny Gold chanted together without prompting. They exchanged knowing smiles. Benny congratulated himself on having acquired some virtue in the estimation of this awesome woman. There was nothing contrived about it either: he was genuinely fond of dogs and children.

The Major was concentrating his attention on the debut of the tardy Miff. Because the door was literally at the top of the stairs anyone approaching could choose to open it from several steps below floor level. Miff had done just this so that he appeared in stages. He proved to be a very fat man of better than medium height. The size of him was emphasized by his gradual heaving into view like some cinematic Sancho Panza riding in over a near horizon—except there was no donkey: it was all Miff.

Once over the threshold the Director paused for breath, shedding a tight-fitting Raglan style overcoat in a loud brown check. Underneath he had on an ultra-conservative black jacket and striped trousers.

'This is definitely not my coat,' he volunteered deliberately. He mopped a high-domed, nearly bald pate and radiant forehead. The fleshy countenance which at first had seemed dangerously red from exertion was now paling to an equally alarming off-blue.

The nose—like the affronted expression—was patrician as, in a sense, were the extra chins. The Major put the man's age at no more than fifty-four: Mr Gold figured he'd been lucky to reach fifty-six.

'It's 'scraceful,' puffed the subject of these speculations whose age was actually fifty-one. 'Disgraceful,' he repeated, looking about him defiantly.

Since Miff's gaze finally fixed itself on Hercules the Major was happy to concur with the sentiment—up to the point where the speaker absently produced a dog biscuit from a side pocket and gave it to the animal.

'Bank manager belligerent. Trustees loftily indifferent. God, what a mess!' The Director began a tentative advance across the room while attempting to light a cigarette. He now noted the presence of the two visitors. 'Who are you? Some kind of debt collectors, I shouldn't wonder.'

'This is Major Copper, who's here by written appointment,' said Miss McSlope, who had remained seated. The two men had risen. 'And this is Mr Gold. You arranged to see him by telephone. Both had appointments at ten o'clock for election interviews.'

'Bad luck.' Miff shook hands, appearing unaffected by his secretary's obvious stricture. 'Ring the bank and say

someone there's stolen my overcoat. They'll send it
round.' He looked at the one he was holding. 'They can
have this one back. Don't worry about being late,' he
cautioned Copper and Gold magnanimously. 'Should
have stopped you coming at all. Fact is . . . fact is . . .'
Unsteadily he began pacing the width of the room,
drawing hard on his cigarette. 'Fact is, without a miracle
the Rudyard Trust is shutting shop.'

'You surely can't mean . . .' The Major—the first to
react—felt Miff must be exaggerating for effect.

Benny Gold mused that the arrangement had sounded
too good to be true but he felt a pang of disappointment
all the same.

'I mean we've run out of money, which because of
Marmaduke Rudyard's crack-pot Trust also means we
have to wind ourselves up . . . or should it be down?' Miff
gave a loud hiccup and promptly flashed an accusing look
at Hercules.

Miss McSlope seemed totally unaffected by the news.
Benny marvelled at her fortitude. The monocle was
firmly in place. 'This *is* your coat,' she said severely. 'Your
new coat.' She picked up the garment and hung it in a
cupboard near the door.

CHAPTER 3

'Rudyard was an Edwardian philanthropist. Also fancied
himself as an advanced political philosopher,' began the
still agitated Miff.

Having recounted why there was no purpose in his
interviewing his callers individually, he had, on impulse it
seemed, ushered them into his own office and seated
them in worn leather chairs on either side of his desk. It
was clear he felt further explanation was due.

Instead of sitting himself, the Director was making and re-making the circuit of the quite small room, touching some objects as he went and brushing others with his substantial frame. There was a scent of alcohol building up in the air: naturally it was Copper who first noticed it.

'Great public benefactor,' Miff continued. 'Hedged everything around with legal barbed wire. Scared of a Socialist take-over even then. That's why a lawyer has to do this job. It's in the Trust Deed. I'm a lawyer.' The last fact was made defensively as though the speaker expected it to be challenged.

Judging from the wear marks on the carpet, he was a compulsive indoor walker. He was also a chain-smoker. Whether he was a regular mid-morning tippler was open to conjecture. He paused unsteadily and lit another cigarette although he already had one burning in the ashtray on his desk. Benny, who worried about such things, hoped Miss McSlope had extinguished the one left burning in the outer office.

'The National Health Service still succeeded in grabbing most of the Rudyard foundations after the War. I wasn't here then, of course.' Absently he dropped the smouldering match into the waste-bin as he passed Benny Gold. 'Not that it would have made any difference,' he cautioned modestly while bumping into a floor safe.

'Hospitals, weren't they? The other places, I mean.' The Major had done some homework.

'Yes. Rudyard made a fortune from patent embrocations. Felt he should be recognized as a medical luminary. Built small hospitals for the deserving poor all over the place. The Off-Gents—er, Officers and Gentlemen—came later. Same legal protections. More difficult to break. So we've survived. Just.'

Miff gazed quizzically at Gold, wondering how he had come to start the fire he was tending at the bottom of the waste-bin.

'You mean the hospitals got shaded into community ownership. The clubs for officers stayed independent,' said the Major, twisting his neck to follow Miff and wishing the chap would stay in one spot.

Miff nodded at Copper, gave Gold a reproving look and deliberately kicked the now smokeless bin out of reach. He then stationed himself behind the desk and began inhaling and exhaling deeply between phrases.

'The initial endowment was fifty thousand pounds . . . Large sum in 1903 . . . Some of it went into land and buildings, of course . . . Apart from that the only new funds . . . come from resident fees, down payments and bequests. The Trustees . . . they're not supposed to tout for gifts . . . Not that anyone's . . . anyone's likely to give us any . . . Too many more deserving causes . . . We'd need half a million . . . Interest on that would see us right . . . if only for a bit.'

'But the Trust was expected to be self-supporting,' put in the Major.

Miff had stopped the breathing exercises. He was now taking his pulse. He looked up from studying his watch. 'That was the idea, but running costs have gone up out of all proportion. We increase the fees every year. Still nowhere near the real cost. Lot of members have to dig into capital to pay them.' He registered dismay, then put his watch to his ear.

'Which means they have less to leave the Trust when they peter out.'

'That's right, Major. And we are supposed to be a charity.' He looked suddenly relieved and began winding the watch. 'Stopped,' he explained. 'Our traditional kind of member . . . er . . .'

'Wouldn't care much to enter a State home but is too hard-up to afford a private one.' Copper eased them over a delicate point.

'The properties must be worth a lot. They're in pricey

places.' Benny Gold spoke for the first time.

'Buildings worthless. Sites, yes, they're valuable all right. All three clubs in districts with soaring land prices. Prime commuter-belt stuff round London. High housing densities,' Miff announced with a lucidity suggesting he had said it all before — and often.

'So why not sell out and set up again somewhere cheaper?'

'Because, Major, the Trust doesn't allow it. We can't sell an acre. We've got nearly thirty. We can't build either, except for own use.' The speaker lowered his substantial bulk into his chair: exercise and deep breathing appeared to be over for the time being. 'And that's not all.'

There was pain in the expression though it wasn't clear whether this was due to some sedentary discomfort or the mental anguish that prefaced the next announcement. 'If the Trust runs at a loss for more than three years the Trustees have to liquidate it, disband the clubs, divide the proceeds between Marmaduke's direct descendants.'

The Major looked dumbfounded.

'That's so uncharitable,' said Gold without vehemence. 'Who could have made such crazy rules?'

'Rudyard himself: who else?' Miff almost shouted, not quite disguising a hiccup. 'The fool seriously believed if expenditure exceeded income it'd be because there weren't enough takers. Not enough retired officers and gentlemen having to resort to charity. Not even two hundred and fifty of 'em in the whole of bloody England.' He blinked sharply.

'That's the number you can take? But I was told there were vacancies.'

'Yes, Mr Gold, many. We've been purposely running down — facing the inevitable. And all because our fees are beyond the reach of people who ought to qualify — not, as Rudyard would've imagined, because capitalism has triumphed.' This time the punctuation was a hiccup unawares.

'And the Trustees have no discretion?' Major Copper obviously knew about discretionary trusts: Benny was impressed.

'None. Trust Deed's clear and precise. I'm a lawyer. Did I tell you? Professionally have to admit no doubt about the Benefactor's intentions.'

'And you can't cut back? Save a little here and a little there so you don't make a loss,' asked Gold tentatively.

'We could starve the inmates . . . the members.' Miff corrected in deference to the intended status of his audience. 'Fire most of the staff. Cut Headquarters' personnel to two and make 'em work in a garret for a pittance. Except we've done that already.' A glint suddenly appeared in the despairing eyes. 'Would you care for a small whisky?'

In answer to affirmative nods Miff pressed a button on his desk, then stared expectantly at the closed door of his office. When nothing happened he levered himself out of the chair and marched into the outer office. Although he closed the door after him the two visitors caught first the tone and then the words of the heightening altercation ensuing outside.

Miff returned lighting a cigarette. 'That buzzer's out of order,' he remarked taking his seat again. 'Wonderful woman,' he issued more loudly than was necessary. 'The coffee will be here shortly,' he finished without dissembling.

'Marmaduke Rudyard's descendants. Maybe they won't take the money? They could give it back.'

Miff favoured Benny Gold with a patronizing smile. 'There's no money in the family. Marmaduke left very little. What there was was dissi . . . dissi . . . lost. Business failed.' He shook his head. 'There are four . . . er . . . recognized descendants. Two are for grabbing the money.' He paused to subdue a hiccup. 'One we can't find. The other's on our side.' Copper and Gold clearly were to consider themselves enrolled under Miff's colours. 'Wants the Trust Deed changed by Act of Parliament. It would take that, I'm afraid.'

'Bully for him,' said the Major.

'Her—it's a woman, Florence Spotter, spinster, aged sixty-five, granddaughter. Writes and illustrates children's books. Can't do anything by herself, of course.'

'And the others?'

'There's Everard Crow-Patcher, great-grandson. Won't budge. Middle-aged, divorced, re-married—an American woman older than himself and probably for her money. She didn't have any. They can't wait for the Trust to be wound up.' This slanderous summary was uttered without emotion. 'Then there's Stephen Spotter, also a great-grandson and nephew of Florence's. Bit younger than Crow-Patcher. Last heard of years ago working for a bank in Hong Kong. Doesn't answer letters. May not get them, though they haven't been returned. We keep trying.'

'He could be on our side,' the Major put in, conscious the odds were less than even in the circumstances. 'There's someone else who's against?'

'Prudence, unmarried daughter of Rudyard himself. Aged eighty-six. Florence Spotter lives with her in Surrey. Looks like a bit of Balkan royalty and behaves like it.'

'And she's in favour of closing the clubs her father founded. What good can the money do her?' Benn¡ found the filial disloyalty hard to credit.

Miff shook his head. 'She's convinced she's doing the right thing.' Suddenly he looked up with the most ingratiating of smiles. 'Isn't that so?'

Miss McSlope, the object of the question, had entered with a tray of coffee cups in time to be included in the last exchange. 'Miss Rudyard considers it her bounden duty to follow her father's wishes in all things,' she said.

'That's why she didn't run off with a chauffeur in 1914, or so they say. Never regretted it, apparently,' Miff put in gratuitously.

'We may still hear from Stephen Spotter,' Miss McSlope continued, disclosing she had been following the rest of the conversation through the partition wall. 'Miss Rudyard interprets her father's intentions as clear from the Trust Deed.' She put the tray in front of Miff and returned to the outer office. Benny followed her movements and words with deepening respect.

Miff coughed. 'Miss Rudyard really is immovable.'

'She is exceedingly old,' ruminated the Major.

'Oh, she could outlast us all, I assure you. In any case we're nearly over our time limit already. Our financial year ends next month. The new balance sheet will show a loss for a third year in a row. And that'll be it . . .'

'Unless Mr Spotter turns up.' Benny had no difficulty remembering the name. He and Rachel had once had a dearly loved mongrel terrier with bow legs called Spotter. 'He might be on our side.' The dog had been the friendliest of creatures.

'Wouldn't necessarily alter the picture.' Miff took a sip of coffee, swallowing it as though it came in large lumps. 'If the residual beneficiaries—that's the family members— aren't of one mind, the Trustees won't consider promoting any Parliamentary Instrument. They've said so.'

There was a pause. 'Could you give us the address of the two ladies? Oh, and Mr Crow-Patcher?' asked the Major with a supporting nod from Mr Gold. Miff looked hesitant. 'We could look them up, of course.'

The Director reached for pen and paper, scribbled some words, and handed the paper to Copper, all Buddha-like, without disturbing his head or trunk. He gave a deep sigh.

'You've mentioned four descendants. Are there more?'

Miff looked at Copper indicating he wished the question hadn't been put. 'Marmaduke had two sons and three daughters. Both sons killed in the First War. Both unmarried. Mary, the oldest child, married a Percival Crow-Patcher. He eventually became a General. They had a son and a daughter, both dead. The son was Everard's father.' He dropped his voice. 'The daughter, Fay, black sheep of the family. Died in Switzerland, 1961.' The last fact was uttered as though to provide final proof of waywardness. 'Prudence Rudyard was her aunt, but they were nearly contemporaries, very close apparently till Prudence saw the light.'

'After not running away with a chauffeur in 1914?'

Miff nodded at Benny. 'They say Fay did run off with a stockbroker in 1920. Prudence won't enlarge. Says Fay was disowned.'

While he was speaking, and with some dexterity, Miff had removed a small silver flask from a side-pocket presumably hoping the object was hidden from view in his podgy right palm. Next, shielding his cup behind his left forearm he began shifting his gaze between his two companions like some spectator at a tennis tournament. Then, with only a momentary glance at the cup, he poured a liberal dose of whatever liquid was in the flask into his coffee, snapped back the silver top, and slowly returned the vessel to his pocket.

There was a moment's silence. If it was apparent to the two astonished observers that Miff had just laced his coffee with alcohol, Miff himself was wholly determined not to acknowledge the fact. He glanced once more from Copper to Gold, then back again, before raising the cup to his lips and taking a long draught.

'And Mr Rudyard's other daughter?' It was Benny who spoke.

'Victoria, the middle one, born 1887,' Miff replied with exaggerated bonhomie. 'She married the Reverend

George Spotter, an Evangelical Anglican of no distinction, in 1910. Daughter Florence you know about. Son Michael killed in '41. Wife dead too . . .'

'The parents of the missing Stephen?'

'Quite right, Mr Gold.' He blinked, then stifled a yawn.

'If only Miss Rudyard and Mr Crow-Patcher could be persuaded to alter their views,' Copper offered ruminatively.

'Not a possibility, I assure you.' Miff's eyes had half closed. 'Good of you to take an interest. Don't know what to do for the best. Bad day.' He shook his head sharply. His eyes opened, then closed again. 'Damned pills don't help.' He was breathing heavily. Grunts began juddering the hefty frame. The mouth and chinfolds beneath had become fixed in a sullen pout.

It was 11.06 a.m. and Clarence Miff had gone to sleep — without, of course, having given a direct answer to the Major's key question.

CHAPTER 4

'Might be some kind of sleeping sickness,' said Benny Gold charitably. He and the Major were seated side by side in the subdued interior of Le Café Américain, Victoria Street, awaiting delivery of their modest orders.

It had been Benny's idea — tentatively offered — that they should take an early lunch together, ahead of the office workers.

Major Copper shook his head. 'Saw a good deal of sleeping sickness in West Africa before the War. More likely some metabolic imbalance.'

'Oh,' Benny murmured: he hadn't heard metabolic imbalance mentioned in Open University broadcasts so far. 'Miss McSlope said it wasn't serious if he does as he's told.'

'Like give up booze, perhaps. She was pretty close

about it, didn't you think?'

'Very loyal. That's nice these days. She said he shouldn't drink when he's on pills.'

'Puts him to sleep. We could see that.'

'It's what the row was about when he went out for the whisky.'

'Our whisky,' the Major put in pointedly. 'He had his own.'

'You figure he was tipsy all the time?'

'Yes,' came the flat answer. 'Well, perhaps that's unfair. But didn't it strike you he was when he arrived? Thought it was rummy the way he kept moving about. Works off the effects. In his case keeps him awake as well. Curious the way some of them can sound sober. What he was telling us was perfectly clear. Hardly justified the journey, of course.'

'An alcoholic. "The heredity factor is now considered key in the incidence of alcoholism." ' It was something he had memorized from the 'Developments in Medical Science' Series. The Major failed to react to this snatch of higher wisdom. 'Explains why he's got such a lousy job. Can't pay much,' Benny added.

'Probably explains the pills. Part of a cure. They say boozing runs in families.'

Benny let it pass. 'Poor geyser. Educated man. Professional qualifications and coming down in the world. Get a nose for that sort, cabbies do. Dress the part but three eyes on the clock and bad tippers.' Perhaps he shouldn't have said that. He picked up the menu. 'Prices are very reasonable. We could have chocolate gateau for afters. My treat.'

'No, we said we'd go Dutch.' The Major smiled. 'I'll bet they don't get chocolate gateau at Rudyard Clubs, Mr Gold.'

'Do me a favour? Everyone calls me Benny. Short for Benjamin.' He thought for a moment. 'Funny giving us the whole story like that. Makes you feel responsible.'

'Involved. Must have been his interview with the bank manager. Needed to unburden to someone, not just McSlope.' He cleared his throat. 'My name's Roderick.'

'Oh. Well it'd be nice to help 'em out in some way . . . er, Roderick. Imagine, there's two hundred old gents going to be turned out in the street.'

'It won't be like that. They'll have to make provision. But in the long term you're right, Benjamin.' The Major disliked diminutives. 'It'd be good to take the initiative . . .'

'Grasp the nettle.' Benny found he enjoyed being addressed by his full name: only his mother had ever called him Benjamin. 'Show officer-like qualities they used to say in the RASC.' His gaze became pensive behind the rimless glasses he had put on to read the menu. After a moment he sighed and gazed about the room. In his mind he had been to El Alamein and back. 'Nothing we can do to raise half a million, of course. Need a Monty for that—a Field Marshal, Lord Montgomery. There was a leader. Served under him in the Western Desert.'

Through the vagaries of army postings the Major had never seen combative service in the whole of his military career. It seemed incredible but it was a fact. He had even volunteered for especially hazardous duties. Somehow he had always proved unsuitable or ended up the officer surplus to requirements—through twenty years in the infantry, a period which had included a quite lengthy World War.

Say what you like, it had certainly affected his career prospects. It was the reason, he believed, why he had never had any real career prospects. Yet here was Benjamin Gold, cab-driver, who could say he had served as an officer under Monty in North Africa.

Indisputably, Major Copper would enjoy showing initiative rescuing two hundred old gentlemen . . .

'There's something *he* could do about it.' He had spoken almost involuntarily, pointing to the picture of François Cruba he had noticed earlier on the front page of *The Times*.

The ex-President of Ngonga had been photographed opening a children's playground in South London. The Chairman of the Race Relations Committee was standing beside him.

Benny read the caption. 'He's loaded, huh? He gave the money for the playground?'

'It wouldn't have cost that much.'

'It says the Local Authority gave the land. The ex-President provided the equipment. So he gets the credit. Smart. Good for business—whatever his business. He'd help the Rudyard Trust?'

The Major frowned. 'I know a bit about Cruba. Been giving his son Pierre extra tuition in maths. A Crammer in Park Crescent. They give me odd jobs.'

He'd been lucky to get that one—called in when the intended tutor had gone sick. Then he and the boy had clicked so he had been asked to carry on. It had meant two hours' work every Saturday for six weeks. 'Never met the father. He's very involved with charities.'

'Public benefactor. Maybe he's a tiny bit Jewish.' Benny's quip only half registered.

'Sounds unkind but he goes for the most noise and the smallest donation.' Copper hesitated to add the information had been volunteered by Pierre Cruba.

'Tight with the wad?'

'In some ways. The tuition for his son, that was different. The Crammer's one of the best. Expensive and difficult to get into. The tutors are very well paid,' he continued ruefully. 'When there was doubt about their fitting in Pierre at short notice I gather Cruba came round offering to buy the place. The whole College. Wrong thing to do, actually.'

'In England you don't try so hard.' Benny put in knowingly.

The Major nodded. 'Still, illustrates my point. He'll shell out on things that matter to him.'

'But you don't think he'd cough up half a million for an old gents home.'

'He's got the money. He'd need to know the cause was going to be popular.'

'Showy.' Benny was looking again at *The Times* front page.

'Yes. It would have to be good for his public relations.' He recalled why the phrase came so easily to mind. 'Of course, he'd do a lot for his son.'

His companion wasn't sure where the train of thought was leading. 'You mean we could get at him through the boy?'

The moustached upper lip did its involuntary twitch. 'Something like that. It might be worth a try. Then again, we mustn't forget the Trustees.'

'You got the name and address. Special kind of bank.'

'The Trustee Department of a Merchant Bank. Pretty remote sort of bunch, I'd expect. Not involved. Probably do everything by the book' — exactly what the Major had been doing all his life. 'Ought to try them first, I suppose,' he added instinctively.

'Without letting on to Mr Miff?'

'That way he can't be blamed.'

'I'd rather go for Prudence and Florence.'

'Oh, them too. All in good time.'

'Right you are, Roderick.'

'Tally-ho, Benjamin. Ah, here come the omelettes.'

At two-thirty the next Monday, Copper and Gold were seated with Happy Brown at a table in the brightly furnished main office of Happy Public Relations Ltd.

With trepidation the Major had telephoned Miss

Brown late on the Friday afternoon. On the strength of their brief acquaintance he had asked if she would help with composing a letter he and his friend Mr Gold wanted to send to a merchant bank.

Miss Brown had come fresh from organizing a successful lunch and press conference for an important client. She had been in the mood for good causes. After hearing the Major out she had asked a great many questions, complimented him and Mr Gold on their enterprise, promised to help, turned down the offer of a fee, and arranged the date. They had been relieved about the fee.

'See if this fits,' said Happy, handing them copies of a draft letter. She was elegant and businesslike in a dark brown cashmere sweater and tweed skirt in a lighter shade. The sweater was V-necked, the sleeves pushed back. The slim hands and wrists were unadorned, like the shapely neck. She carried her head high. Her hazel eyes were wide and intelligent. Her hair she wore to shoulder length in loose, natural waves.

'I'll read it out if you like,' she added as both men reached for their glasses.

Benny Gold was delighted to study and listen to the beautiful Miss Brown. The Major still put on his glasses — to see her better.

' "Dear Mr Edwards . . ." '

'Who's Mr Edwards?' asked Benny in surprise.

'He's in charge of the Trustee Department at Grenwood, Phipps.'

'You knew his name,' said Copper admiringly.

'After I'd rung them and asked for it.'

'Makes a difference. Adds authority.'

'Professional touch,' confirmed Benny.

The two nodded at each other.

' "Dear Mr Edwards, I am writing on behalf of FORT, which stands for the Friends of the Rudyard Trust." ' She

looked up. 'I think that sounds quite well, don't you?'
There was no hint of dissent from the awed, assembled
Friends.

' "FORT," ' she continued, ' "has appointed me as
Honorary PRO and invited me to tell you about its aims."
Paragraph.' She cleared her throat.

' "At the outset, my clients want to stress they are
acting on their own initiative without involving the
Trust's management, employees or resident members.
Simply, they know about the problems which face the
Trustees and wish to offer their help in avoiding closure
of the Rudyard Clubs." '

Happy paused again to invite comment. She received
only approving expressions.

'It goes on: "Specifically, FORT will be prepared to
raise funds, organize petitions, lobby members of
Parliament, contact opinion-formers, arrange press,
radio, and television coverage, and generally assist the
Trustees in their admirable commitment to have the
Benefactor's instruction to wind up the Trust set aside by
Parliamentary Instrument.

' "FORT will, of course, seek immediate support for its
aims from all Marmaduke Rudyard's descendants . . ." '

'I don't think they're exactly committed. The Trustees,
I mean,' the Major interrupted belatedly. 'Mr Miff said
they mentioned it some time ago—and only informally.'

'Exactly, but they damned well ought to be
committed,' Happy rejoined. 'The purpose of all that
waffle is to wake them up. Make them realize they have a
hot public issue on their plates—that they'd better decide
now to get on the side of the angels.'

She smiled at Benny of the cherubic countenance. 'We
know they'd move if all the Rudyards backed them. We
need them to move with—' she referred to her notes—
'with Florence Spotter alone, if necessary. By the way,
we'll need to have known from Miss Spotter about their

inclination to move at all, not from Mr Miff. You've arranged to see her next week. Make sure you clear that with her. In case they ask. I think that protects everybody.'

'Yes. That's what I think too,' said Benny earnestly.

The Major nodded agreement.

'There's a bit more.' Happy read on: ' "Following the receipt of some formal acceptances we shall shortly be sending you the list of prominent public figures who have consented to serve on the Council of FORT . . ." '

'We shall?' Benny's pleasure at the news was tinged with surprise.

Happy nodded. 'No problem there. We haven't asked anyone yet but you'll have retired Admirals and Generals queuing up to serve if you want them. Running FORT will be like campaigning against sin.' She smiled, then glanced back at the typescript. ' "Meantime we shall look forward to hearing from you, we hope with your approval and a message of encouragement. Yours sincerely." ' She looked up. 'Is that about what you wanted to do with the first broadside? Make them show their colours?'

'Oh absolutely. By Jove, first rate.'

Benny was nodding too, indicating that if the ignorance of all three in matters relating to Trustee responsibility did them small credit their enthusiasm at least was commendable.

'Can we give a copy to Miss McSlope?' asked Benny. 'It won't be strictly right, I know, but . . .'

'Not yet. After we've approached the Generals, perhaps. It might embarrass her,' Miss Brown advised. 'I think it's rather sweet the way she protects Mr Miff.'

'Me too,' said Benny with feeling.

'She doesn't want him to lose his job by stirring things up. That's what she said,' the Major observed.

'So soon he loses it anyway,' commented Benny with more logic. 'Can't wait to see the Trustee's answer.'

*

It took two days for Wilfred Jonkins at Grenwood, Phipps to decide how to deal with the letter from FORT—after resisting the temptation not to deal with it at all.

Jonkins was an Assistant Manager in the Trustee Department at the Bank, a position he had occupied for more than fourteen years. The portfolio of private trusts for which he was responsible were usually small and untroublesome.

His retirement lay only months ahead—an event he anticipated with ambivalence. If it meant he was to spend each remaining day with Mrs Jonkins, then he was firmly against the change. If his partly formulated plan to escape by himself to a low-price apartment in sunny Florida materialized, then he could hardly wait.

That the low-price apartment was in the middle of a swamp inhabitable only if residents remained indoors through the greater part of the year with the air-conditioning set to freezing was a factor yet undisclosed. Jonkins's current researches were restricted to reading a biography of Gauguin.

Mr Edwards was in charge of the Department, but he also had other responsibilities. He was away at the start of a five-week trip abroad. Jonkins could have acknowledged the letter saying it would await his superior's return. On balance he decided if the cranks who had written actually did obtain some sort of public airing for their objects it would be as well that Grenwood, Phipps should be on record with an unexceptionable view. His reply to Happy Brown read:

Madam,

We acknowledge your letter of 26th April.

As Corporate Trustees for the Rudyard Trust we commend your interest in the future of the Clubs. However, we need to correct a misapprehension on your part. We have no present commitment to seek alteration to the terms of the Trust Deed, nor in law or ethics could we have. Any initiative in this context would need to come from the residual beneficiaries, namely the direct descendants of the late Marmaduke Rudyard.

Yours faithfully,
WILFRID F. JONKINS

He had checked in the file. Miss Florence Spotter had written six months before saying she would be in favour of having the wind-up stipulations set aside. She had also proposed selling land to overcome the financial problem. If only such things were as simple as lay people would like to make them.

No doubt it had been Miss Spotter who had briefed this lot of busybodies. Jonkins re-read his earlier answer to her, pointing out that she was only one of the residual beneficiaries and that he would inform her if any others wrote expressing views similar to her own: none had.

He ordered Miss Brown's letter to be put before Mr Edwards on his return, together with the reply. He debated about sending copies of both to Mr Treasure, decided the survival or extinction of a £50,000 Trust was hardly meat for the attention of the Chief Executive.

He did nothing further before returning to Gauguin with a quiet mind.

If Jonkins's reply had offered even a spark of hope to its recipients events might then have taken a very different turn.

If Major Copper and Mr Gold had not been so pompously rebuffed the cavalier course of action that had meantime opened before them might never have been adopted.

If Happy Brown had been more irritated — and,

frankly, less busy—she might have pressed both members of FORT to let her persevere with Grenwood, Phipps. In fact she was quite relieved when they asked if she minded letting the campaign lie while they got to know Miss Spotter better.

In short, if only Jonkins had tempered justice with humanity then murder might well have been avoided.

CHAPTER 5

'Milk or lemon, Mr Goldstein?' Miss Prudence Rudyard demanded in a wavering contralto. She rallied on the surname, pronouncing the invented suffix in the German manner. She regarded Benny with mounting incredulity through her lorgnette—an accoutrement he found much more unnerving than a monocle. He was certain she believed he was the Major's chauffeur.

'It's Gold . . . tea . . . I mean lemon. Thank you very much.' Benny reddened with confusion. He had been confused since their arrival at Rudwold Park, as arranged, at four o'clock for tea.

He had borrowed the cab they had come in from a sick friend. They had found the house beyond a burnt-out lodge and along a twisting, menacingly overgrown drive curtained by immense rhododendron bushes. It was on the south side of Callow Hill beyond Egham, some twenty miles from London.

Rudwold Park was half an imitation castle begun by Marmaduke Rudyard in 1904 and stopped in 1905 when he failed to acquire the peerage it was intended to embellish. The blocked ennoblement was due to his having competed with the King for the affections of a married lady that neither had any moral right to be suborning.

What happened about the lady is not material: hopes

for the peerage sank without trace, not even to be revived
in the following reign. Despite his good and public works,
Marmaduke's rift with the old monarch did nothing to
endear him to the new one, who had him marked as a
womanizer: even a modest knighthood was twice vetoed
at the highest level. He died in 1921 plain Mr Rudyard—still
with half a castle which he had come to abhor.

The complete east- and south-facing aspects of the
house—all Norman tower, turrets, oriel windows and
battlements—had some redeeming features: the cement
rendering incised to look like stone was not one of them.
Ivy had long since been allowed to obscure this masonic
solecism.

The back of the building left in honest red brick was
more convincingly medieval than the front. Even so, it
had no embellishments like the southern colonnade with
its semi-circular arches overlooking what had once been a
well-kept formal garden, nor the crumbling, crenellated
porte-cochère on the entrance front—very grand though
Perpendicular, which tended to undermine what
integrity the building possessed.

They had parked the taxi beyond the shelter of the
portico, which looked ready to fall down, and picked
their way back to the front door, avoiding pot-holes ankle
deep in water from a midday storm.

It had been Florence Spotter who had cheerfully
greeted them at the door. Before that it had been
impossible for them to ignore—and to fail to
identify—the eighty-six-year-old Prudence Rudyard
standing in full view at a ground-floor window and stonily
marking their staccato progress.

Since the lady had given no sign of acknowledgement
the Major, respecting the old etiquette, had purposely
offered none himself: one who might be choosing whether
to be at home had, for the moment, better be assumed to
be out.

Copper had some difficulty in explaining all this to
Benny much later—Benny who while almost following
the other's lead had given a no more than waist high and
tenative lift of a forearm in greeting. He had frozen the
movement guiltily when the lady within turned about and
walked away from the window.

Miss Spotter was short and wiry, wavy grey hair
matching the colour of twinkling eyes. She had the
bounce of a keen if aging gym mistress. 'Come in, come
in,' she cried while appearing to conduct an invisible
orchestra through something rousing from the doorstep.
'You're dead on time. Found us all right in our
unenchanted castle. *So* good of you to come.'

The writer and illustrator of *Trudy the Tuna, Sally the
Salmon, Wally the Winkle* and other *Fishy Stories for the
Under Fives* was appropriately dressed in a turtle-necked
sweater over well-pressed aquamarine slacks.

Introductions over, Florence had disposed of coats,
offered the freedom of the wash-room and delivered a
brief history of the house. She then added the more
personal intelligences that her Aunt Prudence was hard
of hearing and a trifle unpredictable.

All this had been accomplished while conducting the
visitors from the front door, along the marble-tiled, oak-
panelled hall to the drawing-room.

Florence had paused before the double doors on the
left allowing the two to admire the grand central staircase
opposite. The broad stone steps rose in a single sweep to
the centre of a wide, cantilevered gallery above.

There was a large silver bowl on a mahogany plinth
standing at the head of the stairs displaying an
arrangement of daffodils, tulips and spring foliage. 'All
my own work, but God helped a little,' Miss Stopper had
answered when the Major remarked on the flowers.

It was explained that only the ground floor of the house
was used. The three main rooms to the south of the hall

comprised Miss Rudyard's bedroom—once the library—
the drawing-room, and the dining-room in the base of the
round tower. The rooms in the east wing to the north of
the entrance were Florence's own domain.

Keeping the house on at all satisfied Prudence
Rudyard's caprice and, she apparently insisted, her
father's earnest wish. Florence was disinclined to demur
at this stage in her aunt's life.

The drawing-room was a vast chamber, dark, and
almost unfurnished. Only at the eastern end near the first
of five velvet-draped Venetian windows stood four chairs,
almost certainly late Chippendale, a card table, possibly
early Woolworth, a two-bar electric fire with one bar
burning, and a steaming electric kettle on top of a giant
colour television set showing a race meeting with the
sound turned off.

Leading the way across the highly polished floor,
Florence had explained that Miss Rudyard had stored
most of the good furniture for fear of fire or theft but had
kept some chairs and other things for entertaining:
evidently fairly modest entertaining.

The card table was laid with the 'other things'—a
Georgian silver tea service and some bone china cups and
saucers. There was nothing to eat.

Miss Rudyard, sitting with her back to the window,
had acknowledged the introductions with a bow of head
motioned the men to be seated and gone back to
counting the spoons. She occasionally glanced at the
television.

Shrunken rather than diminutive, she was an aged
grande dame and very aware of it. She wore a high-
necked, ankle-length dress in heavy pink brocade with a
large cameo at the throat. On her head was a pink-
feathered toque. The regal effect of this ensemble was
marred by the worn woollen cardigan over the shoulders
and the ancient sheepskin boots protruding grotesquely

from beneath the long skirt.

It was Florence who had made the tea and turned off the television: it was she also who rescued Benny from his confusion with the milk and lemon. 'Sugar, Mr Gold?' she enquired with a smile.

'No, thanks . . . Sweet enough,' he blurted in gratitude, then wished he hadn't.

'Then he won't require a spoon,' boomed Prudence, who had been listening carefully for the reply. She leaned forward and snatched the implement from its saucer with astonishing alacrity. 'People steal them. The servants . . .' She looked about her in search of servants: Benny did the same. 'Not what they were. Guests little better.' Benny nodded earnestly because she was staring at him.

'Oh Pru! Mrs Smith is the soul of honesty. She's our cleaning lady,' Florence added for the benefit of the others. 'And the Major and Mr Gold are the first guests we've had for ages. Except the Vicar. He doesn't steal spoons. At least I don't think he does. Shall I ask him? What a jape that'd be.' She rocked to and fro on her chair, still holding the sugar bowl.

'Have you had a chance to reconsider closing the Rudyard Clubs, Miss Rudyard?' the Major enquired boldly and very distinctly.

'Nothing to consider. Not my responsibility. My dear father had perfect judgement' — except in the matter of royal mistresses.

'Come now, we chewed it over again this morning,' Florence put in loudly. 'You said you'd listen to these gentlemen.'

'They're not poor. Came in a taxi-cab. I saw it.' She pointed at Benny. 'You were driving.'

'Mr Gold used to drive a taxi before he retired, Pru. He borrowed one for today.'

It was not clear whether Miss Rudyard had chosen to hear. 'My father founded these clubs for indigent officers and gentlemen.'

'Not indigent, Pru—retired.'

'Not rich though. Not people with expensive conveyances at their beck and call.'

Either she considered Benny to be the prosperous owner of a fleet of taxis or merely the driver of the affluent Major sneaking a free tea.

'There are two hundred deserving members . . .' Copper began, articulating carefully.

'Know how many inmates there are now?' Prudence burst in tremulously. 'Two hundred. Numbers dropping all the time. Father said it'd happen if we put down the Bolsheviks. He was right. Everard will tell you. Where's Everard?'

'My second cousin, Pru's great-nephew, Everard Crow-Patcher, promised to join us as you asked, Major. Not sure he'd do much for the cause. Anyway, he's creaked. Rang to say he couldn't make it.'

'What's that?' demanded Miss Rudyard. 'You're mumbling again, Florence.' She slipped a teaspoon into a cardigan pocket.

'I'm telling them about Everard. He's not coming.'

'Everard? Everard?'

'Stanley's son.'

'Can't come.' She gazed around the group in triumph. '*He's* a deserving gentleman. No means of getting here, I suppose.' She then added accusingly, 'No motor-car.'

'Dental appointment, Pru.'

'Not a disappointment at all,' the old lady protested. 'Never had a chance poor lad.'

'What a hoot. He's forty-four,' Florence interjected quietly.

'Badly hurt in the Crash—in '31. There'll be money for him in this Trust.' Miss Rudyard made a performance of studying the gold watch pinned to her dress. 'Now I must see cook about dinner. The Prince of Wales often drops

in unexpectedly. We cannot afford to be taken
unawares.'

'He did once,' Florence put in. 'Not this Prince of
Wales. The last one, in 1925. Thought we were a golf
club. There's one just down the road. Didn't stop, of
course.' She smiled apologetically. 'She wants us to go. It's
one of her programmes.' She turned to her aunt. 'If I see
cook I'll send her in. Want to see the cartoons while
you're waiting?' She turned on the television set.

'Don't mind,' muttered Miss Rudyard. 'I'm sorry you
cannot dine. My best wishes to His Royal Highness.' She
rose unsteadily, did a kind of curtsey to the Major and
glanced malevolently at Benny before sinking back into
her chair. Meantime two spoons and the sugar tongs fell
from her person with a clatter on to the bare floor.

'She's not batty. Just gets things mixed up. Don't we all?'

Florence had led the others around the stairs, past her
bedroom, and seated them in her well lit studio.

'Everard wasn't born in 1931. She was talking about his
father. And of course we don't have a cook. Used to. Now
we just have Mrs Smith and the electric floor polisher.
Sounds like a children's story, doesn't it?'

The room was as full with impedimenta as the other
one had been empty. There were chintz-covered
armchairs and a huge sofa, a fine, leather-topped
partners' desk, tables of various sizes, and books,
drawing-boards and typescript pages piled on every
available surface. There were more books on shelves and
more drawings stacked against the walls. Under the north
window was a draughtsman's easel and a rickety swivel
stool. But what captured the eye on entry was the
collection of watercolour landscapes hanging on the
walls.

'The pictures. They're a delight,' cried the Major.

Florence blushed. 'All mine, I'm afraid. Nothing

pinched from the family collection. Nothing so good . . .'

'That I find difficult to credit.'

'Me too,' said Benny loyally, though he was still too overawed by the house in general to have savoured anything in detail: the drawing-room had been the stateliest he had ever entered without paying.

'My watercolours sell well enough. Not as well as my fishy books, alas. Prudence doesn't care for watercolours.'

'Well, a few of these would do wonders for the other room,' Copper volunteered with feeling.

'That was the ballroom?' enquired Benny who had had difficulty keeping his feet there.

'No, the drawing-room, but it looks jolly like a ballroom, Mr Gold. The ballroom was never built. It was to have been on the north side of the house. This was the gun-room and next door, where I sleep, was the billiard-room. Rather romantic having a turret staircase over there, don't you think?' She pointed to a round-headed, studded oak door in the corner. 'My bathroom's above— with a rather Spartan sort of guest-room. It's the only bit of the upper floors we use.'

'You could let your hair down from the turret like in the fairy stories.' Benny had been a tireless reader of bedtime fairy stories through two generations.

'For my lover to climb up? What a lark.' The sixty-five-year-old spinster clapped her hands together and gave a loud, infectious chortle.

'You said on the telephone you'd do anything to keep the Rudyard Clubs going, Miss Spotter.' The Major's tone was serious.

'My dear Major, anything.' She was trying to suppress a giggle. 'A rope-ladder might be more practical, Mr Gold.' She and Benny laughed aloud as Florence demonstrated the shortness of her hair.

The Major was not amused. The others looked reprovingly at one another.

'Sorry, Major. This is no time for hilarity,' said Florence, steeling herself to think of indigent old gentlemen incapable of mounting even step-ladders. 'Tell us what we can do. Pru's quite dug in, as you've seen. It could have worked—your coming here, I mean.'

'But Mr Crow-Patcher . . .'

'Everard feels guilty. I'm sure he feels guilty about the whole thing, which is why he hasn't turned up. Apart from that, he and I haven't hit it off since he left Cicely.'

'I was in Sicily,' offered Benny, feeling he should atone by saying something.

'No, no. Cicely, his first wife . . .'

'You feel even if your aunt relented, Everard's a dead loss?' the Major put in quickly to avoid any more comic cross-talk. 'If he feels guilty surely he might . . .'

Florence shook her head. 'You don't know his second wife, Dina. American. Hard as nails.' She sighed. 'So you see, it's all rather hopeless . . .'

'Not completely,' said Copper.

'You mean Stephen Spotter may yet materialize and be on our side? Two against two. You think the Trustees . . . ?'

'Not even that, Miss Spotter.' The Major hesitated, glancing at Benny before continuing. 'You see, we have a plan of action that could save the Clubs without involving the family at all. At least, not in an obvious way. Only if one member . . . that is, only if you wanted to help.'

Benny was nodding furiously. 'To help us raise half a million so the books balance again.'

'You could do that? It's a huge sum. I think I could manage a little, but . . .' Florence's voice faltered.

'No, dear lady. It's not your money we need. It's . . . it's . . .' This time it was the Major who was lost for words.

'Help in other ways. Like there's two ways of killing a

chicken? So we're using the other way. Only our way's not strictly kosher. Like it's a tiny bit irregular,' Benny stated firmly.

'We believe we have a potential benefactor, Miss Spotter. Someone who'll provide the money — not willingly perhaps . . .'

'But Major, why should anyone give money unwillingly?'

'So taxpayers pay willingly?' Benny opened his palms in a gesture of surprise. 'Or people being blackmailed? I mean, that's an extreme case, but . . .'

The Major cleared his throat loudly.

'Is there anyone we could blackmail?' enquired Miss Spotter earnestly. 'It's a jolly good cause. It'd need to be someone rich and very, very evil. An absolute blackguard who should be made to make up for his sins. You've someone like that in mind?'

'Certainly not. Figure of speech by Mr Gold.'

'I suppose blackmail is against the law, Major.'

'Exactly, Miss Spotter.'

'So is . . .'

What ever it was Benny had intended to say he left unsaid after an urgent signal from Copper, who had stood up, walked to the north window, then turned to face the others.

'Our plan is a last resort, Miss Spotter.' The easel was beside him. On it was a half-finished drawing of Olly the Octopus engaged in a clog dance — in eight clogs. In his mind's eye the drawing had already become a campaign map indicating encircling movements against the enemy. He straightened his back hoping the light behind might be accentuating the trim silhouette. His feet were spread apart, hands clasped behind his back.

'To recap, then. The Rudyard Headquarters staff is powerless. We've tried the Trustees and drawn a blank. With no disrespect to you, Miss Spotter, there's precious little hope of help from the family. Yet we have a just cause . . .'

'A humanitarian one,' Florence interrupted, nodding at the Major and then at Benny.

'Indeed, ma'am, which is why we've been offered help. Source unusual.' The Major had begun rocking backwards and forwards on the balls of his feet. His voice had risen a shade: the intonation had become more nasal, reminding Benny of someone. 'Our helper's a young man. Very young. Fine boy, Pierre Cruba. Son of ex-President Cruba of Ngonga. Listened to our problem. Immediately came up with a solution.'

'He's getting his father to give us the money. And they are very rich?' Miss Spotter had scarcely heard of Ngonga and never of President Cruba.

'Not as simple as that.' Benny had cut in. 'We need help with him and that's why we said to each other, "If Miss Spotter is kind and helpful like she sounds on the telephone . . ." '

'That we'd enlist your aid, dear lady.'

'Well, enlist away, Major. I'm all ears.'

'We need what in Intelligence we call a safe house,' continued Copper, whose knowledge of Intelligence was gleaned entirely from television. 'A house well insulated from the outside world. A place where a chap could lay up for a day or two. No fear of discovery. In fact, with one reservation, house like this.'

'Montgomery! General Montgomery. That's who you sound like, Roderick. Doesn't he sound like Montgomery, Miss Spotter? You should have heard him at the Alamein Reunions.'

'Who, the Major?'

'No, the General.'

Copper shot Benny an irritated glance and, ignoring the interruption, continued, 'Fly in the ointment, of course. Your aunt.'

Florence shook her head. 'Not at all, Major. If you want to come here for a bit she'd never need know.'

'Not us, Miss Spotter. It'd be Pierre Cruba.'

'Well, whoever it is can come round the back of the drive, in through the window behind you, sleep in the room upstairs, and so long as he keeps to this side of the house and grounds Pru'd be none the wiser. She never goes out. The people she sees are the ones who come to the front door.'

'And your cleaning lady, Mrs . . . er . . .'

'Mrs Smith. Nine to twelve daily, and not weekends. She's only in here one morning, and never upstairs. Pru and I generally eat separately. I prepare it all.' She smiled eagerly. 'Come, do tell me. Why is the stay secret? Is the young man planning to run away?'

'Not exactly, Miss Spotter. You're close though, isn't she Roderick? Very good. Very quick.'

'To be quite truthful, dear lady, the young man is planning to be, er . . . to be kidnapped.'

CHAPTER 6

Yvonne, the third Mrs Cruba, gazed sleepily around the master bedroom in her big South Kensington home. Her eyes focused on the digital alarm clock on her husband's side of the six-foot-wide bed.

It was not quite a quarter to seven. The morning sunshine was piercing through the curtains. For Mrs Cruba the sunshine was symbolic. It was such a special Saturday morning: Maytime in London, and she was very much in love.

It had been hot during the night. They had discarded all the bedclothes except the sheet: now she pushed that aside too.

She stretched her firm, ebony-coloured body, looking it over with pride. She never wore a nightdress.

'*Chéri?*' Winding both her legs around one of his, she began tracing the folds of his face with the tip of her forefinger.

He stirred but did not open his eyes. 'The time?' he asked as she withdrew her exploring lips from his, which up to then had remained unmoved.

'*Sept heures moins le quart, chéri. Chéri?*' she finished insistently and began lightly scratching the hairy part of his chest.

'In English,' he muttered automatically. 'Go back to sleep, woman. Hell, it's too early.'

She sighed, rolled on to her back and began to make soft moaning noises. That did no good either—not that she really minded for the moment: not after last night.

There was plenty of time. She had ordered breakfast downstairs for 8.30. The maid, who lived in the basement, would not rise before 7.30. Pierre, on the other side of the house, slept as long and as soundly as this one beside her: they were very much alike in some ways—both handsome, intelligent and engaging.

Her English was near perfect but it was not a language she cared to use in bed. They both urged her to use English all the time while they were in London: she smirked.

She enjoyed lying awake in this room. It was a rich room. The whole house looked rich: it had been done over to her taste before they moved in. That German diplomat's wife had called it *nouveau riche* when she thought Yvonne was out of earshot. That was before the cow had seen this room. Pity—the mirrored ceiling must have really given her something to talk about.

Yvonne tried never to think of going back to Ngonga. Here there was everything *she* wanted—well, almost everything—entertainment, parties, the house, the money, the social position.

If she hadn't married François Cruba she would probably have lived here anyway—here or in Paris; possibly New York for part of the year. She had done modelling assignments for *Vogue* even before she had left the American School in Paris five years ago.

She was still being pressed to work for designers on both sides of the Channel—and in America. People said she personified 'black is beautiful'. She sat up, posing at the mirrors around her dressing-table: people were right.

She smoothed one hand over her stomach. It was tight still and there were not going to be any stretch marks to spoil it—not for a very long time if she continued to have her way.

She swung round, kneeling on the bed, staring down at his tranquil face. She wished she understood him as much as she adored him. After the power he'd enjoyed of course he had to return to Ngonga if the chance came—she accepted the inevitability of that. His fulfilment, his true destiny, had to lie in Africa. Yet there were times when he insisted only the two of them mattered. She wanted so much to believe he meant that, because there was no long-term future for them in Africa or anywhere else unless . . .

'When does that plane land?' His eyes had opened a fraction.

She lay down close to him again. 'Ten o'clock. Sometimes they're early this time of year.'

'Tail wind. Personally I hate night flights.'

'I enjoyed this one.'

'Hussy. You have plans for the morning?'

'Immediate or long-term, like half an hour from now?' She bit into the flesh of his shoulder.

'I mean after,' He chuckled. 'After breakfast.'

'Taking Pierre to Harrods.' She moved across him to bite the other shoulder.

'Pierre asked you to go with him? That's nice. You two made a truce?' He looked into her eyes. 'You're getting heavier.'

'Pig.' She grimaced. 'He needs me to sign the account.' She glanced again at the clock. 'And why do we still waste time? Soon you'll be fussing to take precious Pierre jogging. Mmm . . . such stamina. I'll see you get a good breakfast.'

'I'm invited, Madame Cruba?' He pulled her to him.

'It depends how well you behave before then, Monsieur Opac.'

Later they all three breakfasted together—Yvonne, Pierre—and Gérard Opac, the ex-Trade Minister of Ngonga, who normally occupied the intercommunicating apartment at the top of the house.

Opac was even early at Heathrow where he drove to meet François Cruba off the plane from Washington DC.

'It isn't the driving. It's just I don't sleep so good.' Benny Gold looked around the breakfast table at all four members of the Potts family in turn. 'Anyway, I like cornflakes. We both like cornflakes best, don't we, Kathy?' He could always rely on support from his seven-year-old granddaughter. She nodded vigorously.

'You usually have All-Bran, Grandpa.' That was Peter. He was nine. Peter always knew better.

'So Grandpa decided on a change today.' George Potts wished his wife hadn't raised the subject in the first place. They all knew her father had made a mistake with the cereal packets: it wasn't a criminal offence.

'But, Dad, you were tired yesterday too.'

George tried to signal his wife to drop it.

'For a couple of nights it's been too hot to sleep. So I should take to a wheelchair?' Benny countered.

'*I* was hot,' claimed Kathy loyally.

'Heat-wave in mid-May. Takes some getting used to.

Tonight I'll be acclimatized.'

'Bet it cools down again. I've turned off all the heating,' said George ruefully. 'Always the way.'

Denise was unconvinced. 'I still think the driving's too much. More coffee, Dad?'

'Fifty years I've been driving a cab. Eight, nine hours a day. Longer sometimes. So all of a sudden it makes me tired doing a few mornings a week to help a friend? And I'm enjoying it yet.'

'Fifty years ago I don't believe you were seventy years of age, Dad.'

'Mummy, how could Grandpa have been seventy when he was . . .'

'Peter, eat. Mummy was using a figure of speech,' said his father.

'So now seventy is too old to drive? You can be Prime Minister at seventy. President of the United States of America at seventy . . .'

'Chairman of British Steel.' Peter sometimes had his uses.

'That's right, Peter. And Churchill saved his country when . . .'

'Churchill wasn't driving a cab, Dad.'

'He didn't have a licence. Count your blessings Churchill didn't have a cab licence. He might have been pushing a hack instead of saving the country.'

Benny and George enjoyed the older man's joke; Kathy pretended to even though she didn't understand what they were all laughing at.

'Maybe they won't renew your licence this August.'

Benny shrugged his shoulders at Denise's comment. 'Three years ago I passed the medical A1. Perhaps last year it wouldn't have been so easy. So I got lucky. The medical's every three years. Today I'm fit again.'

'It's worth the trouble and expense? Renewing it again.' George enquired, trying to sound casual.

'Expense? What expense? It costs 15 pence to renew a London cab-driver's licence for three years. 5p a year. Some expense, I don't think. You know what it costs to be a cab-driver in New York? Thirty, forty thousand dollars. That's a once for all payment, but *that's* an expense.' He nodded sagely. 'So I should pass up the privilege for 15p?'

'I got 15p. Can I be a cab-driver, Grandpa?' Kathy asked.

'Have; not got,' her mother put in automatically.

'You could do worse, chicken,' said Benny, then, figuring that wouldn't please Denise, he added, 'But then you could do a whole lot better.'

'Is Harry Katz still sick?' asked George.

'He's mending.' It was Katz's cab Benny was using. 'He's glad of the money we split till his back gets better. They say he'll be driving again in a week or so.' He grimaced playfully at his daughter. 'He's only seventy-four yet.'

'Dad, you're incorrigible.' She smiled. 'So you won't be here to lunch?'

He shook his head. 'Spending the morning picking up rich tourists in the West End. I should be so lucky'—or so impious if he had really intended working on the Sabbath, he thought. It was strange Denise hadn't noticed. 'Later I'm meeting the Major for a snack.'

'You bringing him back for tea again, Dad? He's welcome.' Denise approved of the Major.'

'Not today. Expect me when you see me, OK?' He knew, deep down, they would be glad to have a Saturday to themselves with the children.

'OK, Dad. But no overdoing it.'

'And don't do anything I wouldn't do,' added George.

Benny smiled bravely. If he wasn't about to do something George wouldn't do he'd be sleeping nights.

At weekends breakfast at the Paragon Private Hotel

started officially at 7.30 if you liked cold coffee, 7.40 if you preferred it hot. The Major had been back in his room well before eight. He had not waited for his egg or the second lot of fresh toast. All this sacrifice had been in a good cause. Today, Exercise Rudy took precedence over creature comforts—a phrase that loosely embraced breakfast at the Paragon.

They had settled on Exercise Rudy because of the first four letters in Rudyard and because Benny had a cousin called Rudy who owned a successful shoe store in Toronto—the significance of which had escaped Copper and appealed to Benny because it gave him a chance to mention a prosperous relative. Both had felt that the royal cypher 'ER' seemed appropriate for an undertaking by two men who had held the Queen's Commission—or would have done if the Monarch at the relevant time hadn't been a King.

The Major had returned hot-foot to his room to be sure the radio weather forecast at 07.55 hours was no different from the one he had heard at 06.55: it wasn't. One left as little as possible to chance. He could now be reasonably certain there would be no rain to slow up traffic at the critical zero hour—nor, according to the BBC, for the several uncritical days immediately following zero hour. He again considered the unchanging, cloudless blue sky through his open window and gave a calculated nod.

He next checked his special equipment—dark glasses and a supply of 10p coins for telephones and parking meters. There was no call in the plan for using either: once more, he was ensuring against all contingencies.

The glasses looked appropriate for the day and, he thought, subtly altered his appearance—even his character. Without them the tweed cap, dark blazer and grey flannels made him immediately recognizable as an English Gentleman dressed for the weekend. Add the affected dark glasses and it would be easy to mistake

him—he felt sure—for an American or even an Arab
wishing to be taken for English. It was all in the eyes.

The only problem was the glasses he had bought to
encompass his whole disguise were so dark he had
difficulty seeing anything through them. Well, nothing is
ever perfect, as his dear mother . . .

He took off the glasses to look at the time. It was 08.21
hours exactly. He had checked their watches after the
dummy run the day before. This was an action of no
lasting significance since Benny had forgotten to wind his
later and had started it going again in the morning a
minute—or it might have been two—after hearing a
church clock strike.

Benny would be outside the hotel to pick him up at
08.45 hours. Their ETA in Hans Crescent was 08.55
hours—that being the street skirting Harrods on the east
as Hans Road does on the west and Basil Street does to the
south. The store's main frontage on Brompton Road had
no bearing on Exercise Rudy.

By 09.00 hours they were to be parked in Basil Street
where they could observe all Harrods' eastern and
southern entrances. Mrs Cruba was invariably an early
shopper and this morning with extra encouragement
from Pierre would arrive not later than 09.15 hours. Her
light blue Mercedes Coupé with CD plates she would
leave in the Crescent or in Basil Street where Copper and
Gold could see it: Pierre had guaranteed this so long as
the two already had the taxi at the agreed vantage point.

Pierre would leave Harrods alone through the southern
exit fifteen minutes after going in. He would then walk
west along Basil Street until they drew abreast of him with
the cab. He would cross in front of them, getting in
through the near-side door.

Benny could then turn right into Hans Road—one way
to Brompton Road—or head straight on for Walton
Place, depending on how the traffic looked, joining

Cromwell Road further along. Either way they would be set for the M4 Motorway and the fastest route to Egham.

Their ETA at Rudwold Park was 10.30 hours.

As he came down the Paragon stairs Copper debated again whether they were putting too much of a burden—too much responsibility—on Florence Spotter.

Pierre Cruba was showing huge resource. In their talks on the telephone one sometimes got the feeling the lad could be masterminding the whole operation. Well, bully for him.

'Good morning, Major Copper, sir.'

' 'Morning, Mr Chauder.'

'Is it a taxi again today, sir? Would you like me to telephone the rank, Major? The Major takes taxis everywhere,' Chauder added in an undertone to a departing guest he was trying to shame out of querying any more of the unsubstantiated extras on the bill.

Damn Chauder: of course, he had been standing on the hotel steps the morning before at exactly the same time at the start of the dummy run. It was Benny who insisted on coming to the Paragon—in case it rained and the Major got wet waiting on some corner.

The fellow knew perfectly well Copper couldn't afford taxis in the ordinary way—and certainly not two days in a row. He had to think fast. 'Don't bother, thanks very much, Mr Chauder. A parent, d'you see? That's it. Parent of one of my pupils. Kind enough to send transport. Here in a jiff, I expect. Wait on the porch.'

'You do that, Major sir. Be my guest. Have a chair. There'll be no charge. No charge whatsoever—today.'

There was always the chance the other guest might have used one of the cane chairs on the stoep, thus incurring a justifiable charge not entered on his bill.

The man, a short Iranian, had studied the Major carefully while weighing the owner's words. Now he produced a wallet. Chauder smiled to himself. He knew how to deal with foreigners.

Outside Copper eschewed the seats and began pacing
up and down the pavement. He was much too early—but
so was Benny who pulled up behind him unnoticed.

'Taxi, guv?'

The Major started. The bright tartan cap, the dark
glasses *and* the false red beard took some digesting.

As Copper got into the cab Benny swivelled around,
pulled the glasses down his nose, and smiled expectantly.
'So how about the disguise?' He paused. 'It's Scotland
forever—already.'

CHAPTER 7

'There he is,' cried Benny over his shoulder. He started
the engine of the taxi just as a long, black Daimler
limousine double parked beside them. With a car
immediately in front, another behind and now one
suddenly alongside they were totally hemmed in.

'Tell that fool to move,' the Major ordered from the
rear of the cab as though he were a paying customer. He
could see Pierre Cruba standing hesitantly outside the
store entrance a hundred yards ahead. He hoped the boy
had spotted them—and their predicament. The plan had
worked perfectly up to this moment.

Benny had the top half of his body hanging out of the
window as he gesticulated to the driver of the otherwise
empty Daimler. 'Can you shift it, mate, please?' he
pleaded. 'I want out.'

The sallow-faced uniformed chauffeur stared dully at
Benny for a moment, then, lethargically, he indicated
with a backward jab of his thumb that he was waiting for
something to happen behind.

Copper too thrust his head out of a window. Two cars

back a big American saloon was drawing away from the kerb—or trying to. It seemed the woman driver had several feet in which to manœuvre but was behaving as though there were only inches. She hit the car in front: possibly there *were* only inches.

The Major got out and stalked around the back of the limousine to remonstrate with the driver.

'When Boadicea gets 'er chariot out, I'm backin' in there.'

'If you let us out you can back in here.'

Sallow-face wasn't buying. 'Too small for this heap. Why's 'e in there anyway? Taxi rank's over there.' He pointed at Benny and then at the official rank they had avoided using because it offered the wrong view of Harrods. 'Wants it all ways, 'e does. 'Sides, 'e's on a double line. Blimey!'

They both looked back sharply. The woman driver had hit something else—noisily. An upstairs window shot up in the house closest to where she was bumping about. A young man wearing a superior air and a blue silk dressing-gown leaned out. 'I say,' he observed, 'that's my Renault.'

'Bad luck, mate. Should have bought British.' This was sallow-face again, more or less to himself.

'You're causing an obstruction.' Benny had climbed down from the cab the better to support the Major's protest. In brilliant sunlight his beard looked not only false but also threadbare.

Sallow-face was unimpressed. 'An' you're parked illegally. So what?'

'So you're both in trouble.' A buxom traffic warden with a blonde moustache, slight but more convincing than Benny's beard had joined them from the pavement.

'I say! Miss! Miss!' The man in the dressing-gown had also now materialized in the centre of the road and was competing for the warden's attentions. 'Will you kindly witness what that banshee's done to my Renault?'

'Your what, luv?' She looked him up and down, wetting her lips in what to the Major seemed uncomfortably close to lewd anticipation.

'My . . . My bumper,' stammered the man. He tightened the dressing-gown around him in a prudishly defensive gesture on being made aware that this and open slippers completed his sartorial equipage.

'Smashin' legs, in't 'e?' the warden remarked conversationally to Copper as she moved back to the American saloon.

Sallow-face let in his clutch, meaning to slip away quietly but stalled his engine.

Copper and Gold made for the taxi.

'Jeremy, you're a double-edged bastard!' This considered insult was hurled from the original thrown-up window by a raven-haired temptress dressed in a skimpy negligée — but only just. 'You've let the Ayatollah out.'

A group of mute onlookers was now assembling. Gazes turned back from the window to the hapless Jeremy. One or two people looked about for an escaping Moslem. A man in Gas Board uniform went on scrutinizing aspects of the negligée.

The woman in the American car got out, slammed the door and, ignoring everyone, walked away briskly east — in the direction of Sloane Street.

'Isn't he in Fiona's room?' Jeremy quizzed Raven-hair while starting in pursuit. 'Here, I say, what about the damage to my car?' he called, dropping a slipper and having to come back for it. He looked appealingly towards the warden. She reciprocated warmly.

'He's not in Fiona's room,' bawled Raven-hair. 'The Cardinal's in bed with Fiona.'

The onlookers remained silent except for the Gas Board man. 'Cor,' he said.

An elderly nanny with a shocked expression hurried

two little girls onward through the crowd. Sallow-face succeeded in moving the Daimler a few paces until progress was impeded by the slow-moving traffic building up in Basil Street.

'She's got a permit, luv.' Blonde moustache was addressing Jeremy and pointing to a sticker on the windscreen of the American car. 'Where's yours, then?'

'I'm visiting. Surely it's allowed on Saturday mornings?'

'Depends what you've got in mind, luv.' She paused for a well-timed round of subdued sniggering from the appreciative audience. '*Parkin's* not allowed. Not without a permit it isn't. Not in the Residents' Zone.'

Benny squeezed the front of the cab into the road between the rear of the Daimler and a small van. A Siamese cat darted out from under the taxi.

'It's the Buddha. He's out too. Jeremy, you are the most utter swine.' Raven-hair began hurling things through the window—mostly articles of men's clothing which Jeremy bobbed about collecting. The crowd was delighted.

The van driver waved the supplicating Benny forward.

'Thank God we're moving,' said the Major, who was on the tip-up seat immediately behind Benny, peering over his shoulder. 'Can you see Pierre anywhere?'

'I'm here, sir,' said the olive-skinned, curly-headed fifteen-year-old sitting well back on the far side of the cab.

'Bless my soul,' cried Copper. 'How did you get in? Benjamin, he's here.'

Benny looked around briefly. The boy he saw was handsome, well developed and big for his age—and he was grinning broadly.

'Got tired of waiting, sir. Thought it best to walk back to you. So many people about. No one noticed. I'm all packed for a short stay, sir.' Pierre patted a large Harrods' carrier bag on the seat beside him. 'How d'you do, Mr

Gold,' he called.

'How d'you do, Mr Cruba . . . er, Pierre. Well done, my boy.'

'Oh look, there's my stepmother.'

They were moving past the south store exit Pierre had used. Yvonne Cruba was standing outside looking perplexed and waving to the doorman who was seeing someone into a car.

'Down on the floor,' hissed the Major obeying his own injunction and feeling rather foolish when he had done it. 'All clear. Back on the seat, Pierre. Don't think she saw us.'

Benny had crunched himself down behind the wheel so that he could scarcely see over it, but he had made good progress: they were half way along Wilton Place.

Just ahead on the left a small and elderly clergyman was standing at the kerb. 'Stop, stop, Mr Gold,' Pierre demanded urgently. Benny complied promptly.

The boy leaped out of the cab and ran to the priest whom he then literally propelled across the road. The two appeared to engage in some mild form of altercation when they reached the other side before crossing back again together. Pierre pushed something into the clergyman's hand, and pointed to the cab before hurrying back to it alone.

'What was all that about?' asked the Major once they were under way again. He had watched the performance with growing impatience through the rear window.

'Insurance, sir,' answered the boy lightly, then added with an embarrassed chuckle, 'Actually, he didn't want to cross the road at all, but he was pleased with my gift for the poor.'

'What sort of insur . . . ?'

'I should stop somewhere else?' Benny called from the front, interrupting the Major's question. 'Brompton Oratory? Hammersmith Synagogue? Maybe they could use a little money too.' He shook his head and smiled as they turned west out of Beauchamp Place. In situations like this the boy took time for good works: eccentric, but nice.

'No more stops, thank you, sir.'

'When d'you think your stepmother will raise the alarm?' The Major sounded edgy.

'Yvonne? She won't. We'll have rung my father before she'll think of it, sir.' Pierre's tone was entirely confident, something both men found strangely reassuring since it was they who were supposed to be in charge. 'We split up after we'd been to the radio department. I said if I wasn't waiting in the car in half an hour I'd have gone to the Science Museum.'

'We've just passed it,' called Benny.

Pierre nodded. 'Actually, she came out much sooner than I thought.'

'I think she was going to ask the doorman if he'd seen you,' said Copper.

'He hadn't. He wasn't there when I left. Pity. I wanted him to see me.'

The Major stiffened. 'What if he'd seen you get in the cab and taken the number?'

'Nobody takes cab numbers,' Benny called over his shoulder. They were waiting for the lights to change at Gloucester Road. 'You ever take a cab number, Roderick?'

'I suppose not.'

'Now you have to speak up.' They were in motion again and accelerating.

'I said I never had,' bellowed the Major.

'Right,' Benny bellowed back. 'In a cab you're anonymous. All black and two numbers on the back to confuse everybody. Except policemen.' He smiled benignly at a motor-cycle patrolman passing them in the outside lane. 'Nothing unusual, Officer. So what's a little kidnap between friends?' he added when the policeman was nearly out of sight: Benny was getting heady.

Pierre had emptied the Harrods' bag on to the seat. He also took some things from the pockets of the grey trousers he was wearing beneath an open white shirt and navy blue sweater.

'I brought a spare toothbrush from home, and some socks and hankies. Nobody'll notice they're missing. Had to buy other things.' He indicated pyjamas, undershorts, a coloured shirt and an anorak. 'But they're all things Yvonne knew I was buying. This was expensive.' He produced a miniature Japanese cassette recorder from its box. 'It takes this.' He delved into the pocket of his shirt and brought out a cassette which he slotted into the machine. 'It records as well as plays, of course.'

'Top of the Pops, I expect,' observed the Major, eyeing the mechanism with forced geniality.

'Oh no, sir. This is programmed with all the phone calls we'll be making to my father. I couldn't bring my other recorder. They'd have noticed. It's the same as this only with lots of attachments. Not so portable. Yvonne promised me this for my birthday.'

'Programmed?'

'Yes, sir. Listen.'

The cab was filled with the sound of a high-pitched, mechanical voice. '*I have a message about Pierre. I have a message about Pierre,*' it intoned. Each syllable was treated as an incantation, the consonants emphasized but clipped. '*Please bring President Cruba to the phone,*' the monotonous, unworldly howl continued.

'We may not need that bit,' said Pierre, stopping the machine. 'My father often answers himself, especially at weekends. If he does, we skip to the next part . . .'

'Sounds like a Chinese soprano in a very high wind,' commented the Major. 'Whose voice is that?'

'Mine, sir. But you'd never guess, would you? It's been

electronically buffed. Like in the science fiction movies.'

'Daleks, you mean?' called Benny from the front.

'That's it, sir.'

The Major had once watched a TV film involving Daleks, but not for very long. 'But I thought those voices were made with instruments. Gadgets.'

'If you've got the right gear, sir. This is just simulation.'

'And quite horrible.' Copper beamed. 'I see the point, though. Clever stuff, young Cruba. Anyone know you dabble in this kind of thing?'

'I don't, sir. Not usually. This is my first go. Nobody knows. Want to hear some more?'

'Yes,' cried Benny. 'Put it up loud.'

Pierre pressed the switch. The voice continued, *'President Cruba, your son is safe. If you want him to stay that way do not contact police. Do not let anyone else contact police. We shall know if anyone does.'*

'You have to say that, sir.' Pierre put in. 'They always say it. My father'll believe it too. He thinks all police forces are infiltrated by criminals. He won't risk my skin.' The boy's tone was entirely without emotion.

'Can't hear,' called Benny.

'Mr Cruba won't go to the police,' the Major shouted back. Benny nodded. Pierre set the tape going again.

'President Cruba, please be ready to make notes. This is Saturday. By 2 p.m. Monday you will deliver a sworn declaration to the Director of the Rudyard Trust for Officers and Gentlemen, 52 Strutton Ground, that the half million pounds you will deposit in the Trust's account at the National Bank, Victoria Street Branch, by 3 p.m. Tuesday is a voluntary and irrevocable gift to the Trust. We will repeat that.'

'Those are the proper words, sir?' Pierre had stopped the tape. 'It's what you said on the phone. What Father has to do and so on.'

'Exactly, Pierre. You must have taken careful notes.'

The Major had spent five hours in the Law Section of the Public Library getting everything right. He had given the boy a thorough briefing to be sure he would know what was involved: he hadn't expected Pierre to have taken quite so much of the initiative. 'The voice only has to add you'll be returned safely. I suppose that's on the tape?'

Pierre cleared his throat. 'Actually, sir, there's a bit before that.'

'He's very thorough, this young man,' called Benny, who had been straining his ears to keep up. 'So there's something we've forgotten, Pierre?'

'It's the part about the fifty thousand pounds for my mother.'

'Your mother?' Copper and Gold echoed nearly in unison.

'In cash. To be handed over on the Duke of York steps at ten-thirty Monday night. Except we'll get it before then.'

Benny pulled the cab into a lay-by beyond the Hogarth Roundabout, left the driver's seat, and joined the others in the back. 'You want to start again, my boy?' he asked. 'The bit about your momma?'

'It's simple really, Mr Gold, Major. You have a good cause. I too have a good cause. My mother.' The boy paused. 'My father treated her very badly. Not over money. In other ways. She won't take money from him. She's too proud. But she needs money. She deserves much more than fifty thousand.'

'But if she won't take it . . . ?' began Benny gently.

'A gift from an anonymous admirer. That's what the note will say—the one we'll send with the money. She'll have to take it. There'll be no one to give it back to.'

'You don't think she'll guess?' asked the Major slowly.

'She might. It's not likely.' Pierre smiled, then added, 'If she thinks it's my father, I don't believe she'll ask him about it, sir.'

'I think I understand, Roderick,' said Benny pointedly.

'Hmm.' The Major looked from one to the other. 'Pierre, our good cause is a worthy charity which you kindly volunteered to help. Did you have it in mind to help your mother as well from the beginning?'

'No, sir. I got the idea later.'

'I see. It's true, of course, Mr Gold and I may eventually benefit from the Rudyard Trust but our main purpose is charitable.'

The boy looked down. 'My good cause is my mother whom I love very much, sir. Honestly, I shan't benefit at all.'

Benny shrugged his shoulders. 'So it's two good causes. If we're helping one we have to help the other, Pierre. Is that right?'

This time the boy looked up into the faces of the two men. 'I've already promised to help the Rudyard Trust.'

'And you'll honour that promise even if we don't agree to help your mother?' The Major's voice was stern.

'Yes, sir.'

All three were silent for a few moments, then Copper and Gold exchanged nods.

'So now we're helping your mother,' said Benny with a resigned smile.

'We've never discussed her, Pierre. Of course I know she lives in London. And all this . . . the kidnap plan . . . it's because of her?' Copper asked.

'Only indirectly, sir. When you rang and asked whether my father might bail out the Rudyard Trust I knew he wouldn't. Old people . . . er, older people aren't his scene. We needed to put him under pressure.'

'Which is why you suggested the kidnap.'

'Yes, sir. For the Trust. I added the bit for my mother later. It's quite safe. You see, she's always helping other people, and it's just stupid she won't take money from my father—not when she knows it's from him.' The tone had become impassioned.

'And she knows nothing about . . . about our plans?' the Major enquired carefully.

'Nothing, sir.'

'But what if your father tells her you've been kidnapped?'

'He won't, sir. She's away till Tuesday night. I'll be safe home by then. He won't tell after the panic's over — not ever. It'd look too much as if he or Yvonne haven't been looking after me properly.'

There was a guileless expression in the boy's eyes which the Major, for one, was inclined to discount. It seemed Pierre was well able to care for himself, and for the wants of others — including his mother and the members of the Rudyard Clubs.

Again there was a momentary silence broken by a sigh from Benny. He shrugged his shoulders, removed his beard and carefully pocketed it. 'So while I'm sitting comfortably, can I hear the rest of the tape now?'

CHAPTER 8

They had parked the cab out of sight behind the disused lodge at Rudwold Park. The Major, Benny and Pierre had then made their way through the rhododendrons to the north end of the house. A low-silled, casement window to the studio was open in readiness. Pierre climbed in first.

'Hoorah!' cried Florence, jumping up from where she was seated at the desk. 'Mission accomplished. Welcome to the intrepid three. Welcome Master Pierre Cruba.'

The boy bowed, shook hands, then, turning, gave another slight bow and said, 'How do you do, sir.'

Neither Copper nor Gold had noticed the heavily built

man who now rose from the sofa across the room. The Major gave a start: Benny made to return to the window.

'Fear not,' charged Miss Spotter, sounding like the Angel of the Lord, early for Christmas. 'Allow me to introduce my long-lost nephew, Stephen Spotter.'

'You're not a policeman?' Benny's words came as more of a supplication than a question.

The big man gave a loud guffaw and strode forward, hand outstretched.

'How d'you do.' The Major had collected himself sufficiently to observe the formalities.

'Don't worry. Stephen's on our side,' volunteered Florence, which Benny, for one, considered was just as well in the circumstances. 'I've been telling him about the whole jolly Rudyard problem and how you clever men are solving it. He's absolutely behind us.'

'You bet,' said Spotter with another guffaw. He let go Copper's numbed hand and grasped Benny's in the same vice-like way so that the little man nearly cried out. Then the stranger turned to the boy. 'So you're Pierre. Met your father once. Great guy and tough with it.' The accent and idiom were adopted American. 'I guess you're a chip off the same block. Gather you set up this whole deal.'

Stephen Spotter was bronzed, fortyish, well over six feet, and good-looking in a rugged sort of way. The Major thought he could easily be a film actor—the kind that wins through in epic war dramas, surviving to get the girl against appalling odds and worse scripts.

'Well here I am. Ready to help you good people any way I can.' The man was scoring well for dialogue in the context of Copper's speculation. 'There's just one technicality, I've explained to my aunt here. For business reasons my being in England has to stay under wraps for a while.' He looked grave.

'Isn't it exciting Stephen flying to our aid?' Florence was doing her best to enthuse the others, who so far

seemed less than buoyed up by the unexpected event.
'We're quite safe, by the way. Prudence is poorly.
Spending the day in bed. She's thoroughly chuffed,
though, at seeing Stephen. Do sit down everyone.'

'A fine age. A fine old lady.'

'Yes, Mr Spotter, but unfortunately not ready to help
like you,' said the Major pointedly. He purposely chose a
straight-backed chair, high enough to lend dominance.

A still disquieted Benny joined Stephen on the long,
low sofa but at the opposite end, and perched on the edge
of the seat. Pierre remained standing: he was studying
Florence's paintings.

'I take it Mr Miff tracked you down at last.'

'That's right, Major. In Houston, Texas. Letter got
there with more forwarding addresses than an alimony
writ. Must have been following me about best part of a
year.'

'You move around in your . . . in your business?'

'Oil's my business, sir. The funding of oil exploration.
Kind of keeps you moving.'

'Stephen puts up the money to dig oil wells,' said
Florence with pride.

'Not exactly, Aunt,' but the disclaimer scented more of
modesty than protest. 'I'm what you'd call a Mr Fixit. I
organize finance groups—consortia, and I do it fast.'

'I always thought oil exploration was in the hands of big
international companies.'

'That's what most people think, Major. Not so.
There're a whole lot of individuals and small outfits
involved too. Ad hoc groups cobbled together when
somebody gets a geological hint there's oil under his back
yard.' The big man smiled expansively. 'That's where I
come in. I'm the cobbler. But you have to be fast to stay
ahead of those multinationals . . .'

'Who perhaps can't move as quickly . . .'

'As Johnnie who gets to the spot with the right

connections and know-how. You've got it, Major. That's me. So long as there's oil for the finding, I'll be there.'

'It's estimated the calorific value of the world's known deposits of peat equals the world's known deposits of oil. I think,' Benny chipped in bravely.

There was a moment's silence.

'Fancy ' said Florence uncertainly.

'You don't say?' Spotter eyed his sofa companion quizzically. 'Peat,' he paused again. 'You Irish?'

Benjamin Gold shook his head. 'It was on the wireless. The Open University.'

'So you've been difficult to reach, Mr Spotter,' the Major offered quickly to head off any more learned irrelevancies. 'No fixed address,' he added lightly, before regretting he had used a phrase most commonly applied to vagrants in the criminal courts.

'That's about it. Guess I've been a bad boy not keeping in touch. Aunt Florence said my last known address was the Bank in Hong Kong. Jeez, I left them fifteen, sixteen years ago. Since then it's been Indonesia, Australia, the US, Mexico, South America, Africa, the Mid-East. You name it.'

'But he dropped everything to get here when the letter arrived,' Florence affirmed indulgently.

'Caught the first plane. Came straight over from Heathrow an hour ago. Took a chance there'd still be family living here. But that's what I mean. A cry for help's like somebody smells oil. Either way Steve Spotter gets travelling.'

'Did the letter explain we need more of Marmaduke Rudyard's descendants to help stop the closure of the Clubs?'

'Sure thing, Major. No problem. Why, I figured to balance the books myself . . .'

'Oh good,' Benny exclaimed.

'. . . if necessary, that was. Seems to me, though, you

fellows have the immediate problem well in hand . . .'

'We could easily cancel . . .'

'No, no, Mr Gold. We press on with your plan. Then when we have the—er—the contribution from Pierre's father in the bag, that's when Aunt Florence and I mount our offensive. Shouldn't be rushed.'

There was another moment's silence.

'You married, Mr Spotter?' asked Benny in the hope a prolific union might have added a string of charitable progeny ready to support father in the cause.

'Not right now,' and as if following the questioner's line of thought Spotter added. 'No kids either. Not that I know of.' He finished with what Copper considered a wicked leer.

The spinster aunt accepted these intelligences with a smile both coy and forbearing. 'Stephen means to shame Everard over to our side.' Perhaps this made up for the lack of legitimate progeny as well as the shameless uncertainty about there being any of the other sort. Even so, the assertion hardly matched Florence's earlier view on the enduring quality of Crow-Patcher obduracy. 'He even has hopes about Pru. She's certainly fallen for him.'

Perhaps Pru was not the only one, thought the Major. 'You're aware how we intend to extract—er—collect what you call the contribution from Pierre's family?' It had crossed his mind that Miss Spotter might have been more circumspect than appearances suggested.

'A harmless case of kidnapping?' Appearances had been right after all. 'Well, since Pierre here is in on the act I guess everything's kosher.' Benny winced as Stephen continued: 'Got a conscience about how your old man put together his loot, Pierre? Feel it ought to be shared out with the more deserving? Does you credit, son.'

'Not quite, sir.' Pierre's tone was polite, but he was evidently angry. 'My father is an honest man . . .'

'Oh, don't misunderstand me . . .'

'We couldn't be sure he'd want to help with the Rudyard Trust. He gives to a lot of other causes.' The boy had ignored Spotter's interjection. 'This way's certain.' He paused. 'Of course he can afford the money.' He glanced from Copper to Gold. 'Also there's another smaller money matter we're dealing with. You say you know my father, sir?'

'We ran into each other years ago in New York. Briefly.' There seemed to be little inclination to enlarge on this.

'And my mother?'

'No, I don't believe I had that pleasure.'

'Even though Pierre's co-operating most magnificently, Mr Gold and I are at some risk—with the law, I mean, and so on.' The Major changed the tack of the conversation. 'If you could still see your way to rescuing The Trust yourself, Mr Spotter, we'd be happy to cancel . . .' Ever since Pierre had introduced the business of the £50,000 for his mother the dangers in Exercise Rudy seemed to loom larger by the minute.

Stephen looked grave. 'I'd like to do it. Fact is, untying more than a million dollars right now would be complicated for me. Oh, I know it's chicken feed.' Benny found himself nodding in agreement though he couldn't have said why. 'It's a matter of interlocking funds. Difficult to extricate ready cash without rocking other people's boats. All a question of confidence, if you see what I mean.'

Benny steeled himself into admitting he didn't see at all. 'I think Mr Miff, he's the Director, said the Trust's loss wouldn't be more than forty thousand this year. If we could find that much straight away . . .' He looked appealingly at Copper.

'Mr Gold's right,' the Major took over. 'The half million was intended as long-term capital—to earn interest. If you and Miss Spotter, and perhaps the other descendants, if you agree to get the terms of the Trust altered we'd only need enough to balance the books now — to tide the Trust over till it can sell land . . .'

'Wish I could help.' Spotter looked deeply disappointed. 'Fact is, I just have to keep my being here a total secret for a while — for a few weeks at least, maybe a month or so. A call on any one of my banks, even for forty thousand pounds, that could give the whole game away. You have to know the oil business to understand, fellows.' He shook his head sagely. 'For Steve Spotter to lay out nearly a hundred grand, in dollars that is, in London. Wow! If that leaked there's at least ten people who'd figure they were being double-crossed. Cut out of something. Sorry.'

'Must be jolly tricky being a tycoon,' Florence put in: Copper and Gold exchanged dejected glances. 'I'm sure Stephen will do what he can . . . in the circumstances.' She applied smiles all round. 'You mentioned something else, a small money matter you're dealing with, Pierre. Perhaps Stephen can help with that?'

The two older men allowed Pierre to explain about the unscheduled call he was making on his family's financial reserves. They assumed in advance that Spotter was as likely to help with this as he was to volunteer paying off the National Debt. They were right. After hearing his excuses they listened dully as Florence recited a sentiment only too dear to both of them — that collecting money from François Cruba in person invented unspeakable extra hazards.

Pierre went over the plan revealed on the tape-recording, convincingly defending its feasibility. As agreed with Copper and Gold, he did not go on to say exactly how the arrangements would be implemented: earlier, in the taxi, they had all thought it best to keep this to themselves. Spotter, like Florence, was thus deprived of the total confidence, but unlike his aunt showed no misgivings, praised Pierre's ingenuity, and insisted on hearing the tape three times.

'You'll be staying here, Mr Spotter?' the Major enquired later.

They had finished consuming coffee and homemade biscuits. Pierre had installed his effects in the room above. Stephen had returned from his second courtesy call on the ailing Prudence. It was nearly noon — the time it had been agreed to call the ex-President.

'I wish you would stay, Stephen,' Florence put in earnestly. 'It'd be perfectly easy to make up a bed on that sofa, and when Pierre's gone you could have . . .'

'No, won't hear of it, Aunt.' The big man beamed. 'You folks have enough on your plates without complicating things with an unexpected guest. If you're sure I can borrow that car of yours for a few days . . .'

'With pleasure, my dear. I have the bicycle, you see. The car's not very grand. Not what you'll be used to . . .'

'Suits me fine. I can rent one of my own later. At this moment in time it's better I don't have to fill out rental documents. You'd be amazed how word gets out.'

Neither Benny nor the Major showed the least bit of amazement: both wondered why Stephen Spotter had risked coming to England at all if news of his presence was going to stand the whole oil industry on its head.

'About a hotel . . .' The Major was about to suggest the Paragon as guaranteeing anonymity if not much else.

'No problem.' Spotter interrupted. 'Fixed it already. Place at the airport. Don't need regular identification for that. Used a phoney name. Sorry to sound so cloak and dagger. Believe me, it's necessary.'

There was a general murmur of assent as the Major announced: 'Time for Phase Two. That is the only telephone in the house, Miss Spotter?' He pointed to the instrument on her desk.

'Indeed, indeed. Pru won't have one near her, but it's

so essential to my work. You see . . .'

'Quite, so we'll make the call, then Mr Gold and I'll be off. Since we're using Pierre's recorded message I suppose we could have left earlier. Still, it'll be good to know everything's going as planned.'

'Reassuring,' said Benny, but with the look of a man who feared the worst.

'That recording. It's safe for length?' asked Stephen. 'It won't give them time to trace the call? Don't know how long it takes in this country.'

Pierre was attaching a small microphone to the telephone. He shook his head. 'Longer than people think, sir,' he answered with authority. 'In any case, they're going to be so surprised by this first call nobody's going to think of things like that. The other taped messages we'll be using are all short.' He glanced at the Major. 'OK to start, sir?'

'Carry on, Pierre.'

The boy seated himself in the chair Florence had vacated, lifted the receiver and placed it on the desk with the voice-piece next to the cassette machine. He began dialling the number of his home.

The other four had stationed themselves near enough to catch both sides of the coming exchange. Pierre was ready to depress the switch on the machine.

The ringing tone sounded only once. A female voice — a recorded female voice — broke the silence in the room as dramatically as if it had been amplified several times.

'The lines from Reading are engaged,' said the voice on behalf of Telecom. 'Please try again later. The lines from Reading are engaged. Please try again later . . .'

CHAPTER 9

Just south of Old Brompton Road lie The Boltons. The name is plural: the place is singular. Two elegant Victorian crescents face each other across an oval garden with St Mary's Church in the middle.

The tall, ornamented stuccoed houses on both sides are very grand and mostly in pairs: only a wag would call them semi-detached. St Mary's, in grey Kentish ragstone, demurely falls short of the immaculate in the midst of so much Walpamur whiteness.

Mark Treasure parked the Rolls and strode briskly across the lower end of the oval to a walled house standing by itself—one of a very few especially superior villas near the junction with Tregunter Road.

It was one-forty when he rang the bell. Less than an hour earlier he had been summoned to the telephone while leaving the eighteenth green at Swinley Forest Golf Club, twenty-five miles away.

He had been ruffled at missing lunch but not nearly so much as if he had been called before holing the twenty-foot putt that won the match.

François Cruba had said, in confidence, it was a matter of life or death. The man was not given to dramatics.

The fast drive had been unremarkable except for the comic turn in the taxi. Even that he would not remember without prompting, but it had been funny at the time.

It happened that the banker, driving in the outside lane, had drawn up beside a London cab at the first set of traffic lights after leaving the M4 Motorway. The single passenger in the cab—a man in very dark glasses—was occupying the tip-up seat immediately behind the driver, a choice singular enough to have attracted Treasure's idle notice. The two occupants of the cab had appeared to be arguing.

Suddenly the cabbie, who had been sporting a loud tartan cap and a red beard, shrugged his shoulders and removed both cap and beard to the evident consternation of his passenger. After hurried words, both heads had turned shamefacedly to meet Treasure's by now frankly intrigued gaze before reverting more quickly to facing front.

The cabbie had then sheepishly replaced the cap but not the beard. The passenger, who had slipped the glasses down his nose to look at Treasure, had slipped them up again, and while staring resolutely and stonily forward had removed his whole person very slowly and along a level plane past the window to the rear of the cab.

Curiously, it was not the imbecilic piece of mime nor even the red beard that had lodged in the observer's mind; rather it had been the seraphic and engagingly apologetic glance the cabbie had darted in his direction just as the lights were changing.

'Mark, *mon ami*, we're deeply in your debt.' It was Gérard Opac who had opened the door. 'François's in the library. Yvonne's with him.' He hurried Treasure up the eight wide and carpeted steps into the even wider hall, all marble and oak panelling. 'You want to clean up?'

The banker shook his head. 'I could use a cold lager.'

'Get it myself. Why don't you go in? The old boy's pretty cut up. Can't wait to see you.' The handsome African swallowed. 'Pierre's been kidnapped.'

Treasure's surprise at hearing Cruba referred to as 'the old boy' was quickly eclipsed by the frightening announcement that had come next. Even so, it was something that returned to colour his thinking in the days ahead. Opac spoke English as surely as he did French with little trace of accent and entirely without idiomatic stumbles.

*

'The police must not be involved. Not in any circumstances.'

Cruba had spoken with heavy deliberation. He was standing before the empty Adam fireplace, hands clasped behind his back. His characteristically shifting gaze darted perpetually between the three others present. He did look older than his years—old, worn and tense but more alert than many a younger man might have been who had stepped off a night flight from America to learn his only child had been abducted. Treasure gave marks for this.

It was fifteen minutes since the banker had arrived. He was seated in a deepbuttoned leather chair beside the hearth. Yvonne was opposite—statuesque and distractingly attractive in a slit-skirted, white silk dress that had fallen open over her crossed and very shapely legs, something Treasure had been trying unsuccessfully to ignore. Opac had chosen the window-seat in a rounded bay on the other side of the book-lined room.

'No police? Not even after . . . ?'

'*Jamais*. Not ever, Mark. No police. No publicity. If we come from this with my son safe, from then we make better precautions. If these people are political they may be after publicity but they won't get it from me. If necessary, we deny everything. *Le tout*. No kidnap. No ransom. No pay-off.'

'And if they're not political?' asked Treasure.

'Then still we don't tell every criminal syndicate from Los Angeles to Rome that François Cruba pays on request . . .'

'Which is what you're doing, *chéri*.'

Cruba hesitated only briefly at his wife's interruption. 'This time we're paying because there won't be a next time.'

'You mean you'll have Pierre protected?'

'Yvonne also. Round the clock if necessary.'

'It'll be difficult, François.' Treasure still found it hard to affect a warm personal relationship with this man. He'd have felt easier addressing him as 'Mr President' rather than by his first name. Cruba looked and behaved like a political head of state. He was dynamic, and despite a lack of height, a dominating personality: he was also invariably decisive—sometimes impetuously so.

'Difficult,' the banker repeated. 'Irritating for the person—or persons—being protected, and in this country usually unnecessarily, and at worst counter-productive.'

'You mean it calls attention to those worth protecting. It . . . it sets them up?' This was Yvonne.

Cruba ignored his wife. 'It wouldn't have been unnecessary this morning,' he uttered flatly, then put out a hand to stop Treasure's reply. 'I know what you're going to say, Mark. This case is special. You don't have the kidnapping in Britain. I know that too. It's partly why we live here. All the more reason not to encourage this Corsican type of lawlessness. Tell the police now and the press will hear sooner or later—probably sooner. We could easily get drafted into a police operation that goes wrong—wrong for Pierre . . .'

'I don't think the police would stop you making the payments, if that's what you wanted,' Treasure pressed. 'They'd be looking for a sporting chance of collaring the villains afterwards.'

'Which means the story comes out. And there's no assurance it wouldn't come out too soon, even if it's desirable it comes out at all. I would need persuading on that point.'

'Of course it's political. Unofficial but political.' This was the first comment Opac had made. 'It's to show up François's wealth. That he's filthy rich. That's all—this time.'

'*Vous savez . . . pardon*, Mark . . . you know very well,

Gérard, I don't follow that theory.' Cruba's tone was impatient.

'They're Ngongan. They're Communist. They're approved by the Patriotic Front, our so-called Government, but not openly backed by them.' Opac too sounded impatient. 'That's why they need the fifty thousand cash—to cover expenses. So they can prove their independence if they're caught. It's part of a much bigger plan. Something I've been expecting, but not that it would start in this way.'

'A plan to demean and impoverish me before liquidating me. Nonsense.' Cruba lifted both arms in the air and brought them down sharply in a gesture that emphasized his abject disagreement. He turned to Treasure who at the same moment saw Yvonne glance poker-faced at Opac. 'Gérard's wild theories we can discuss later. Perhaps these people are political.' He shrugged his shoulders. 'Or they're Robin Hoods—or something else we haven't guessed. For the moment there are more important considerations. Mark, you can arrange things financially? The cash, the transfer to the charity, the sworn declaration . . . that's from a notary, uh?'

Treasure nodded. 'And which we can arrange to have revoked later and the money returned. In a case of obvious duress . . .'

The ex-President shook his head violently. 'Mark, we must understand each other on this. We are playing it their way—this time. We're paying. No tricks. These people are not fools. On Monday or Tuesday they leak to the newspapers I make a gift to charity of half a million . . .'

'They've said they'll do this?'

'No, but I believe they will. We are asked to confirm. What can we do? Say yes, then next day demand the money back because it was a kidnap ransom?'

'We wouldn't need to say that.'

'But *they* would, my friend, to be sure. Then follows the great media and police investigation. No. No. No. That part is settled. Now, you say Grenwood, Phipps are Trustees for the . . .'

'Rudyard Trust for Retired Officers and Gentlemen.'

'*Sans doute* a coincidence, but a convenient one. We can assume with safety it's not a front for kidnappers, though why . . . ?' He left the sentence uncompleted.

The last thing Treasure wanted to do at this moment was to confirm unwarranted assumptions. Inwardly he was embarrassed that knowledge of the connection between the bank and the charity was all the information he had to work on. Under oath he could not have sworn the Officers and Gentlemen hadn't become kidnappers, blackmailers or even white slavers. Simply, it seemed wildly unlikely that the Rudyard Trust could be knowingly involved in anything crooked.

Even so, there could be an angle—a twist that meant the blackmail money was to be openly 'laundered' through a respectable charity to suit some wholly uncharitable purpose. Treasure didn't believe in latter-day Robin Hoods: he didn't even believe in the first one. Nor did he much care for private charitable trusts—often more trouble than they were worth.

The Grenwood, Phipps Trustee Department was well enough managed, but in the nature of things it was small and only marginally profitable. Treasure had as little to do with it as possible. Now, with a sinking heart he remembered Edwards was away in Australia: it was Jonkins who would be responsible for the Rudyard. Jonkins, that deeply boring man who looked like Crippen, he was the one Treasure would need to see as soon as the present interview was over. He would also have to reach Freddy, of course, but the need to establish the enduring *bona fides* of the Rudyard Trust would be the first concern.

'I'll have the legal declaration brought here for witness and signature late Monday morning,' he said. 'The cash for Monday night they want in used five- and ten-pound notes?' In the banker's view it was the £50,000 that gave the lie to the 'rob the rich to give to the poor' theory: a ten per cent collector's surcharge seemed greedy. There was a half-formed speculation of his own that fitted the case better, but it was one he was not ready to share with anyone else.

Cruba had nodded. 'In a document case which I pass to someone . . .'

'Man or woman unspecified?'

'Correct. Someone who approaches me and says the password "Wellington" . . .'

'As you go on up the Duke of York steps from the Mall to Waterloo Place. You're not intending to do that yourself of course.' Treasure's tone was purposely matter-of-fact.

'Why not? That's what they tell me to do. Also it's the one part of their instructions I'm happy to carry out. It will give some satisfaction to see one of the cowards who have stolen an innocent child.'

'*Mais, mon amour, le danger!*'

'There will be no danger, Yvonne. To deliver half a million pounds the next day they must keep me in good shape. No. I will do it. They say a taxi will arrive here at 10.15. The driver will have been told to take me to the Mall . . .'

'An accomplice. One of the gang.' Mrs Cruba broke in and looked to Treasure for support.

'In the circumstances probably not,' the banker admitted. 'It'll be easy enough for them to ring for a cab as though they were calling from here. It's normal to give the destination. Don't think I'm advocating François goes, but I don't think arresting the cab-driver would do much good.'

Cruba smiled grimly. 'Mark is right, my dear. They've thought it all through. You notice they've made provision for counting the money. It's a large sum in that form but they have until the next afternoon to make sure it's right. They'll still have Pierre. You'll make sure they're not short-changed, Mark?'

'If you won't have the police involved, you have to let me go with you.' This was Opac.

'No one goes with me, Gérard. You will attend the dinner at the Reform Club in my place. I will phone myself and plead indisposition.' The ex-President turned to Treasure. 'A private Anglo-French event. The retirement of an old diplomatic friend who is *persona non grata* with the rabble now ruining my country. It would be doubly discourteous to drop out at the last minute without providing an admirable substitute, and escort for Yvonne.' He treated the last phrase to an extra emphasis.

'I shan't go,' said his wife.

'We shall see.'

'The Reform is barely two hundred yards from the Duke of York steps . . .' Treasure began.

'So if I get into trouble I know where to run for succour.' Cruba spoke briskly. 'I think all is agreed.'

'About your . . . about Pierre's mother?'.

It was Opac who answered Treasure's question. 'We've been trying to contact her. She may be away. We'll keep trying, of course.'

'Of course,' Cruba echoed, frowning.

CHAPTER 10

It was a little after 2.30 when Benny Gold decided he wasn't hungry after all. He considered the hardly touched beefburger and the serving of chips on the plate before him: then he thought of the starving children in Bangladesh. Benny was always making life hard for himself.

On the other side of the plastic table for two the Major was making better progress with his order. As Benny had noticed before, his friend consumed everything put before him whatever the time of day: also he never refused anything free.

'More coffee, Roderick?' There was no charge: you just had to signal the waitress to refill your cup. The Major nodded. He had his mouth full. In any case they hadn't spoken much. The tables were very close together and people could overhear. It was only now that the place had emptied of lunchtime traffic. It was a chain restaurant in the Earls Court Road not far from Copper's hotel.

'Perhaps I shouldn't have had the onion garnish. Onions don't agree with me.' Benny hesitated. 'I still wish the mother hadn't come into it.' He looked about him, then dropped his voice to a piercing whisper. 'I mean getting the money for her.'

The Major swallowed, then nodded again. 'Shouldn't have agreed, of course. Very awkward at the time, though. Anyway, it's done now. Can't go back.'

'We could, Roderick.'

'Not on our word. Not at this stage with the whole thing in motion,' he said with gloomy resignation.

'The first plan was so simple.' Benny leant forward. 'What if they tell the police . . . nab us Monday night?'

'Both wanted?' broke in the waitress from behind Benny's back, making him jump. 'Coffee for both?'

'Only for my friend.' He had had too much coffee already. Coffee was bad for him. He should have had tea: they didn't serve tea.

The Major smiled at the girl, waiting till she had refilled his cup and left before he spoke. 'You heard Pierre. Nothing will make his father call in the police. In any case, anybody out to catch us would go to the Duke of York steps—where we won't be going.'

This time it was Copper who checked there was no one within earshot before continuing. 'You collect Cr . . . the subject, drive up the west side of The Boltons, which is one way going north, brake at the top as though you're deciding whether to go down the other side or up to Old Brompton Road. I jump in from the right . . .'

'When you know there's no one following me.'

'Right. I sit with my back to you facing the subject. I tell him there's a change of plan, give him the password and take the briefcase.'

'It'll still look odd. People don't get into occupied cabs. Not without the driver objecting.'

'Which is why you look round surprised, slide open your partition . . .'

'And you say without turning round, "OK, driver, I'm making the trip instead of my friend. Let him off at the church." I close the partition . . .'

'Drive the fifty yards down the other side of The Boltons while I tell the subject to take off his glasses, if he's wearing them, to get out when you stop, and walk back *up* The Boltons without looking round if he cares about Pierre's safety.'

'Anyway, he can't read numbers without his glasses.'

'So we're doubly protected. Three times really. You said people never take cab numbers.'

'He might want to take this one,' Benny answered dismally.

'Except we'll be round the bend and into Tregunter Road . . .'

'And if someone comes looking for the cab next day I answered a call from the cab rank phone at South Kensington. Orders to take a party from The Boltons to the Duke of York steps.'

'But after you started the original passenger got out

after being joined by a friend who took the cab on . . .'

'Changing destinations to Paddington Station.'

'Brilliant, really. Gets you off the hook completely.' The Major beamed as though it had been his own idea. 'Still not sure about wearing the lady's stocking over my face.' His tone suggested he considered this nearly obscene.

Now it was Benny's turn to promote confidence. 'It works in the movies. It'll be dark outside, and in the cab. No one's going to see you except Cruba—I mean the subject. If you wear the stocking, your old deer-stalker *and* the dark glasses he'll never recognize you again.'

'If I wear that lot I'll need a strong torch as well.'

'So do without the glasses.'

'Hmm.'

Benny changed the subject. 'You think Stephen is as rich as he says?'

They had avoided discussing Spotter until this moment.

'No.'

'Phoney?'

'Something of the sort. Pierre obviously didn't trust him. Glad the boy headed us off telling him the whole plan.'

'About not going to the Mall?'

'Right. Pity Florence spilled the rest of the beans before we got there.' The Major frowned. 'Still, he's basically an ally.'

'Long term?'

'Long term.' Copper nodded.

Both wished Mr Stephen Spotter had materialized before Exercise Rudy had started. Both faced the growing conviction that the grasping of initiatives was work for younger men.

Benny loosened his tie. 'It's hot, huh? You wouldn't like half my burger? I haven't touched . . .'

'If you're sure you don't want it.' The Major leant across and stabbed the object cleanly with his fork.

Lean and gangling Everard Crow-Patcher, aged forty-four, great-grandson of Marmaduke Rudyard, grandson of General Percival Crow-Patcher, son of Stanley Crow-Patcher, country lawyer — all deceased — fitted the appearance of a used car salesman. This was appropriate since his present occupation was selling used cars — though not very often. Indeed, the motor trade was only the most recent of several callings to which Everard had responded since being asked to leave the regular army following a misunderstanding over mess funds.

After closing the street door on the departing visitor he had waited a minute, then glanced out again before returning to the living-room of the small, first-floor flat in Guilford Street, Bloomsbury.

His second wife, Dina, previously Mrs Herman Schultz of Jersey City, was still presiding over a tray of used tea-things. He noted, though, that in his absence she had made time to pour herself a vodka and tonic. It was a little after five o'clock.

'Well, bully for Cousin Stephen,' she rasped, patting her hair which had the colour of ripe corn and the texture of wire wool. 'Now there's a guy I could make a play for. Should have offered him a drink. Bit early.' She regarded the glass in her hand. 'Gimme a cigarette, there's a doll?'

'He's a second cousin, actually, and you're a bit old for him, my sweet. He can't be more than forty.' He smirked and stroked his thick moustache.

'Drop dead.' Dina had just turned fifty. 'Such a physique. Reminded me of my Herman before his first episode.' Mr Schultz had passed away six years earlier, defeated by conditions mostly associated with being over-weight. 'Loaded too.'

'No. Only sounded rich.' Now there Stephen did

resemble the late Mr Schultz, Everard reflected bitterly. 'Something fishy about him. Sensed it from the start.'

'Takes one to find one.'

He ignored the barb: gratuitous insults peppered their exchanges and were without significance—like their endearments. 'He didn't come just to tell us we should ignore rumours about the Rudyard Trust. About moves to rescue it.'

'Well, he did a big enough spiel on it. Made me feel kinda warm.' It had also encouraged her to believe there might be foundation to her husband's claim to an expectancy after all.

Everard could hardly admit to a more desperate hope in the same vein. Any day his wife could discover he had mortgaged what remained of her securities with a now overdue bank overdraft.

Apart from his meagre and erratic earnings they lived off the interest from Herman's estate—a widow's *dot* somewhat smaller than Dina had knowingly implied when Everard had engineered their whirlwind marriage four years before—or thought he had.

At the time he had been available as a cultural escort for wealthy tourists—by his own report a gentleman 'filling in' while an inheritance materialized. In reality he had been broke, with a backlog of alimony payments. She had been, by her own report, a wealthy tourist and inconsolable widow—in reality one with a quite modest income, a penchant for younger men, a strong desire to remarry and none at all to return to Jersey City.

In many ways they deserved each other.

'He came on very strong about not supporting Florence.' He poured himself a gin.

'That crazy bitch.'

'Actually, the dotty one's Prudence but we don't say so because she's in favour of winding up the Trust. I've told you that before. Several times.' He gazed at the ceiling, drew his lips back and sucked air in noisily through clenched teeth. This indicated an exercise in massive toleration or else that he was thinking deeply.

'I wish you wouldn't do that.'

'Florence is quite sane,' he continued, now staring at his wife over the top of his glass though his eyes showed he was preoccupied with a more important subject.

'If it's your Aunt Florence who wants to keep the cruddy Trust going through Act of Parliament, she's got to be the crazy one.'

'She's also a second cousin, not an aunt,' he corrected absently. 'Prudence is an aunt — a great-aunt, actually.' He was taking in air again. 'What I don't understand is why it's such a big secret he's here. Stephen, I mean. Why we mustn't let anyone know he's in England— especially the old girls, not for a couple of days.'

'It's like he said. He's a big shot in the oil business. My Herman used to say those guys played it very close.'

'Did he indeed? How very perceptive of him. Must have known a great many of them to come up with anything as profound as that,' he observed, cynically concluding that the nearest Herman ever got to a big oil man was probably a heavy petrol pump attendant. 'Well, if Stephen's playing his own close little game, we can do the same.'

'How d'you mean?'

'I mean there's something cooking we haven't been told about. I'm going to pay a call on the old girls. Owe 'em a visit anyway. Go in the morning. In the BMW if I don't sell it tonight.'

'You won't if it's before dark,' she countered sarcastically. The nine-year-old car had been his only stock in trade for some time: a good light accentuated some bad respraying resulting from extensive accident repairs.

'Anyway, I might flog it to Florence. She needs a new car.'

'How would you know?'

'I sold her the one she's got.'

'That's a pretty good reason.'

He shook his head. 'It's looking worn. It was parked up the street. Stephen drove away in it.' He sucked in some air. 'Just doesn't fit.'

Greywick Court Mansions is a substantial, Victorian four-storey block of flats still invested with a sort of dignity—the kind condemned aristocrats of the better sort used to exhibit on the scaffold. In a decade tenants of the Mansions will be obliged to yield up their spent leases and the freeholder will knock the building down to put up something more practicable.

Meantime, for most of the tenants the cavernous halls, the labouring lift, and the grandiose, unheatable accommodations provide homes at a relatively low basic cost. For many the close proximity of Westminster or Whitehall makes compensation for a modest extra investment in thicker winter underwear.

The dog Hercules often covered the level quarter-mile to Strutton Ground in ten minutes—less with a following wind. This was one reason why Greywick Court suited the ailing spaniel's indulgent and—for the present—impecunious owners.

Half an hour after leaving Guilford Street, Stephen Spotter pressed a doorbell on the second floor of the Mansions, and above a card announcing that this was the residence of Mr and Mrs Clarence Miff.

The heavy, unattended street door below had opened to his touch. The wires from an early model, automatic-entry system had been hanging loose from their casing outside: a porter's booth just inside the hall looked long since abandoned—successive relics of a genteel past.

There was a low canine moan from inside the flat. It rallied rather than peaked as the door was opened.

The middle-aged woman stared searchingly at the caller. The light in the hallway of the flat was a good deal better than it was on the landing. The woman fumbled for her monocle.

Spotter hesitated. 'Mrs . . . Mrs Miff?' he enquired with astonishment.

'I am Mrs Miff, yes. You are . . . ?'

'I don't believe it. Edna. Edna McSlope. After all these years. It's Stevie.' He paused, still not quite certain. 'You *are* Edna? Fay Crow-Patcher's daughter? I thought you were dead. Nobody's mentioned . . .'

'Merely disowned, like my mother.' It took a moment for Miss McSlope to compose herself. 'I'm sorry I didn't recognize you. You were a little boy . . .'

'At Nice after the war. I was eight. I guess you were twenty . . . or thereabouts . . . and er . . . and very beautiful.'

'Come in, please. I was a little taken aback. I'm sorry.' She stood aside for him to enter. 'How did you come to find me?'

'I didn't. It's your husband I came to see. Figured I'd drop by on the off-chance. Say, do they all know the Director of the Rudyard is married to one of Marmaduke's great-granddaughters?'

She motioned him along the passage towards an open door at the end. Hercules fell in behind. 'If by they you mean the rest of the benighted family I haven't the first idea. You see, none of them has ever asked.'

CHAPTER 11

'Kidnaps at Harrods and skulduggery among the officers and gents. Darling, you have had a day,' exclaimed Molly Forbes, the attractive actress wife of Mark Treasure. She was curled up in a broad wing chair, a cold chicken leg in one hand and a glass of champagne in the other.

It was 11.15 p.m. They were in Treasure's study at their house in Chelsea's Cheyne Walk. Molly was unwinding after a 5 o'clock matinee and an evening performance of a boisterous Congreve revival which, thanks largely to her performance, was playing to capacity audiences. He was sharing the half-bottle she had brought in with her supper tray a few minutes earlier. Treasure had been taking a telephone call when his wife had appeared: Freddy Hinterton had just received the mid-afternoon message to call back as soon as possible.

'You forgot to mention an unforgettable evening with Wilfred Jonkins.' The banker sighed, surveying the open files and folders on the desk before him. 'He didn't leave till after ten.'

'Seemed a harmless little man.' Jonkins had arrived just before Molly had left for the theatre. 'Not a bit put out about suddenly having to work on Saturday.'

'Possibly made up for doing nothing the rest of the week. Lord, what a mess!' He looked up, then smiled. 'That's a new negligée. Nice. Oh, and Freddy just had the nerve to suggest meeting at midnight somewhere near Hampstead Heath.'

'Freddy lives near Hampstead Heath.'

'Yes, but we don't. Anyway, all this cloak and dagger stuff is quite unnecessary.'

'Which is why I heard you arrange to meet in Lincoln's Inn Fields at ten in the morning.'

'Because I humour the fellow.' He sniffed. 'Freddy was sailing all day.' The tone was a touch resentful.

'That was sinful of him when he could have been helping you over the kidnap. Any news?'

'Not on that, but I don't like this Rudyard set-up. Oh, and I was right remembering the family had an incentive

for folding up the Trust. What's difficult is finding
anyone desperately interested in keeping it going.
Desperate enough to stage a kidnap, I mean — the kidnap
that's still top secret, all right?'

'Aye, aye, sir.' Molly saluted with the chicken leg.
'Cloaks and daggers will be worn, after all. What have
you got on the Offs and Gents?'

'That for three or four years numbers have been
dropping. Not enough people can afford the ante or the
weekly rates, or both.'

'Wouldn't that be quite common these days?'

'Yes, in a way. But the entrance fee, the initial capital
payment, is five times what it was a few years ago, and the
weekly charge for new members over two hundred a week
when you'd expect it to be about a hundred.'

'Because the Trust is supposed to be a charity not a
chain of three-star hotels? Mmm. But couldn't one have
known this before now? Isn't there an annual report or
something?'

'A Director's Report bewailing soaring costs plus an
auditor's report showing decreased income and mounting
expenses. As you said, nothing unusual in that these days
if you accept the facts as presented and don't dig.'

'But you've been digging?'

'Jonkins has on that phone, for information we
wouldn't normally come by. You see, the Director, who
has to be a qualified lawyer, has enormous discretion.
Normally we, the Trustees, accept what he says and does
without question. It's he who interviews new applicants,
fixes the ante, the weekly charges . . .'

'But surely there's a voluntary council of do-
gooders — people who raise extra money for improvements
and so on . . .' Molly was on the Council of one of the
national children's charities and several local charity
committees.

'No, there isn't,' Treasure interrupted. 'The Rudyard is

a closed operation. You'd expect outsiders to be involved but they're not. Most charities of that type have the kind of set up you're used to, but not this one. Which partly explains why it seems we've been slack in overseeing it.' He might have substituted Jonkins or Edwards for 'we', but with trouble looming the conscientious Chief Executive of Grenwood, Phipps knew exactly where the buck had to stop. 'I should have twigged what was happening. Would have if I'd bothered.'

'Nonsense,' said Molly, as much out of instinct and experience as out of pure loyalty: mentally she was revising her tolerant view of the evidently slothful Jonkins. 'Anyway, what's been happening that could have been avoided in these inflationary times?'

'An overkill. The fees have been put up far higher than necessary to meet expenses—so high they've virtually stopped the inflow of new members. As old members die . . .'

'Oh dear, how sad.'

'Well, we are discussing old gentlemen's homes. As members die they're not being replaced. Hence the dramatic fall in numbers and new income. Most of the present inmates joined long enough ago to be paying the old rates . . .'

'Fixed for ever when they came?'

'Exactly. Result, increasing losses over the last three years, which under the Founder's rules means the Trust should be wound up—a hazard that's nothing to do with the auditors, of course, but one the Director has been promising to do something about. It seems he's been using the wrong strategy.'

'Cue for Robin Hood to the rescue? This kidnap business?'

'Not sure yet. I still don't believe the boy's in any real danger.' It was an instinctive feeling he had had from the beginning.

Molly dipped a Jersey strawberry in sugar. 'Where's Jonkins been digging?'

'Well, for a start there's precious little written information from the Director, man called Miff. From time to time, though, candidates for membership apply direct to the Trustees by mistake—quite a lot of them. It's a predictable enough error. Grenwood, Phipps is the first name listed under the Rudyard entry in this.' He held up a copy of the *Directory of Grant-Making Trusts*. 'We pass the enquiries on to Miff but we keep copies. The most recent ones are in this file. About eighty from last year, another sixty since January. From seven to ten this evening Jonkins has talked to as many of the applicants as he could reach by phone—them or relatives—to find out what happened to them. He managed to get nineteen. Enough as it turned out.'

'Because they all said the same thing?'

Treasure nodded. 'All interviewed by the Director. All asked, among other things, about their capital resources and their incomes. All eventually told the size of the required down payment and the weekly rates—different in almost every case.'

'Depending on what each totted up to? That's accepted charitable practice isn't it?'

'Sure. But every time the sums involved have been a hell of a lot more than any of these people reckoned to afford. Not one bought the deal. Either they're still where they were or they've taken some other, cheaper option.'

'You don't have copies of any written offers?'

Treasure shook his head. 'I don't believe there are any. Miff seems to do it all verbally. He gets the candidates either to accept or reject on the spot, or else to write or phone a decision later. Most say they phoned, which possibly means some did and others just forgot the whole thing. Some declined at the interview. Very few said they wrote a refusal.'

'Which leaves a very slim volume of written testimony, m'lud.' Molly lit a State Express cigarette. 'I still don't see why this Mr Miff's been so busy doing himself out of a job . . .'

'And denying droves of deserving old gents from getting into retirement homes.'

'You've spoken to him?'

'No, I'm going to have Jonkins deliver the declaration about the half-million to him Monday afternoon. I hope it comes as a surprise. Once the boy's safe, of course, we can take the place apart.'

'You think Miff could be involved with the kidnap?'

'Highly unlikely, But I'm not taking chances. Don't have much on his background. Been with the Trust eleven years. Lawyer. Widower, re-married. There was a mix-up five years ago over a member's joining fee. A suggestion a special headquarters deposit was asked for in cash. It was a misunderstanding by Miff's secretary. She left shortly afterwards. Replaced by someone older and more experienced.' He glanced at some scribbled notes. 'A Miss McSlope. No, I'd guess the kidnap is an entirely separate firm. Either people who genuinely want to rescue the Rudyard but by a totally irresponsible method, or else someone whose sole interest is in the fifty thousand.'

'Who's only pretending to involve the Charity? Oh, that's very devious.'

'And possibly quite clever. Anyway, we'll know after Tuesday. Meantime, I'm not having Miff disturbed. Incidentally, Jonkins knows nothing about the kidnap. He thinks the panic's because someone's alerted me to the fact the Trust's in imminent danger of being closed down. I've told him now I have the bare facts I want a day or two to consult with others.

'On Monday he's going to think you've raised half a million.'

Treasure chuckled. 'I suppose so.'

'Isn't it extraordinary no one's got anything going to save the Rudyard Trust before now? I mean the relatives of members . . .'

'Seem to have been purposely kept in the dark. There've been no appeals because, being absolutely legal about it, the Trust Deed says specifically the Trustees musn't sanction extra fund-raising from any source . . .'

'But surely relatives . . . ?'

'I know. They could easily have been told about the situation. Would probably have coughed up without being asked.'

'Still would.'

Treasure nodded. 'One of the Founder's grand-daughters wrote us some time ago saying the rules should be altered to keep the Clubs going. We should have responded a lot more enthusiastically than we did. Then more recently a group calling itself the Friends of the Rudyard Trust wrote offering all kinds of help. Well-intentioned ex-officers, I'd think. They were firmly choked off by friend Jonkins. His boss Edwards is away . . .'

'Seems to me Mr Jonkins has been behaving neither like an officer nor a gent.'

'Afraid you're right. Anyway, I've told him he can follow up the Friends tomorrow. I think we can safely assume what you'd call a group of earnest do-gooders haven't been kidnapping West African heirs.'

Given all the circumstances it was a reasonable assumption: or was it, he wondered.

It is more than three hundred years since Lincoln's Inn Fields recalled more of the country than it did of the town. On the edge of the old City, it was the first of London's great squares, with a large public garden in the centre. It is said King Charles the First came to inspect

Lindsey House—in the new Palladian style—when it was completed in 1640. It still stands on the west side and Treasure had parked the Rolls beside it as arranged. If Freddy was late the time would be usefully employed contemplating the most historically significant house in London—and bathed in morning sunlight.

Freddy arrived shortly after ten in an early Range-Rover spattered in well-caked mud. He had commended the choice of rendezvous. It was far from the habitat of men from the FO—and, it transpired, almost everybody else on a Sunday morning.

The Soane Museum stood closed behind its abstract, Neo-Classic façade. The pedantic Greek portico of the Royal College of Surgeons opposite looked equally deserted and sternly less inviting. The Great Hall of Lincoln's Inn itself dominated from over the wall on the east side, it's Elizabethan elegance no less agreeable for being a Victorian simulation.

The two men had walked twice around the square while Treasure related all he knew about the kidnap.

'I think it right not to tell the police,' was Freddy's first reaction.

'We've no option. I've given Cruba my word. Our word,' Treasure added pointedly. 'What you're getting is privileged information.'

'Quite so. My lot can't possibly object to Cruba giving half a million to a charity that can't be a front for something subversive. Grateful to you for keeping me in the picture.' Freddy hesitated. 'It can't be subversive? The charity.'

'Well, if it is now it won't be from Wednesday. Once the boy's safe we'll have all assets frozen before we do anything else. The half-million will stay part of the capital of the Rudyard Trust.'

'You offered Cruba the chance to have the gift revoked? Duress and all that.'

'He won't risk it in case of some kind of reprisal.'

'And the fifty thousand cash? Not that that matters to us.' Even so, Freddy had asked the question.

'Opac guesses it's to cover expenses.'

'You have a different theory?'

'Could be a professional fee.'

'What sort of profession?'

'Charitable fund-raisers. They usually work for ten per cent of the gross. This lot are on to a new method.'

'You're right, of course. Fifty thousand is ten per cent . . .'

'Of half a million. But if we're up against a fresh style of fund-raiser, who the devil commissioned them?'

'This Friends of the Rudyard Trust group you mentioned.'

'Unlikely after they'd announced their existence.' Even so he had been on the telephone to Jonkins an hour earlier telling him to stay clear of FORT after all. 'There is another explanation for the whole caper, of course.' Treasure pressed on before Freddy had time to ask what it was. 'Can you cover Cruba when he gets to the Mall tomorrow night? I mean with M16 people. That Diplomatic Protection lot perhaps? You wouldn't have to mention the kidnap. Just invent a reason for having him watched for a few hours.'

'Oh . . . umm . . . it's very difficult . . . arranging things like that these days without stirring things up.'

'Come on, Freddy, this is an emergency. Involves a very important person—important to you, anyway. I thought at the very start you were giving him protection. Wasn't it part of the deal?'

'He refused it.'

'I wondered about that. Seems not to trust policemen. I think you'll find he's changed his tune when this is over.'

'When it's over,' said the other pointedly.

'Which may be too late. Look, he won't have to know.'

'He doesn't *have* to deliver the money himself.'

'Well, *he* thinks he has to, and what's more he's going to. I think he needs some kind of protection.'

'You said he believes he's perfectly safe till Tuesday. Till after the half-million's cleared.'

'If it ever is.'

'What d'you mean?'

'That the fifty thousand cash could be the beginning and the end of the operation.'

'That the charity bit is a blind?'

The banker nodded. 'Which could mean we're up against sophisticated crooks with small aspirations or an elaborate prank engineered by young Pierre Cruba himself for kicks or reasons of his own . . .'

'Good Lord.'

'Or else someone's after Cruba not his money. Wants the thing to look like a kidnap . . .'

'But why?'

Treasure shrugged. 'What about making a political assassination look like an abduction gone wrong? It's a long shot, that last one, and it's not something I'd mention to anyone else. But just to indulge a whim, could you get Cruba protected tomorrow night?'

'Yes.' This time the answer came without hesitation.

'Good.' The banker smiled. They had stopped in front of the Royal College of Surgeons to let a car pass into the courtyard. 'Never know. Might save us a post mortem,' he concluded cheerfully.

CHAPTER 12

The heat wave and dry spell persisted over the week-end but came to a dramatic end on Monday evening. An hour before sunset an awesome darkness fell over London and the Home Counties. The distant rumblings that had been bumping around during the afternoon suddenly gave place to thunderclaps of shattering volume followed by hideous stabs of lightning. After this impressive overture the rain came just after eight — in torrents.

Had it not been peak viewing time, droves of house-holders might prudently have disconnected TV sets from aerials. As it was, most surrendered themselves to fate and an eleven-year-old movie about an airliner with a demented pilot and a defective undercarriage flying through fog while a time-bomb ticked away in the hold. The other channels were offering less escapist attractions.

It had been an unusually profitable Monday evening for taxi-drivers: Dusty Miller, one of the fortunates, had just dropped a fare in a quiet corner of Hereford Square.

He had been busy since the start of the rush hour. Now it was quieter. He glanced at his watch. It was 9.35: too early for theatreland. He switched on his two-way radio.

Miller was a member of an owner-drivers' association that supported a radio control service. So far this evening there had been no point in listening, with would-be passengers at practically every intersection.

'. . . Boltons to Duke of York steps in the Mall.'

He snapped over from 'receive' to 'call'. 'Nine-Charlie-Five to Control. I'm in Hereford Square. I'll take The Boltons. Tell 'em two minutes. Repeat the number, please. Over.' He was already turning right out of the Square towards Old Brompton Road.

The caller who had hung on desperately for con-firmation thanked the taxi service despatcher, then whistled with relief. The plan had balanced on cabs being easy to get between nine and ten on Monday evenings.

A few hundred yards from Hereford Square Benny and the Major had been waiting in their own cab parked under the trees on the east side of The Boltons, above the church. They could see very little through the steamed-up windows. The rain continued its merciless hammering on the roof.

'Everything's going to take longer,' said Copper.

'We can give it five minutes more, Roderick.' Just after he spoke Benny heard, then dimly discerned another cab splash past.

'Suppose so, but it's not going to stop.' The Major cursed himself for not bringing his umbrella after all. 'I'll just have to get wet. You shouldn't be that long.'

'We can cut out my observation time at the bottom if you want.'

'No. A minute of reconnaissance is worth a year of something or other. Can't remember the quotation. Fits, though. Better we stick to the plan. If you see anything suspicious you've got time to check.' He pulled the piece of stocking over his head. 'Damn. Wrong way round.' The comment was muffled. He had made a hole for his mouth for the unconceded reason he might otherwise choke with repugnance.

The Major hated using the stocking. As for the one Pierre had provided, a used one, a bit cut off one of Mrs Cruba's cast-off tights—he shuddered again at the thought. That morning he had bought a brand new pair of tights at the supermarket staring out the girl at the check-out as he had paid for his single purchase.

After some rearranging the large hole in the nylon now accommodated his mouth instead of his left ear, but the two small slits he had cut for his eyes kept closing. He pulled on his deer-stalker and felt in the pocket of his raincoat for the dark glasses, only to be worn in emergency.

'Right. I'm off.' He threw open the cab door. The handle banged against a parking meter.

'Steady on,' said Benny, mindful of Harry Katz's property, but half apologetically since he wasn't the one now standing in the rain. He started the engine. 'See you in a bit.' The cab pulled away from the kerb.

The Major turned about, taking the same route he would shortly be directing Cruba to follow. It was arranged he would take up position half way down the west side of The Boltons where he could watch for Benny's return. Then, when he was satisfied there was nothing following the cab, he was to move fast to the top of the oval again, ready to jump aboard when Benny stopped at the junction.

He was definitely not expecting the taxi to be heading towards him before he had even reached his vantage point.

The headlights were on low beam: if there was trouble Benny would have put them on high. On the other hand, he had firm instructions to drive very slowly if all was well, and here he was coming around the crescent like a scalded cat.

There was no time to look for possible pursuers. The Major wheeled about, then splashed back along the pavement as quickly as he could. He deplored Benny's misplaced good intention to get him in out of the wet even at the cost of precipitating heart failure. He could tell without looking when the clattering cab was abreast of him. Wet and breathless, he staggered into the road, arm outstretched, to grasp the door handle.

Far from stopping, or even slowing, the cab accelerated, swinging left towards Brompton Road. The Major stood rock steady while he was showered with the several pints of well-oiled rainwater accumulated in one of the Borough's deeper and wider pot-holes.

Dusty Miller had no reason for stopping. He had not even seen the party who darted out at him until it was too late to signal he was engaged, and he certainly could not be responsible for the fate of dim-wits who waited on wet roads without the expectancy of getting soaked.

The Major rarely swore. 'Bloody hell!' he cried aloud. It was only then he thought to read the number of the retreating cab—to twig it might not have been Benny's cab. As he turned around the point was confirmed: he very nearly fell over Benny's cab which was stopped immediately behind him.

'Get in quick, Roderick,' Benny shouted with a lack of caution that defied understanding and the observance of proper military discipline. How was Cruba to credit they were strangers if they addressed each other by their first names.

But Cruba was not in the cab. 'What happened?' demanded Copper from the back seat while starting to shed the more immediately sheddable parts of his sopping outer clothing: the stocking received the highest priority.

'He's in the cab in front. Saw him get in with a briefcase—the sort we expected.'

'You don't know him. It could have been someone else.'

'He was black.'

'Oh Lord.'

'I mean he was exactly like his pictures. I was quite close. He came out of the house with the case . . .'

'There's been a mistake.'

'You think he sent for his own cab, Roderick? Maybe he thought he had to send for his own cab to take him . . .'

'To the Duke of York steps. That's where we go,' ordered the other, irritated to find the lining of his raincoat was wetter than the outer part and perplexed over the reason. Benny set the cab in motion.

In the rain and confusion neither Copper nor Gold immediately noticed the Rolls-Royce halted some distance behind. The chauffeur, Henry Pink, had delayed on instructions before pulling out to follow the first cab—and for too long: a second cab had insinuated itself between him and his quarry at the critical moment. Now the interloper was effectively blocking the narrow road by stopping in the middle of it to take on trade.

'It's all right, he's moving,' said Treasure from the back of the Rolls. 'If we've lost our chap, head for the Mall. Fast as you can, Henry.'

All direct routes from Kensington to the Mall finish by passing Buckingham Palace. From there the broad, straight processional way sweeps down to Admiralty Arch: the Duke of York steps are on the left near the end.

Each of the three drivers had his own variation on what constituted the most direct route to the Palace and they were none of them in sight of each other after they left The Boltons. Henry Pink had no interest — or thought he hadn't — in Benny Green who, as it happened, took an earlier turn eastwards than the chauffeur chose. Dusty Miller was too far ahead of the field to be picked up by either of the others — some luck at the first set of traffic lights saw to that, though the still blanketing rain and the busier streets in the central area would have made serious pursuit nearly impossible.

The vehicles arrived at their common destination in the same order in which they had left. Miller made the best time, Gold was a good second, and Pink nowhere — ten minutes behind Benny due to a traffic diversion set up only seconds ahead of him at Hyde Park Corner where an underpass had flooded.

François Cruba paid off his driver, turned up his coat collar and walked deliberately across the wide approach to the steps which are staged in three broad flights of ten steps each. Above them towers the Column to the Grand Old Duke, dissecting Carlton House Terrace to left and right, with Waterloo Place behind. At the Mall level the long Terrace basements feature as elegant flanking wings to the grandiose Column approach.

As Cruba began his ascent seventy-three members of the North Kent Art Society, mostly female, mainly coatless and wholly resolute, began to disgorge from the lighted portal of the ICA Gallery a few yards to the right.'

The special Private View of a new exhibition was over, the lecture digested, the refreshments consumed, the Society's hired coaches, parked in Waterloo Place, ready to depart. The members had waited some time for the rain to ease. When it did so a little an optimist at the front had cried, 'Come on everybody, it's nearly stopped,' and everybody had believed her.

Only half-seeing, for the steps are badly illuminated, the art lovers fresh from the brightly lit gallery attacked the climb with all the British group enthusiasm engendered by rain, Cyprus sherry, ruining dresses, flattening back-combing and a stimulating sense of adversity.

'Are you all right, Marjorie?'

'Chins up, Doris.'

'Take my arm, dear.'

'Like the Black Hole of Calcutta.'

'Talk about glorious May.'

'Must be easier going down . . . Look out, girls, there's a bull loose.'

'Cheeky monkey, shoving like that . . .'

'Take care, there's another one going up. Do you mind . . . ?'

'Some people . . . There, somebody's fallen . . .'

'Is it Gertrude?'

'Careful, everybody . . . careful . . .'

'There's two down.'

The agonized bellow from the centre of the steps momentarily froze the chatter.

'Oh my Lord.'

'Are you hurt, dear?'

'Stand clear. Somebody's ill.'

'It's the man underneath.'

'Treacherous in the wet. There ought to be more light.'

'He's not moving.'

'Could somebody send for an ambulance quickly?' asked Major Copper. He had caught Cruba's body from behind as the figure between them had darted away. He had not had the strength to do more than lower the other, face downwards, into the wet. He had already been winded himself after taking the climb too quickly. It must have seemed they had collapsed together. 'An ambulance,' he repeated loudly.

'On my way,' volunteered a Mr Edgar, one of the few male members of the group. He was already half way up the remaining flight of steps.

'This lady's a nurse, aren't you, Rene? Where's Dorothy with that torch?'

'Dorothy, over here with the torch, dear. That's better . . . Oh Lord . . . there's . . . there's something . . . there's a knife in his back.'

'No, leave it in.' This was Rene, the nurse. The Major nervously took his hand from the handle. 'Better to leave it in. It may be holding the bleeding.'

He could see the blood on his hands even in the feeble light of the pencil torch. It never occurred to him to run: this was Pierre's father.

He was still kneeling beside the quivering, moaning victim a minute later when the two policemen came clattering down.

Treasure was furious about the time they had lost. He was out of the Rolls the instant it stopped. His eyes were well enough used to the darkness: the rain had stopped and there was no difficulty defining the silhouette of a stretcher party at the top of the steps — and no resisting an awful presentiment.

The figure that had separated from the knot of people and hurried down towards him was Freddy Hinterton.

'I was watching for your car.' The man from the FO for

once had no inhibitions about acknowledging his friend.

'What's happened?'

'Somebody stabbed Cruba.'

'He's dead?'

'No. Not yet anyway. Taking him to the Westminster. Opac's with him.'

'What about your men? Were they . . . ?'

'Too late. It happened so early. Must have been ten minutes ago. We weren't expecting . . . Mark, I'm sorry. Let the side down.'

'Did *anyone* see?'

'Not any of my lot. They've dispersed, by the way. Bit self-conscious about public appearances. You understand? Officially they weren't here.'

Treasure nodded. 'And other people?'

'Plenty about. Police are gathered in strength sorting them out. A group had just come out of the Institute of Contemporary Arts.'

'Any real witnesses?' The two had walked to the foot of the steps.

'The coppers are hanging on to an elderly chap, military type, moustache, no raincoat. He's standing on the right. Can you see?' The clouds were rapidly clearing and moonlight was now fitfully lighting the scene.

'I think so. He saw the stabbing?'

'Worse, he may have done it. Seemed confused.'

The siren of the departing ambulance was a kind of reassurance.

'How have you explained . . . ?' Treasure began.

'Said who I was, that I was passing, stopped to help, and recognized Cruba.'

'Who fetched Opac? You know he was at the Reform?'

'Yes. Don't know who got him. Seemed to pop up. We've hardly spoken.'

'Has that chap got the money? Cruba left with it in a case.'

'I don't think so. Oh, look, they're taking him away. They're from Cannon Row.'

The Major was being led up the steps by a man in plain clothes. Treasure made to go forward to join the official-looking group, then stopped, catching the other's arm.

'Listen, I think I'll stay out of this, at least for the moment,' he said. Freddy, now more composed, looked relieved. 'If the kidnap's gone wrong they'll be phoning The Boltons. There's only Yvonne there. Do the police know . . . ?'

'About the kidnap? I don't think so. Not from me . . .'

'Then don't tell them. Get as much information as you can. Ring me at Cruba's later.' Treasure turned on his heel.

As the banker neared his car Pink nodded towards the round little man who had been standing by the taxi parked nearby.

'Excuse me . . . Mr Treasure, isn't it? Grenwood, Phipps? Your chauffeur said . . . That is, he was good enough . . . Can you help me, Mr Treasure? I don't know what to do. It's about Pierre . . . Pierre Cruba.'

'Please go on.' The utter distress in the man's tone was reflected in his face—a face that Treasure seemed to know: that and the tartan cap.

'They say there's been an accident on the steps.'

'I understand Mr Cruba's been assaulted. You know anything about that?' Now he remembered—the comedians in the taxi on Saturday: it was the cap that triggered it.

'No. Nothing,' Benny nearly shouted. 'And the police have taken Roderick, that's Major Copper? I saw him go with someone . . .'

'Slim, older man, no raincoat? Yes, I think he's been taken for questioning. May have been a witness.'

'Oy, oy, oy. The Major said if anything went wrong I shouldn't get involved. Stay out of it. Leave it to him, he said. Only if they find out about Pierre? Mr Treasure, you're the boss — above Mr Edwards — and I'm telling you there was no harm intended. It's just everything's gone wrong. Like Mr Cruba took the wrong taxi . . .'

'At The Boltons. The Major got into yours. We were just behind.' Treasure decided to back a hunch — that the man before him was no desperado. 'Is the Major anything to do with the Friends of the Rudyard Trust?' he enquired; another hunch.

'Roderick and me. We *are* the Friends of the Rudyard Trust. We wrote to Grenwood, Phipps, Mr Treasure.'

'And we weren't much use. But Pierre Cruba's helping you raise money?'

There were tears in the other's eyes. 'On my daughters' lives, Mr Treasure, that's the truth. Now we'll be up for murder I shouldn't wonder.'

'Mr Cruba isn't dead. Could you take me to Pierre now? Can I get him home tonight?'

Benny nodded vigorously. 'It's only half an hour from here.' Then his face clouded again. 'I should leave the Major at a time like this?'

'Frankly, I don't think you have the option,' Treasure commented briskly and implying an official justification for his own design which was entirely unwarranted. 'D'you want to park that cab somewhere? We're not awfully good at following taxis, and anyway, I'd rather you stayed with me until further notice Mr . . . Mr . . ?'

'Gold. Benjamin Gold, sir.' Benny hesitated. 'Lieutenant, Royal Army Service Corps, sir. Retired, of course,' he added lamely.

CHAPTER 13

'Sorry to have brought you such rotten news Pierre,' said Treasure. 'Remember the hospital stressed he's come through surgery remarkably well . . .'

'And now he's in intensive care.'

'People usually are for a bit after an operation. The Westminster really is one of the best outfits in the country.'

They were alone in the bedroom above Florence Spotter's studio. Treasure had the only chair: the boy was sitting on the end of the bed.

'You think he'll live, sir?'

'Since he's survived so far, I'd say every chance.'

'It was my fault.'

'If that's what you choose to believe. From what I've been told about you, you're too intelligent for that.'

'He wouldn't have been there if . . .'

'If someone hadn't altered your plan for him to be somewhere else. Look, your kidnap scheme was well meaning but bloody irresponsible. You'll cop it from your father for that when this is all over, but he won't be blaming you for his being assaulted. It's pretty obvious your plan was used as a ready-made set-up by someone else—we've yet to know who. That is if you don't believe Mr Gold and his friends are hoodlums or terrorists.'

The boy smiled for the first time. The two had never met before. Treasure had insisted on being shown to the room almost on arrival—immediately after telephoning the hospital. He had left a crestfallen Benny Gold below trying to explain things to a bewildered Florence Spotter.

It had hardly seemed the appropriate time to start berating the boy for the trouble he had caused. In any case, his supposedly more mature confederates deserved a good deal of the blame.

'We phoned your house on the way down. Couldn't get an answer. Imagine your mother, sorry, stepmother had already left for the hospital. Strange, though . . .'

'It's usually the maid's day off, Monday. If Yvonne wasn't there.' Pierre finished with a shrug of the shoulders.

'I see. Look, I want you home as quickly as possible. We'll leave pretty soon, but I'm hoping for a call from Gérard Opac or another friend first. I've left urgent messages to ring me here.'

'Couldn't I go straight to the hospital, sir?'

'I doubt there'll be any point. We'll get Mr Opac's view if he rings, but I wouldn't think there'd be a chance of seeing your father till tomorrow.'

'I'd like to be there when . . .'

'I understand. The thing is . . . getting you home will be the surest way of quashing the whole kidnap episode, and that's something I want to do fast.'

'To save my skin, sir?'

'Not specially. Mostly to protect your father's wishes—that and other considerations. If what took place tonight was a political act, the culprit may be aiming to focus the blame on a kidnapper if he knows there's one handy.'

'Not on a mugger, sir?'

'Because they're always handy? A kidnapper sounds more credible. Anyhow, the worst hasn't happened.' Treasure was glad to be discussing François Cruba's survival as something factual: he just hoped the supposition was justified. 'The point is, we can do without the embarrassment of the kidnap story, and we can stop it providing a smokescreen.'

'You don't think it could have been a mugger, sir?'

'Who got lucky and grabbed a case with fifty thousand pounds in it? Too much of a coincidence, don't you think? It almost has to be someone who knew about the kidnap arrangements. Whether he was using them for political or personal advantage we don't know.'

'If it was political why didn't they just . . .'

'Take a pot shot any time? You should know your father's too popular in Ngonga again for his opponents to risk that. The new government would certainly have been blamed . . .'

'Correctly,' the boy put in sternly.

'Mmm . . . Well if that was proved they'd have been risking a counter-coup.'

'Gérard could lead one.'

'Well, that's very speculative, of course.' Even so, it was a scenario that had crossed Treasure's mind already. 'Let's assume it wasn't political. Tell me who knew about the money besides Mr Gold and his Major friend.'

'Miss Stopper knew . . . Er . . . did Mr Gold mention anyone else?' Pierre enquired tentatively.

'I asked the question first. All right, the answer's yes, to stop you breaking a confidence. He mentioned the curious Mr Stephen Spotter who wishes to remain unheard of.'

'Good. Then there's someone called Crow-Patcher, another sort of relative. He was here yesterday morning.'

'Did he see you?'

'No, I nipped up here, not that it made much difference. Miss Stopper told me afterwards she'd let on about the kidnap because she thought he knew already—from Stephen Spotter who'd been to see him. Miss Spotter was pretty angry about Stephen.'

'For blowing your story?'

'No. Well, that too, sir, but mostly for telling Mr Crow-Patcher not to co-operate in schemes to save the Rudyard Trust. Oh, and for telling him not to contact her. Not to let on he knew Stephen was in England—not for a few days.'

'But the chap had been down here first.'

'I know, sir. It's crazy. And when he was here he pretended to be all for saving the Trust.'

'But he didn't actually do anything to help, and when he saw Crow-Patcher he was busy hindering.'

'And he must have known he'd be found out eventually. Miss Spotter could have rung Crow-Patcher, or vice versa.'

'Mmm. What he wanted was a few days' grace. Mr Gold said he talked as though he were immensely rich. An oil baron.'

'I didn't believe him, sir.'

'No, neither did Gold.' Treasure smiled. 'So far as you know, only Mr Gold and the Major knew the trip to the Mall was just a blind?'

'That's right, sir, but one of the others could have twigged it of course, or pre . . . pre . . .'

'Pre-empted it?'

'Thank you. That's right, sir. Sent another taxi earlier, guessing my father wouldn't suspect anything. He wouldn't have, either. He said he was doing everything we asked.' There was shame in the boy's voice as he added, 'That's all he had to say at the end of the taped messages I phoned yesterday and this afternoon.'

'I heard about those,' said Treasure without emphasis. He looked at the time. 'I need a word with Miss Spotter, and one of those calls should be through about now. Why don't you pack up your things and join us downstairs?'

'I haven't heard from Stephen since he left here on Saturday afternoon, Mr Treasure.' Florence was very downcast.

'In your car, and without telling you which Airport hotel he was in.'

'We could check. There aren't so many,' Benny offered.

'Assuming he's using his real name,' said Treasure, who was seated at the desk. The other two were on the sofa.

'Also assuming he's staying in one,' added Benny.

Florence burst into tears at the probably justified imputations. 'He was such a dear little boy.' She produced a large mauve handkerchief from the sleeve of her blouse. 'I'm so sorry.' She blew her nose loudly. 'Such a disappointment. One naturally accepts people at their face value—especially relatives.' She blew her nose again.

'Stephen nobbled Miss Rudyard on the quiet,' Benny explained in an aggrieved tone: he supported the generalization about relatives. 'He said the same things to Mr Crow-Patcher.'

'Indeed he did,' said Florence with a sniffle.

Pierre appeared through the turret door. 'Ready, sir.' He smiled awkwardly at Benny, then sat on the edge of one of the upright chairs, dangling his Harrods' carrier bag.

'So far as we know, Spotter wasn't planning on seeing anyone else?' asked Treasure.

Florence shook her head as the telephone started to ring. Treasure's responses during the call were brief but he smiled encouragingly at Pierre several times.

'That was Gérard Opac. Mr Cruba is out of immediate danger. It's very good news, Pierre. Opac is taking your stepmother home and that's where I'm delivering you. Your father won't be seeable till tomorrow at the earliest. It seems also that Major Copper is free. Cleared by other witnesses. The Police must be pretty certain to have let him go.'

'He's not under arrest!' Benny exclaimed.

'Evidently not.' Treasure's smile signified more charity than he actually felt.

'Your Royal Highness.' The quavering greeting

emanated from the threshold of Florence's bedroom: the double doors had been thrown open dramatically. Poised in the opening was Miss Prudence Rudyard. She threw a deep curtsey in Treasure's direction. It went well enough going down but it subsequently became evident that rising again presented difficulties. There was a moment when a rally to the upright seemed possible, but the moment passed as Prudence sank back slowly to the floor. She was a study in ballooning red velvet — and a white silken toque crookedly embellished with a jewelled tiara.

She looked about her with the jerky neck movements of an affronted broody hen. Benny and Pierre hastened to her aid.

'Pray forgive the tardiness in my appearing, sire,' Prudence recited with a rich tremelo while affecting not to notice she was being assisted from the floor — lopsidedly since Pierre was applying more strength than his partner. 'The servants omitted to advise me of your Royal Highness's arrival.' She directed a meaningful glare at Florence. 'It wasn't until I observed your conveyance and retinue in the drive . . .' She blinked at Benny who was now well below her eye-level but still affecting to prop her up. She shook her arm from his, then turned her attention to Pierre, raising her lorgnette while retaining his still necessary support. 'The Royal Blackamoor, I perceive.' Pierre grinned amicably. 'With your Royal Highness's permission, I'll take that chair.'

Pierre guided his charge to the seat he had just vacated.

'This is my aunt, Miss Rudyard,' offered Florence. 'Pru, this is Mr Treasure, Mr Mark Treasure,' She repeated the surname with especial clarity.

'Indeed? A most remarkable likeness.' Prudence nodded loyally, acknowledging that if the Prince of Wales chose to travel incognito his secret was safe with her.

'Mr Treasure is to do with the Trust, Pru.'

'Naturally he's august. Have I not shown the proper deference to *Mister Treasure*. Oh, very droll,' She savoured her private joke, then enquired: 'You have been offered refreshment, sire?'

'Thank you, yes, Miss Rudyard,' Treasure answered untruthfully. Florence put a hand to her mouth in dismay at the omission. 'We can't stay, I'm afraid,' the banker continued hastily but carefully articulating every syllable. 'I hear your two great-nephews have been visiting you. Mr Spotter and Mr Crow-Patcher.'

'Nobody told me.'

'Stephen and Everard, Pru. They were here at the weekend. You remember?' Florence shouted desperately.

'Not deaf. Want to close down the Rudyard Trust. Quite right too. Very nearly a nasty accident. With the secateurs.' Prudence completed this unrelated sequence by staring accusingly at Benny. 'Florence could have been impaled,' came as an afterthought.

'Nothing of the sort, Pru,' her niece put in quickly. 'She insisted on getting up Saturday afternoon. Took Stephen upstairs to admire the stairway and the hall from above.'

'But not the guest suite?' Treasure asked, raising his eyebrows at Pierre who shook his head.

'I'd stupidly left the secateurs on the balustrade after doing the flowers. Stephen said Pru . . . I mean, someone accidentally knocked them over. I happened to be standing underneath. No harm done. They missed . . . didn't hit anything, I mean.' Florence finished in some confusion.

There was a moment's silence dramatically shattered by a loud hammering from outside.

'The front door,' Florence confirmed. 'But it's after eleven-thirty. Whoever could . . .'

'Probably the Vicar,' announced Miss Rudyard. 'We are not at home,' she added emphatically and much to Benny's evident if unexplained delight.

'I think we'd better be,' said Treasure. 'My driver's sitting in the car for a start. Perhaps if I answered?'

There were two police cars in the drive drawn up, the banker noted, so that there could be no movement from the Rolls in any direction. There were two uniformed officers standing under the porch, and two men in plain clothes with another in uniform talking to Pink in the drive.

'Good evening, sir. Is Miss Spotter at home, please?'

'I'm here, I'm here. Oh, it's Mr Jones.' Florence emerged from behind Treasure. 'Not on your bike?' she added.

' 'Evening, ma'am, No, got a lift tonight,' said Constable Jones, the older of the two, touching his helmet: his uniformed colleagues wore peaked caps. 'We saw the lights. You all right, Miss Spotter?'

Treasure concluded the remark about the lights was palpably untrue if the first observation was supposed to have been from the road. He also noticed the second policeman shift a heel into the door-jamb.

'Perfectly all right, thank you, Mr Jones.'

'And Miss Rudyard? She's all right too?'

'Yes, thank you. We're both in the pink.' Florence burst into a fit of nervous coughing. 'Oh dear. Swallowed the wrong way. Better now. How very kind of you to . . .'

'Could we come in a minute, then?' The policeman, like his colleague, was now keeping his gaze on Treasure as were the others in the drive.

'Yes . . . I suppose so. Yes, please do come in.' It was Florence who was now eyeing the banker most earnestly and evidently beseeching guidance as she spoke.

'My name's Treasure.' He stood aside to let the two into the hall.

'We gathered that from your chauffeur, sir. Paying a late call, is it?' Despite twenty-two years' service on the Surrey/Berkshire border Evan Jones's Welsh accent was as true as the day he had left Tonypandy.

'Picking up a young friend who's been staying with Miss
Stopper. Actually we were just leaving.'

'I see, sir. There was another gentleman who came with
you like?'

'Yes, Mr Gold.'

'And the young friend, sir?'

'Pierre Cruba.'

'We thought it might be, sir.'

'They're both through here, Mr Jones, with Miss
Rudyard. If Miss Spotter doesn't mind, you're welcome to
meet them.'

Florence was only too pleased to have the responsibility
of directing Constable Jones's next move taken firmly out
of her hands.

Treasure, in turn, aware the door to the studio was
open had been offering his proposals in a voice almost
loud enough to have alerted Miss Rudyard herself.

A few minutes later the banker was showing Jones back
through the hall. The second policeman had left already,
though Treasure suspected in time to inspect the other
downstairs rooms before actually rejoining the others in
the drive.

'Well, that's all right then,' said the Constable. 'Not
often mistaken for a royal bodyguard.' He chuckled.
'She's very good for her age, sir, don't you think? And it's
my belief she knows perfectly well what's going on. Just
enjoys a bit of make-believe. And where's the harm in
that?'

'Perhaps now you can tell *me* what's going on, Mr
Jones,' Treasure enquired affably.

'Pleasure, sir. Didn't want to alarm the ladies, of
course. Not over a hoax. Especially not Miss Rudyard.'
He paused at the open front door. 'The Station got a call,
see. Anonymous it was, saying Mr Cruba was being held
here against his will. Kidnapped, like. Had to treat it

seriously. I said a warrant wouldn't be needed. Guessed it was a hoax. Known the ladies for a long time.'

'But you came in strength.'

'CID, the lot. You get very fast back-up in this area, sir,' said Jones proudly. 'Had to be sure the ladies weren't being held under duress, of course. Lonely house, this. Big too. Wonder why they keep it on, really. Anyway, if you're leaving now, sir, we'll wait to see you off. Then we can get the ladies tucked down.' He smiled warmly but indicated he had no intention of moving from where he was.

'We're on our way, Mr Jones. Ready, you two?' Treasure called back into the house with undisguised urgency.

It was obvious the news of the assault on François Cruba had not been included in the so-called hoaxer's intelligences. The banker decided not to volunteer the information which would no doubt filter through to the Surrey Police in due time. Immediately, he was more anxious than ever to have Pierre re-installed in the Cruba household—a more appropriate base for the issuing of whatever denials might be necessary than isolated, mock-Norman castles.

CHAPTER 14

At the time Treasure and party were leaving Rudwold Park a nervous, exhausted Everard Crow-Patcher was paying off a taxi outside the flat in Guilford Street. 'Keep the change.' He thrust a note at the driver.

'Ain't any. Exactly two quid,' came the prompt, laconic response.

'Sorry. Here's another. Take . . .' He noticed the two policemen patrolling up the other side of the road.

'That's all right. Been a nasty evening.'

The cabbie stopped the slow fumble for silver. 'Thank you, guv,' but his late passenger was already out of hearing, having difficulty fitting a key in a street door.

'Everard?' The call had come from the living-room: he had hoped she would be in bed.

He swallowed. 'Coming, my love.' He put the black attaché case inside the hall cupboard, took it out again, paused uncertainly, then put it back where he had it before, behind the Hoover. He'd decide about the money in the morning.

'Everard, you're soaked.

'Dried out nearly. It was raining, or didn't you notice? Nothing like it since the flaming Flood. Shower in a minute. Drink first.' He took off his jacket, poured himself a huge scotch, and dropped into his usual chair. He gulped at the drink. 'Plenty to tell you.' He thought he had the authorized version ready for promulgation.

'You located Stephen Spotter?' He quite missed the disquiet in her tone.

'Where I said. Top of those steps. *And* he was early, but not too early for yours truly; oh no.' His confidence was building.

'He didn't see you?'

'Well, I wasn't exactly waving a flag. Went down to the bottom and waited—in the monsoon. He came past me like a bat out of hell, pelted up the Mall to Spring Gardens—that's at the end by Admiralty Arch. He'd parked his car there—Florence's car—on the corner, and they'd towed the bloody thing away.' He slapped his leg and gave a great hoot of laughter. 'That's how I caught him—well, caught up with him. Police had towed away his getaway car. Thought he'd have apoplexy.'

'But he got the money?' Dina was concerned with the tangibles.

'Oh yes. Your Mr Big was after the piddling fifty

thousand all right. Said he would be. Cruba must have
been there like Santa Claus dishing out largesse to all
comers. Could have handled it myself.'

'No, you couldn't. Would have taken guts.'

He looked hurt, but inwardly he agreed. 'Couldn't be
certain about the police, of course. But they weren't
there. It was just as planned, except the geriatric
kidnapper got nothing.'

'How much did you get?'

'Difficult, that bit. He was grateful, of course, relieved
too, at first, that I wasn't the ever vigilant constabulary.
Didn't recognize me straightaway. Knew there was someone after him. Called his name.'

'How much?'

He ignored the repeated question and continued
earnestly. 'Got him off the street. Not having transport
and all that. Pity I'd sold the BMW. Cheap too,' he
reflected bitterly. 'Anyway, walked him straight to the
Institute of Directors, round the corner. The RAC would
have been better, but too far in the rain.'

It went without saying Everard belonged to neither
establishment. He used all the larger London Clubs and
with what he considered a nice lack of discrimination in
view of the wide differences in the quality of the services
and quite probably the size of the membership fees. The
Royal Automobile Club happened to be his marginal
favourite at the moment. The name lent credibility to his
standing as a motor-trader.

'And you divided the money?' Dina tried a new tack.

'Went to the washroom in the basement. Great hangar
of a place. Plenty of privacy. Always is.'

'How much?'

'I thought you'd be pleased about that.' He reached for
his discarded jacket and from various pockets began
producing bundles of bank notes—slowly, like a conjurer.
'Five thousand,' he announced boldly.

'Not enough. You were robbed.'

'Actually it was Cruba . . .' He let the attempted witticism get strangled by a nervous giggle. Then he looked suitably crestfallen: he wanted her to think he knew she was right, which she was if you didn't count the other bundles in the briefcase. Those he would use for paying off the overdraft. 'It's ten per cent. He took all the risk. I mean I didn't get involved till I knew there was no one else after him.'

'Should have got more.' She was sizing him up with a look that made him think she knew he *had* got more. 'Everard, there's something . . .'

'It gets better,' he injected. 'We made the phone call. I made it, actually, tipping off the Egham Police about the kidnap. Where the boy was. Stephen said he'd have done it. That's what he meant Sunday, saying we shouldn't take any notice if we heard someone was bailing out the Rudyard. He'd intended to ring a newspaper . . .'

'A newspaper! For crying out loud, that Trust would've been in the headlines for ever. Listen . . .'

'Exactly. I said the police'd be better. Publicity the last thing we wanted. He understood. My way news of the kidnap may never get out. Important thing's to be sure Cruba won't need to pay the ransom tomorrow, that there's nothing to stop the Trust being wound up . . .'

'Lover, it looks like Mr Cruba won't have to pay anyone anything again. They just said on the newscast Mr Cruba was stabbed on those steps tonight. They made it sound like tomorrow he'll be the late Mr Cruba. So we'd better figure how to get rid of that money and any more of it you've got stashed away.' He faked outrage at the last suggestion. 'The dough may be marked,' she added. 'We don't want you traced along with your second cousin for murdering anybody. You know how to reach him?'

Everard was sucking in air. His lips were drawn back tightly over clenched teeth.

'Who saw you together?'

'Only about half the members of the Institute of Directors.' He'd never freeload there again. 'Look, I'm positive Stephen didn't stab Cruba,' he insisted with utter conviction. 'There was no reason. The man was waiting to part with the money. Stephen just got in first. He didn't have to stab anybody.'

'He didn't have to. The police are looking for two men—two men and a missing attaché case. Black hide. Did Stephen get rid of it?'

A suddenly ashen Everard nodded. 'He got rid of it.'

Stephen Spotter had heard no news bulletin. He had double-locked the door to his room in the Grosvenor Hotel next to Victoria Station and gone to bed. It was the third and best hotel he had been in since his arrival, showing caution and his improved financial state.

It wasn't late but he needed to be up early to join the holiday charter flight to Dubrovnik from Gatwick Airport. Once in Jugoslavia he intended to settle in for a long relaxing summer. The Americans had no extradition arrangements with the Jugoslavs covering fraud. The chances were the California Court would lose interest anyway after a while. His luck had been in getting bail in the first place—because the Los Angeles jails were overflowing with people awaiting trial for violent crimes. It was an ill wind . . .

It wasn't through luck that he had had two passports. They wouldn't start looking for him outside the USA for a while even when he didn't show up for the trial on Friday, not with the Court holding a valid passport.

As a British national all he had to do was stay clear of the USA for ever—and from the UK for a decent interval. Covering his tracks since Saturday had been easy, and he was mighty glad he'd come.

At the start he had intended just to borrow money from

the old girls. He had never believed there was much to the Miff letter: the wording had been too careful—too 'iffy'. Then everything had come up roses.

When Florence had first spilled the news of the kidnap he had meant to tip off the police as soon as he was clear of Rudwold Park himself. That was before the others arrived and told him about the fifty thousand—his for the taking, if he got in ahead of the Major, and still with time to blow the kidnap before Cruba needed to pay any life-saving half-million to the charity.

And to think he had been conning his way around the world all these years when he was in line for a legitimate stake in a thing as big as the Rudyard Trust wind-up.

It was a long time since he had been in phoney oil exploration—or Texas. His last racket had been insurance. If only he had known about the potential in the Rudyard business he could have been here much earlier, moving it along. Facing facts, though, he wondered if he could have done as neat a job as Cousin Edna: that was some operator—deserving too. He thought back to their first meeting in the South of France all those years ago.

His father had been killed during the war. His mother had never remarried and had worked very hard to keep a home going. They never took proper holidays, but his grandfather, the Reverend Canon George Spotter had been filling-in as Assistant Anglican Chaplain in Nice one August. He and his wife had taken Stephen along.

Just about the first soul to come forward—not for curing but for old times' sake—had been Fay Crow-Patcher, intrepid survivor of several divorces, countless scandalous love-affairs and a German occupation. She was as ebullient and vivacious as the Canon remembered her from the 'twenties—and even more of an embar-rassment to the family and his cloth since she had reverted to her maiden name *and* embraced the Roman faith: maidenhood and piety were not conditions convincingly evoked by Fay Crow-Patcher.

The lady had been given tea and no encouragement to call again: her exposure to the eight-year-old, impressionable Stephen had been minimal. He being afterwards instructed that further intercourse with this intriguing, new-found relative was expressly forbidden, took every opportunity to foster some. This had not been difficult since Fay lived close by, the beach was common ground, and the Reverend Canon and his wife given to staying indoors, out of the sun, composing anti-œcumenical letters to *The Times* about Popish plots.

Thus Stephen alone had met Edna—down for a visit later in the month. She was the sole progeny of Fay's short-lived marriage to a ship's engineer, an honest Scot called McSlope. He had sternly abjured the offered pleasures of bedding without wedding but had been equally insistent about exclusive rights after the ceremony. Fay had had other ideas.

McSlope had been given custody of Edna after the divorce. Any doubts he had harboured about being her real father had been dispelled as she grew older, less like her mother, more like him—and increasingly dour, a propensity he was certain she could not have inherited from any of Fay's frivolous paramours.

The girl had been brought up by McSlope's God-fearing mother. She had not seen Fay from infancy until the visit to Nice that had coincided with Stephen's: by then she was already earning her own living as a secretary in Glasgow.

Stephen's next meeting with Edna had been on the Miff threshold two nights before. He had never told his grandparents nor his mother that he knew her, and thinking back he figured he was now probably the only member of the family aware of her existence. Assuming she was dead had been thoughtless—careless even. The

bare news of Fay's own demise had been transmitted to
him years ago in Hong Kong—at the age of sixty-one she
had broken her neck on the Cresta Run. There had been
no mention of Edna then, and somehow her memory had
merged with that of her irrepressible mother.

It was just dandy that a direct descendant of
Marmaduke, brighter than Crow-Patcher, saner than
Prudence, and clean of philanthropic hogwash (like
Florence) was standing ready to see the Trust obliterated.
All he had to do was sit and wait, and with £35,000 in
used notes to do it with he could afford the interval. He
had done his bit: there'd be no rescue payment for the
Rudyard Trust tomorrow.

Right now he was relenting his generosity to Everard
earlier: £5,000 should have been enough, £10,000 at the
most—£15,000 was ridiculous. So at least he could count
on the guy's loyalty.

Stephen's only serious concern was Clarence Miff. The
man was a loser. Before Edna came along he had been on
the take. He had also nearly been caught—would have
been if Edna hadn't arranged to pay his previous
secretary to take the blame for a 'misunderstanding'. All
this had come out in the conversation Saturday evening
with Miff present but mostly asleep. It was also clear
Edna was genuinely fond of the slob. But why had she
had to marry him, for heaven's sake?

The question was, would Miff fall apart if there was
any deep probing? The whole thing could be plain sailing
unless the merchant bank trustees made problems—
applied themselves to what they should have been doing
for years. Stephen's service with a British colonial bank
had left him with a commendable awareness of other
people's responsibilities.

There were credible answers, for instance, about why
the residents' fees had been jacked up so drastically in the
time since Edna had been effectively in charge. Simply,

Stephen Spotter would rather it were she and not her husband who did the explaining. It would have been better still, of course, if she had been merely his secretary and not his wife. There could be millions at stake, literally, and it looked as though a fifth would belong to him. What if Clarence fumbled things, got faced with charges or irresponsible conduct — even criminally irresponsible conduct?

Stephen put the light on again and sat up in bed. Edna wouldn't face the fact but Miff was a liability — could screw up the whole works. He took a cigarette from the pack on the bedside table. Then, for no especial reason, he switched on the radio and found himself listening to the start of a news broadcast.

Yvonne Cruba lay alone in the centre of the immense bed. She was naked and restless. She pouted at her reflection in a sequence of mirrors. How much longer would he be?

She had played the distraught wife for long enough this evening. She might still have to do the prostrate widow bit tomorrow. Those cheerful medical bulletins were almost certainly meant just to keep her spirits up — hers and Pierre's — till her husband's fifty-fifty chance of survival swung one way or the other.

Should she feel guilty about not feeling guilty? She had been through this before in her imagination: often. Now it was for real and — yes, she could live with it. More: if François died she could live with it, knowing the other possibility had had no flavour — now, this minute, but . . . *Che sarà, sarà.*

She had not asked for the marriage in the first place. She had never been in love until Gérard Opac came into her life. Then what could she do?

The front door was closed noisily. A car drew away from the house. That would be Mark Treasure leaving.

She had begged François not to deliver that money himself: everybody knew that. Instead he had walked into danger—a trap set by his adored, indulged son. Never mind who sprung it: never? Again she steeled her mind.

He didn't knock—just stepped into the room, closed the door swiftly and stood leaning against it. The strain was evident in his eyes—so was his longing for her. It was the first time they had been alone since the meeting at the hospital. There had been doctors, policemen, well-meaning friends—always someone around right up to the time Treasure had brought back Pierre.

Yvonne had slapped the boy hard across the face. Then she had come straight up to the bedroom.

She was not sure why she had hit so hard. She knew why she had hit that sanctimonious woman's son: planned to hit him. It had been a gesture she was sure Treasure would judge logical—emotionally justified. But it had been intended as an act, not something she had expected especially to enjoy.

As for Pierre, he had taken the punishment without flinching but also without any expression of remorse. It was as though he knew she was playing a part in what was a charade for her but a tragedy for him. His expression said he knew.

'I don't think I should stay. Are you all right?' Opac spoke quietly.

She scrambled off the bed and rushed across the room to him, throwing her arms around his neck, burying her face in his chest, pulling him to her. 'Stay. Stay. Then I'll be all right.'

'If he dies . . .' He hesitated, putting his hand under her chin and lifting her face so that she was looking at him.

'If he dies,' she repeated in a whisper, 'if he dies you did it for me. That's all.'

He took hold of her shoulders and held her away from

him. '*You* think I did it?'

She nodded slowly: there was no ignoring the utter conviction in her eyes.

So how long would it be before others . . . ?

CHAPTER 15

Molly Treasure touched her husband lightly on the shoulder. 'Stay where you are. I'll get it.' She took his empty glass and filled it from the second can of lager he had brought from the kitchen. He had been back only a few minutes.

They were in the first-floor drawing-room at Cheyne Walk. Freddy Hinterton was with them: he had arrived half an hour before to wait for Treasure. It was just after midnight: the banker appeared tired.

'Mark, you must be sick of the whole thing. Would you rather I shoved off now? Let you get to bed?' Freddy, with teacup in hand, looked every bit as earnest as he sounded—and pastoral with it.

'No,' Treasure protested firmly. 'I've given you my story, now I want yours: in detail.' He took the glass from Molly. 'By the way, I meant to ask, did you come through the back door disguised as a meter reader?'

Freddy showed polite amusement. 'I don't believe anyone saw us in the Mall and I thought it safer to drop in here than arrange to meet in the morning—especially after what's happened.'

'My Mr Gold saw us. Took you for a top copper.' Treasure smiled at his wife who was now studying a scrawled message in her own handwriting. She had it at arm's length as the alternative to finding and donning her glasses. 'Problems, darling?'

'I forgot to tell you, Florence Spotter rang, in a tizz.

Said to tell you Stephen Spotter asked for Mr Miff's private address before he left on Saturday. Seemed to think it important and . . . oh yes, she didn't have the address.'

'It's in the book. Gérard Opac just looked it up for me.' Her husband frowned; so did their guest. 'And then there were three,' Treasure mused aloud but without explanation. 'Mmm . . . So. Come on, Freddy. To the scene of the crime. What did you find out?'

'There were two men besides this Major chap. They could've been working separately or . . . or . . .'

'Together?' Suggested Molly with wide-eyed, affected innocence.

'Very likely. In collusion. Difficult to decide, really.' Freddy's serious expression deepened. 'One came down the steps. He was tall, in a trench-coat, hat pulled over his eyes. He got the case from Cruba.'

'There was a witness to that?' asked Treasure sharply.

'Not exactly. You see they all sort of had their heads down—or under brollies. It was pelting, as you know . . .'

'Not even the Major? He didn't see this fellow take the case?'

Freddy shook his head. 'He's not sure, Mark, he only knows he saw the chap beetle down past Cruba. Definitely had an attaché case in one hand . . .'

'Like the one Opac said Cruba was carrying—hard-cornered job?'

'That's right. Chap was using it to barge his way through the people. Several said so . . .'

'The people from the gallery?' Treasure asked.

'Yes, but the Major—his name's Copper—'

'Bad casting,' declared Molly.

'Not necessarily. He's kind of on our side now,' her husband put in drily.

'Major Copper,' said Freddy loudly, pausing to re-gather his audience, 'he was quite close to Cruba, five or six steps behind, when the first man went past him going down and someone else came by fast from below. So he says.'

'Short? Tall? Young? Was he white or black?' Treasure pressed.

'Problem there. He could well be the killer but no one got a sight of his features. He was wearing a long plastic mac — voluminous thing, with a hood. Not transparent, though.'

'He had the hood up, and he was going in the direction of everybody else,' Molly speculated. 'And as you said, they were all looking down anyway.'

'That's it exactly. He could have been tall and stooping . . .'

'You mean the Major said he looked short?' she asked.

'He and the other witnesses didn't seem to agree about that, but yes, the Major thought he was probably shortish.'

'And he got between Copper and Cruba . . .'

'When Copper was nearly in touching distance. Assume he did the stabbing, then ran like hell. Copper didn't know what had happened but saw Cruba start to crumple . . .'

'He was sure the first man couldn't have had the knife?' This was Treasure. 'I mean, obviously it all happened very quickly.'

'Copper wasn't sure of anything, but Cruba was stabbed in the back. It's possible, of course, the first man . . .'

'But unlikely, come to think of it. It almost has to be the second chap, unless . . . But go on, Freddy.'

'Copper says he tried to hold up Cruba, couldn't manage the weight, lowered him on to the steps, then saw the knife . . .'

'What sort of knife?'

'No idea. Never saw it. Didn't ask — suppose I should

have done. Copper took hold of the handle. Was going to pull it out.'

'I wonder they let him go with his fingerprints on . . .'

'Natural reflex action on his part,' put in Molly unexpectedly.

'Retired nurse in the crowd stopped him,' Freddy continued. 'Possibly saved Cruba's life, it seems.'

'That's right.' It was Molly again: knowingly. 'Might have bled to death otherwise.'

'How d'you know that?' asked her husband.

'Red Cross classes.' The patrician nose was tilted upwards.

'On how to cope with malicious stabbings? I don't believe it. You only went to one.'

'I expect that was the one.' She made a face at her husband. 'Well, perhaps it was Ngaio Marsh, then.' She smiled at Freddy. 'So the short-tall-fat-thin man of unknown race, creed or colour got clean away?'

'Anyone see which way?' Treasure asked.

'Unfortunately no. Everyone too surprised . . .'

'Or too late,' said the banker without thinking.

'I'm very sorry . . .'

'I didn't mean your people, Freddy. When did Opac appear?'

The visitor looked up sharply. 'Didn't he tell you?'

'Yes.'

There was a pause. 'See what you mean. I think he got there after me. Told the police he was getting his car — it was parked in Waterloo Place. He noticed the commotion . . .'

'Ho, ho,' Molly interrupted confidently. 'So he could have done the deed, skipped and come back again.'

'Highly unlikely, of course,' observed her husband — but thoughtfully.

'He left the dinner before the speeches were over.' Freddy faltered, before adding, 'Sounds boorish, I know, but I rang someone else who was there. Old friend. Strictest confidence and all that.' He looked from one to the other for approval. 'He says Opac slipped out around nine-forty-five. No later.'

'That's about what he told me,' Treasure commented. 'Against Cruba's wishes, he intended to be at the steps . . .'

'So why did it take him so long?' asked Molly.

'He left the dinner *between* speeches. He didn't want to risk upsetting the next speaker by leaving in the middle.'

'Quite proper,' said Freddy. 'Nothing worse than people who . . .'

'He found it was still raining.' Treasure had nodded to show he accepted his guest's intended homily on after-dinner etiquette without the need to hear it. 'He got his coat, then hung about ready to make a dash for the Mall at ten-fifteen.'

'Which sounds about right,' confirmed Freddy as though still anxious to excuse his checking on Opac in the first place.

'Anyone see him "hanging about", I wonder?' asked Molly innocently. 'I mean, was he chatting up the porter at the Reform, or counting raindrops in the porch, or ordering taxis on the telephone?' She paused for effect — and got some. 'Half an hour's a jolly long time . . .'

'Whatever he was doing, according to him, he stayed in the Club, which means someone must have seen him.' Treasure seemed to be thinking aloud. 'Should be possible to find out what time that taxi was ordered. Mr Gold noted the number.'

'Is Gérard Opac a member of the Reform? Would he be known?'

'I don't think so.' Treasure answered his wife. 'But he's an impressive chap, as you know. He was wearing a dinner-jacket . . . and he is black. If he's telling the truth he shouldn't have difficulty finding witnesses. If he's lying he'd have cooked up a better story.'

'Advantage Opac.' Molly smiled and began smoothing the folds from the black and gold silk kaftan she was wearing. 'How was Yvonne Cruba dressed?'

'Trouser suit. Dark linen, I think,' her husband replied. 'Rather stunning. Obviously made an effort despite . . .'

'Desolate with worry, I expect.'

There was silence for a moment after this barbed observation from Molly.

'Good Lord. D'you think it's a case of *cherchez la femme*?' enquired the forty-two-year-old bachelor Freddy in surprise.

'Well if it is, we don't need to search very far.'

'Yvonne is shocked and . . . and not completely rational. Understandable, I should have thought.' Treasure fixed his wife with a look that implied, 'Don't push slanderous insinuations at a time like this.' He received an answering glare meant to read, 'I get all my best insinuations from you.'

'You said she wasn't in when you rang the house after leaving me?' began Freddy, aware that silent exchanges were going on and determined to air a vocal one.

'Opac says he phoned her from the hospital as soon as he got there,' said Treasure. 'She'd cried off going to the dinner herself. Opac was supposed to have taken her.'

'So she threw something over her rather stunning trouser suit and pointed her fleet-footed Merc eastwards—let's hope only once this evening,' Molly commented, watching the expressions on the faces of the men. She paused. 'No, somehow I can't see Yvonne in an off-the-peg plastic mac. Not in any circumstances.'

Treasure frowned. 'Whoever stabbed Cruba did it either for political reasons—and that doesn't dismiss Opac—or else to stop him giving money to the Rudyard

Trust tomorrow.'

'But politically Opac and Cruba are on the same side?'
Molly intended to sound ingenuous.

'What Mark means is Opac may have tried a short
route to assuming Cruba's mantle,' put in Freddy,
worried. 'He stands for all the things Cruba does in the
eyes of Ngongans but he's . . . well . . . clean. He didn't
get rich by dubious means. Cruba's — er — martyrdom
might actually improve the chances of the elected
government being recalled — with Opac as leader.'

'So he'd get the job and the . . . the trimmings?' asked
Molly lightly, and without attempting to enlarge on the
implications in the question.

'Risky but conceivable,' said her husband. In fact, he
had found Freddy's premise difficult to credit — but then
the man from the FO was supposed to be the expert. 'I'd
have thought it'd make more sense if we tried pinning the
crime on the present government . . .'

'Whose agents don't know about the kidnap or the
opportunity it offered.'

'Quite right, Freddy.' Treasure shrugged his shoulders.
'Which brings us to those we might say had a charitable
motive. Members of the Rudyard family — or, more likely,
the inexplicable Miff.'

'Why him in preference to a Rudyard?' This was
Molly.

'Because he seems to have been working harder than
any of them to put the Trust out of business, and because
every Rudyard — excluding Prudence — seems to have
known about the kidnap and where Pierre was being
held.'

'And Prudence doesn't matter?'

'No, darling, she doesn't. One of the other Rudyards
must have tipped off the Egham Police tonight. Any of
them could've done that and avoided the drastic
alternative of trying to murder Cruba.'

'Which leaves Miff,' said Freddy with deepening interest.

'Who we're guessing didn't know about the kidnap but who certainly knew about the imminence of Cruba's gift.' Treasure studied his glass for a moment. 'Spotter may have been to see him with the idea of buying his co-operation over liquidating the Trust. Seems to have been bending everybody else's ear.'

'It'd be natural to assume the Director would be opposed to the thing folding,' Freddy offered.

'In which case the opportunist Spotter was in for a pleasant surprise,' said Treasure.

'If Miff confessed he'd been running down the Clubs,' his wife added.

'Drastic revelations prompting Spotter to cough up a few of his own. Trouble is, if Miff was told about the kidnap he could've rung the police too.'

'There's a middle possibility,' said Freddy slowly. 'That Spotter at some point told Miff where Cruba would be at the right time tonight — on the Duke of York steps. I don't know why Miff is so anxious to have the Trust liquidated . . .'

'But whatever the reason, he learned nine hours ago that years of shameful effort have been wasted.' Treasure spoke deliberately. 'Jonkins delivered the witnessed declaration to Miff himself. It states Cruba is giving half a million tomorrow afternoon — and the gift's irrevocable.'

'Miff's a lawyer.'

Treasure nodded at his guest. 'Probably not a very good one, and almost certainly a crooked one.'

Molly raised a hand. 'Please sir, or sirs, when does a gift become irrevocable?'

'In this case when it's been executed,' her husband replied, smiling. 'We took extra trouble with the drafting for obvious reasons.'

'And if the giver . . . the donor . . . if he dies before it's executed!' Molly pressed.

'His heirs could plead for it to be set aside. If it went to Court they'd almost certainly win—especially if it came out the thing was drawn up under duress.'

'You think we're on to something, Mark?' Freddy's tone was rhetorical.

'Tell you more in the morning. I've a date to see friend Miff in his office at 8.30. Nearly cancelled it while I was with Opac. Original intention was to go over the immediate disposition of the new funds . . .'

'Which won't be materializing.'

'No, Freddy, they won't. Opac was anxious I should see Miff anyway to tell him, get that declaration back, and browbeat him into keeping his mouth shut. I think that's right.' Treasure smirked. 'I'll assess his potential as a murderer at the same time.'

'You'll be careful, darling?'

'Don't worry. From what Jonkins told me, Miff's in no condition for fisticuffs—nor, I suppose, for mounting steps at the double, which bruises our hypothesis a bit. Still . . .' he paused. 'Freddy, what are the police doing about the assault? They seem to have given you all the confidences deserved by a Foreign Office mogul.'

'Oh, I don't know,' replied Freddy a touch bashfully but evidently aware he had pulled rank with some success. 'It was knowing Cruba that did it. The Inspector at Cannon Row Station seemed grateful. Their theory's very simple. Pair of hit-and-run thieves. One got the bag, the other's job to stop pursuit. Common enough crime these days, apparently, the violence not excepted. They're not specially hopeful about catching the culprits.'

'And they didn't know about the kidnap, what was in the bag, why Cruba was there?'

'Not so far as I know. They were naturally concerned the victim was a VIP.'

'Mmm. Of course the Surrey Police are bound to

compare notes with them over what we passed off as a kidnap hoax. May have done already, except these things often take longer to filter through than one guesses.'

'What's the party line—to deny there was a kidnap?' asked Freddy.

'Not to say anything about it unless we're obliged to, and if that happens I hope François Cruba'll be well enough to make the decision himself. His reasons for avoiding telling anyone there'd been a kidnap still hold—more especially if it has to come out he parted with fifty thousand pounds.'

'You think the police might agree to keep silent if they knew?'

'Difficult, I'd have thought, even with a word from the FO. Don't know where my Mr Gold and your Major Copper would stand.' Treasure pulled himself up out of the chair. 'I'll go and ring the hospital. See if there's any change.'

'Then I must leave, Mark.'

The banker stopped on his way out of the room. 'D'you think you could arrange a very confidential word with your Intelligence Chief?'

'What, with the two of us?' asked Freddy with a marked lack of enthusiasm.

'No, just yourself. I don't want to be involved.'

'Yes, I should think so . . . I mean, if necessary.'

Molly wryly judged the speaker was hoping very much the necessity wouldn't arise.

CHAPTER 16

It was raining again on Tuesday morning. There were no natural pyrotechnics to keep cautious secretaries from using electric typewriters: no doom-laden darkness after dawn giving new hope to the banner-carrying 'The End is Nigh' fraternity, foiled again the day before. It just rained.

Clarence Miff and Hercules had made their fitful progress from Greywick Court Mansions to Strutton Ground under the shared protection of a large umbrella.

They were attached to each other by a leather lead, so both stopped while the dog performed his morning offices—in gutters, against favourite lamp-posts, some gates, and selected parking meters. If the urban topography did not allow for the brolly to cover both master and dog at all times, Miff being English, it always covered the dog. The reward was an unblinking, baleful canine stare immediately before and during the not always productive pauses.

For the rest, Hercules had plodded forward along the well-known route in the 'seek and stalk' posture. He kept close to the feet of the ruminating Miff—extremities which because of the animal's failing eyesight (not any less worthy reason) he could scent better than see, even at close quarters.

They reached number fifty-two at five to eight: the changed appointment time was eight o'clock. When he awoke two hours before Miff had contemplated the coming interview with something approaching terror. He was still deeply apprehensive but somewhat more resigned: The brandy had done the trick.

It was early, even for Strutton Ground regulars. The shops were closed: the market stalls not yet assembled. The few human figures in view were hurrying about their business disaccommodated by the rain and the cars hissing through to Victoria Street.

Miff searched for his keys before noticing the big street door was already fastened back in its office-hours position. It surprised him that some other tenant must have arrived already. He undid the leash: Hercules lumbered into the building. The dog always started first up the stairs but finished last, usually a flight behind his master.

The Rudyard Trust Director continued to commune with himself as he began the ascent, inhaling deeply on what was left of the wet cigarette clamped between his lips. How desperately he needed Edna to be right: she usually was, except in this case he was certain it was the plausible Stephen Spotter's judgement she had been using and not her own.

Even after yesterday's visit from Jonkins—even after that Edna had gone on believing in Spotter. He shook his head. It was of no significance to him that neither he nor his wife had heard a news broadcast since six the previous evening: the morning paper, delivered to the flat, he had left there for Edna, unopened.

Hercules was taking his usual breather on the first-floor landing. 'That's a good boy. Keep going,' his master uttered involuntarily.

Spotter was an over-confident fraud. Accepting he had been right about Cruba's fearful donation, how could he have been certain the money would never reach the Rudyard? Had *he* been prepared to do something desperate to stop the transfer?

Nor had Spotter been the one who had schemed and hoodwinked, risked a professional status, lived a lie for years while manipulating the demise of the very institution he was employed to foster. He would never begin to know the mental burden that put on a man; even Edna made too little allowance.

And Spotter had not been the one presented with a sworn declaration yesterday predicting four years' work had gone for nothing. Spotter believed in miracles—but he didn't have a date in five minutes with a tycoon of a clearly different persuasion.

He paused on the second-floor landing. Edna had been

content—even anxious—to let him go it alone at the Treasure meeting. She was convinced the two would be discussing what would shortly prove a fiction—Cruba's gift. There was no reason why Edna needed to be there but several why she should avoid an encounter with the banker until it was unavoidable.

Miff searched for the time-switches that operated the lights over the next flight and the one he had just climbed. Not content with banning permanent lighting in common areas, a parsimonious landlord allowed regulated illumination for less time than it would have taken a dedicated jogger to progress from floor to floor. As a point of principle, Miff always re-lit the way behind for Hercules: it was a small satisfaction, although a comfort that went unrecognized by the dog.

Of course, both the Miffs knew there would eventually be some kind of showdown over the way the charity had been run. They had banked all along on this happening too late to affect the issue: now, who could tell? At least there had been no criminal action involved: Miff had been assuring himself of this regularly for years.

Naturally, eyebrows might be raised when it came out Edna was a Rudyard. There was still nothing in that nit-picking list of caveats in the Deed to stop Marmaduke's relatives working for the Trust. Better: Edna had uncovered a precedent. Edward Rudyard, Marmaduke's youngest son, had been Assistant Secretary at one of the Clubs in 1915 while waiting to come of age to join the army and get killed. He had been paid for the work: the records showed it.

Miff pushed at the door of the third floor WC as he passed. It swung open: the lock had broken again. 'Come on, Hercules. Bikkies,' he called back down the stairwell. The animal was thrusting onwards and upwards: you could hear his paws on the brass-edged steps. His master extinguished the cigarette, then walked along the corridor and up the steep flight to the attic floor. The stairs were differently placed from the others in the building, springing from the end and not the centre of the previous floor. They were unbroken by a half-landing, and had no light of their own.

He opened the door at the top with his Yale key, stepped into the outer office and turned to call again to the dog.

The savage blow to his neck came from behind. It was made with a heavy spanner wrapped in towelling. As he collapsed, he was spun about and thrust backwards down the stairs.

The back of his head hit the middle steps before his spreadeagled body bumped and rolled nearly to the bottom. He lay there quite still, a misshapen, oversized human bundle partly shrouded by a broken wet umbrella; the dog-lead had wrapped itself around one ankle. A hand had caught in the lower balustrading. Two triangular dog biscuits had fallen from his open palm onto the corridor floor.

Hercules sniffed at the hand, and glanced sideways at the rest of Miff. Then he ate the biscuits.

Treasure came upon Miff at eight-twenty-five: the ambulance men were first on the scene after his 999 call.

The leader of the stretcher team was optimistic. 'He's still warm. Could be a pulse. You haven't moved him? Good. Get him to hospital quick, that's the thing.' It was all in the day's work: words of comfort included. 'Easy does it, George.'

As Miff was being expertly borne away a pert police-woman in her early twenties appeared from below. She was followed by a bulky, older male colleague.

WPC Wilson was all speed and efficiency. Treasure's name and address were promptly noted, also his business with the Rudyard Trust. No, he could not positively identify Miff, but he knew who he had to be. No, he hadn't witnessed the accident, only discovered and reported it. Yes, he could supply Miff's address, and yes, he believed there was a Mrs Miff who would be the next of kin.

'We'll have to follow the ambulance, Mr Treasure. It'll be St Thomas's Hospital. See what happens then.' The girl had snapped shut the notebook.

'I think he's a goner,' the banker volunteered.

'So do they, sir.' She nodded in the direction of the departed ambulance men. 'But we all have to keep to the book.'

'I think I should try to reach Mrs Miff myself.' That Treasure was spurred by a sense of responsibility, not enthusiasm, must have been clear from the tone.

'If you'd rather leave that to us, sir,' she offered obligingly. 'Usually better in a case like this. If he's alive we'll get her to him, don't worry.'

'If not?'

'We'll see her anyway, sir.' She glanced up at the open door to the office: a bunch of keys was hanging from the lock. 'Would you be staying on here for a bit, sir?'

'I'll hold the fort till I hear from you.'

'Good. Oh, and is this your dog, sir?'

'Certainly not.' The smell of Hercules was all-pervading. 'There's a tag on his collar. He belongs to Mr Miff. I'll look after him, and the office.'

'Thank you, sir. We'll be back. Shouldn't take long.'

Treasure first telephoned his secretary, Miss Gaunt— always at her desk by eight-thirty. He explained what had happened and left some instructions to be passed to Jonkins.

The files in the outer office yielded nothing of immediate interest except a testimony to their curator's neatness and logical mind.

The floor safe in Miff's office was late nineteenth-

century, the size of a small refrigerator, and operated by
two deadlocks: the keys were on the ring. Measured in
quantity, there was not much inside. It was the quality of
the material that plunged Treasure into a fury of study
and calculation, interrupted by the return of WPC
Wilson nearly an hour later.

'Dead on arrival I'm afraid, sir,' was the pretty ash-
blonde's sombre greeting. Treasure nodded gravely and
motioned her to a seat. 'We've been with Mrs Miff. She's
taken it very well—shocked, of course, but not the weepy
type. She's identified the body. You knew she worked
here, sir?'

'Not until a few minutes ago. Uses her maiden name.'
He nodded at the papers on Miff's desk. 'I'd come to look
over all this stuff with the Director,' he added fairly
accurately and because some kind of explanation for his
having ransacked the open and almost empty safe seemed
appropriate.

'Mrs Miff explained, sir. Said you were the boss man.'
She smiled. 'Anyway, we offered to get a neighbour in,
but she said she'd be OK on her own. We did promise to
take the dog home when we're done here.' The notebook
was out again. 'My partner's seeing the other tenants. Just
a few questions, if you don't mind, sir. You arrived at?'

'Eight-twenty-five. I was a bit early for my meeting
with Mr Miff.'

The bright grey eyes looked up at him. 'Mrs Miff
thought your meeting was at eight.'

'No, eight-thirty.'

'She thought it'd been changed on the phone late last
night.'

'Not by me.'

'She could have been wrong. She said so.' The girl
made a note, crossed, then recrossed her legs. He noticed
they were very good legs enhanced by regulation black
nylons. Somehow one didn't associate black nylon with . . .

'You came by taxi, sir?' Impassively she had rearranged her skirt over her knees.

'No, my chauffeur dropped me.'

'Did he come in or wait outside?'

'Neither. He's meeting someone at Heathrow. Went straight off.'

'Bad luck.'

'I'm sorry?'

'The Air Traffic Controllers' go-slow. Delays again today at all airports. Did you see anyone else when you came into the building, sir?'

'No one.'

'And your first impression of the body, sir?'

'Total surprise . . . and shock, obviously . . . and a nasty feeling he was dead already.'

'And your first action?'

'Was to shout like hell for help. Nobody came. I didn't move him. Neck was at an extraordinary angle. Never seen a broken neck but . . .'

'You don't have to, to recognize one,' the girl put in with the easy authority of an old hand. 'So you thought his neck was broken?'

'Mmm. Anyway, I left him as he was and dashed up here to telephone. Then I came back. Tried to see if he was breathing.'

'Was he, sir?'

'It didn't seem so, and I couldn't find a pulse.'

'And what did you think had happened, sir?'

The honest answer to that question was one he was unprepared to offer anyone at the moment, and least of all a police officer.

'I thought the poor chap had fallen down the stairs and broken his neck,' he said. 'The light there's appalling. He could have tripped over something. The dog perhaps.'

'You thought he'd tripped?'

'That seemed the most likely thing, yes.'

'The office door, sir. Was it closed or open?'

'Open, with the keys in the lock. As it was when you arrived.'

WPC Wilson's partner joined them as the banker was speaking. He was about forty, built like a front row forward, and sweating like one. 'Phew, it's sticky,' he proffered amiably by way of greeting. He sat down in the only vacant chair, nodded at Treasure, then at the girl. 'You OK, Countess? Good little worker, sir. Knows her stuff.' It was the tone of a proud mentor.

'Reckon your friend could've died of a heart attack,' the policeman continued. 'Those stairs are the limit. Been up and down three times. Trying to find anyone in the building before you got here, sir. Nobody.' He removed his cap and wiped the glistening, horseshoe bald pate with a white handkerchief evidently used for the same purpose before—several times. 'I've measured the steps on this flight too. Very high risers.' He stood up, grasped the outside seams of his trousers, did a kind of wriggle with the lower half of his body, and sat down again. 'Excuse me, all.'

'Mrs Miff said her husband was poorly,' the girl put in. She turned back the pages of her notebook. 'He suffered from narcolepsy . . .'

'Means he dropped off all the time, sir,' the policeman interrupted helpfully. 'New one on me, that. Probably you've come across it, sir?' Treasure shook his head. 'Wonder could he have gone to sleep at the top of the stairs?'

Neither of the others was ready to offer a view. 'He was still in his raincoat, sir. Did it look as though he'd gone further than the door?' asked WPC Wilson.

'Difficult to say. I shouldn't have thought so. There's a coat cupboard close by.'

'Climbed those stairs, taken by a seizure, fell back and broke his neck. That'll be the size of it,' said the constable firmly. 'Anyway, post mortem will tell.' He beamed. 'Right, are you done, WPC Wilson?'

'All done,' she answered cheerfully. 'Thanks for your help, Mr Treasure. Someone'll be in touch about the inquest if you're wanted. I should think you will be.'

Treasure walked through to the outer office with the two officers. Hercules, banned to that room earlier, stirred to his feet as they entered.

'Three letters there, sir. Morning mail.' The policeman pointed to the envelopes propped against the Mickey Mouse clock on the desk. 'Brought 'em up with me. They were in a box in the hall downstairs. Wasn't locked,' he added in a mildly admonitory voice. 'Seems Mr Miff was here before the postman. He comes around eight-fifteen. I checked. The deceased must have fastened back the street door too. That's usually done by a gent on the first floor — unless someone else is in first. We've got to come back to see the only party on the ground floor. No answer there still.' The constable smiled. 'No stone unturned. That's us. Good day, sir.'

'Heel, Hercules,' ordered the girl. After a glance at Treasure the dog unhesitatingly fell in behind her — and with a surprising turn of speed.

The banker closed the door. He picked up the three envelopes, decided someone else should deal with them, and put them down on top of the covered typewriter.

He sat again at Miff's desk looking at the neat pile of files he had been analysing earlier. They would need closer study, but from what he had seen he knew what had been happening at the headquarters of the Rudyard Trust. He tried to imagine how Miff must have felt the previous afternoon when it became clear years of effort had gone for nothing.

The man's wife said he was ill. Could he also have been an alcoholic? You almost had to be to knock back a significant amount of spirits before eight in the morning—enough for the smell still to be hanging about your dead body possibly twenty minutes after you had breathed your last. Treasure had seen no point in raising the reek of liquor with the police who seemed not to have noticed it: the post mortem could carry that tale.

Sickness, guilt, frustration, the hope of salvation dashed, the probability of exposure looming—Miff would have been abject despair personified. Treasure was sure the man had taken his own life—only the method perplexed him: the hit or miss possibility in the method. Hurling yourself down one flight of stairs left a good bit to chance even allowing for the strength of the impulse and the firmness of the resolution.

The banker shrugged. He doubted the medical evidence would support his belief: good thing too. Perhaps no one else would come to the same conclusion unprompted—except Mrs Miff.

It was while he was consciously steeling himself to share his view with no one that the telephone rang—beginning a series of events that served to change that view.

CHAPTER 17

Benny put his mouth close to the microphone grille beside the bell-push. 'It's Benjamin Gold with a message from Stephen,' he uttered in a rasping whisper. He was outside the house in Guilford Street.

'Stephen who?' the crackling voice demanded.

It was ten to nine: there were a lot of people about. Benny glanced up and down the street before responding. 'Stephen Spotter,' he croaked. A student nurse hurrying past on her way to Queen's Square looked up sharply in sympathy, diagnosed laryngitis and hoped it wasn't chronic.

Benny raised his pork-pie hat and smiled nervously at the nurse, watched her out of earshot, then re-addressed the grille. 'It's raining something shocking.' He jumped back as a buzzer snarled under his nose.

Everard Crow-Patcher was waiting at the open door on the first floor. He wore a shrunken, karate-style dressing-gown in faded blue, over crumpled green pyjamas. The gown drooped at the front. He had a hand in one pocket because there was only one pocket, giving the whole ensemble a lop-sided look. He was unshaven. His long, thinning hair was standing up in tousled clumps. His eyes were screwed up against the light even though there wasn't very much.

'You'd better come in,' he offered, as though reluctantly acknowledging the only alternative was for the caller to stay outside.

'We're giving the money back,' said Benny less boldly than he had intended, so he said it again, louder.

He had been pointed into the untidy living-room. The curtains were still closed. The air smelled of last night's cigarettes. He was still in his raincoat, holding his hat, and he hadn't been asked to sit. It was Crow-Patcher who sat, abruptly, closing his eyes and passing his hand across his face.

'Who is it, honey?' A fruity, female American voice enquired from another room.

'No one, my love. Just a message. It's nothing.' Everard then lowered his voice to a hiss. 'What d'you mean — we're giving the money back? What money? Who are you, for God's sake? What are you doing in my house — flat?'

'We've been rumbled. All of us. Stephen, you, Pierre Cruba, Florence and us. You see, President Cruba . . .'

'He's dead? I knew it.' Everard paled — even in the light from the unlined curtains he visibly paled. 'It said in the news . . .'

'We don't know. Maybe. It's still touch and go.'

'You're the kidnappers.' This came more in astonishment than as confirmation.

Benny narrowed his eyes like Edward G. Robinson. This was the bit he had practised all the way from Victoria Station after dropping Roderick. 'Uh-huh. But we're in the clear on the killing if we get the dough back. Stephen says you got twenty-five grand.'

'What?'

'Grand . . . it means thousand. It's American for . . .'

'He's a liar.'

'That's what we figured.' He wanted to add, 'The dirty rat', but that might be overplaying things. 'The police . . .'

'The police have got Stephen?'

'Not yet.' That was improvisation: he had meant to say the police knew how much money had been stolen. 'Stephen's at the airport. Our boys are with him right now.' Benny rolled his shoulders backwards which meant his chin got buried in the top of his raincoat.

'Your boys? Your boys? You're supposed to be two old . . .'

'That's what we wanted you to think.' He pulled the coat down so that Everard could see he was smiling confidently. 'The organization—' he paused, reminding himself to breathe deeply to avoid trembling and bringing on his asthma. 'The organization is passing the dough back to the Cruba Family. That way we're clean. Out of the picture. It's a deal at the top.' He looked purposefully at the ceiling. It needed painting very badly. 'Stephen's grabbing the chance. He was seen on the steps last night. He denied it was him. Said it was you.'

'The swine. I was never on the steps.' Now Everard was up and prancing around the room, speaking in a well-articulated stage whisper. 'I was waiting in the Mall on the off-chance he'd pull something.'

Benny nodded sagely. 'We figured something like that.

Also he took the biggest share of the money, I'll bet. He said you split down the middle. We thought he probably kept thirty.'

'Thirty-five.'

'That's what we really thought,' he added quickly. 'It's murder, most likely. Somebody's going to jail for life maybe, and here's a guy cheating over five lousy grand.'

'Keep your voice down.' Everard crept out of the room. There was some shuffling in the hall. He came back with the black case. 'Fifteen is all I got.' He was almost inaudible.

'That case . . .' began Benny, affecting horror.

'I know.' He opened it carefully as though the hinges might squeak. 'There's ten, and here . . .' He put the case aside and pulled several volumes from a low bookshelf to reveal a large brown envelope. 'And here's the other five.' He looked up suspiciously. 'How do I know . . .'

'The notes are marked. Used but marked. We found out in time. Wouldn't have touched them anyway.' Benny shook his head: this was his last card.

Everard's jaw dropped. He pushed the envelope into the case, closed it, and thrust it at Benny. 'I was here last night from eight onwards. My wife'll swear to it. Now get out.'

As Benny pulled the flat door shut behind him, he heard the fruity voice shout 'You did what!'

Florence had warned him about Dina.

He had left the cab on the rank in front of the President Hotel, just short of Russell Square. He dialled the number on a pay phone in the hotel foyer, checking the time while waiting impatiently for a response. It was 09.13 hours. Roderick had them back on the hours business: more important, Roderick was due to ring in himself at nine-fifteen.

'Hello. This is Florence Spotter,' said the voice at the other end.

'Benjamin here. The sum was fifteen—one-a-fife, now recaptured. All's well. Please acknowledge.'

'Oh, well done, Mr Gold. I mean fifteen, one five, acknowledged and understood. Over and up . . . I've lost the instructions . . .'

'Out. Roger and out. Bye-bye, Miss Spotter,' said Benny putting the phone down.

Then he rang his daughter Denise to say how much he and the Major had enjoyed the concert, what a good thing he had been spending the night at the Major's hotel what with the rain and it being late, and how well he had slept, and what a good breakfast he had had.

And may he be forgiven was what he was thinking: lying to his own daughter yet.

The main concourse at Gatwick Airport was a daunting mass of clotting humanity.

Major Copper contemplated the scene with relish. He was glad he had signalled Miss Spotter from a phone on the railway platform: there were queues for everything in the airport. He hoped he wouldn't be here long enough to need the gents. It was up to him now: Benjamin had done well.

Conditions were far better than the Major had expected. Only ten flights out so far, and all of them left over from yesterday—filled with travellers who had camped all night at the airport.

The four rows of check-in desks were operating. Boarding cards were being issued and luggage accepted, but passengers were warned the Traffic Controllers' go-slow was expected to continue through the day. Flights were subject to anything up to twenty-four hours delay.

Passport Control was closed until pasengers on flights actually boarding had left the overcongested departure lounges. No new travellers had been allowed through since seven: better and better.

The Major had garnered his intelligences from the public address system and several frustrated and loquacious holidaymakers delighted to unburden on someone about the lack of information.

He straightened his bowler and advanced on his carefully selected quarry. The furled umbrella and ancient briefcase he held protectively before him.

'Excuse me, Officer. I think you can help me.' The fresh-faced young policeman whom nobody seemed to need offered his full attention. He had spent the last few minutes debating whether he should grow a beard after all. 'Name's Festin. Colonel Festin,' lied the Major. He had once had a friend of that name and rank: passed on years ago. 'Here on a mercy errand. Bad news, I'm afraid.'

'Oh yes, sir? Colonel.'

'Young nephew somewhere in this crowd. Mother's just dropped dead. Terrible thing. Come to fetch him myself. But how to extricate him?' He waved his hand in the air, accidentally clipping a short Japanese on the ear. 'So sorry.' He turned and apologized to a tall female who didn't know what he was talking about.

'Airline, flight and destination, sir?'

'That's the trouble, old chap. No idea. Not the foggiest. Only know he was due to take off from here this morning. I could be all day lining up at those airline desks.'

'The Airport Information desk would . . .'

'That's the worst of the lot. Anyway, I have to know if he's gone already. May need to fetch him back. Have to start with the airlines.'

'Mmm. See what we can do, sir.'

'Knew you'd understand. Always tell the doers from the set of their chins. Same in the War.'

'Follow me, sir.' He decided not to grow a beard after all: his mother would be pleased. The people made way before his resolute stride. Copper followed, affecting what he thought was the searching look of a senior, plainclothes policeman.

A few minutes later a girl was reading the prepared announcement into the microphone on the Information Desk. 'Will Mr Spotter, British Airtours passenger to Dubrovnik, please report to the British Airways Reservations Desk. Mr S. Spotter to British Airways Reservations, please.'

Everyone had been very co-operative. It had seemed sensible to let the constable try British Airways first, it being the biggest. The computer had promptly revealed S. Spotter's travel plans.

Having his 'nephew' report to Reservations had been the Major's idea. 'Sensitive boy . . . Dicky heart himself . . . Don't want him frightened . . . Jumping to the right conclusion, don't you know? . . . Rather be with him when . . . He's asked to be wait-listed on an earlier flight than the one he's on? . . . Tell you what, let him think you want to alter his ticket.'

Stephen had been in the upstairs bar. He grabbed his canvas case, his only luggage: they were switching him to the earlier flight. That was the trick of travelling alone—always that one seat free at the last minute. He hurried down the stairs, feeling good. He pushed his way to the Reservations Desk.

'I'm Stephen Spotter.' The girl gave him her exclusive smile. He was used to that. She then looked over his shoulder and gave her exclusive smile to someone else.

'My dear Stephen. It's Uncle Roderick. A miracle we've caught you.' The emphasis came on the last two words.

He turned about. It was that fool Major and with a cop in tow.

'Never have done it without our friend here. Cut through the red tape like nobody's business.' The Major put his arm around the other's shoulder—very firmly. 'Bit of bad news I'm afraid, old chap.' He looked towards the policeman, who nodded. 'Not here, though. Got to watch that ticker of yours. Arranged a bit of privacy. All laid on.'

'This way, Colonel. Mr Spotter.' The constable set off on another of his parting of the waters acts—but mildly puzzled. Mr Spotter had turned out to be much older than expected and considerably more robust.

Stephen looked about him for means of escape. 'Don't try bolting.' The Major was immediately behind him, breathing words into his ear. 'Do as I say and you'll be off the hook.' He raised his voice. 'Right with you, Officer. Lead on. Lead on.'

The 'bit of privacy' was a small interview room in the Police Control Centre.

'Sit down, Stephen,' said the Major as soon as they were alone. 'Your mother's passed away.'

'To hell with sitting down, and my mother died twenty years ago. What's your game, Copper?' He sat down anyway on a plastic chair across a small table from the Major.

'I'm collecting thirty-five thousand from that hold-all of yours and returning it to ex-President Cruba. That's my game. After I've played it you can resume your journey to Dubrovnik—or Kancheepuram, for all I care.'

'You have to be crazy.'

'No, but you'll be if you don't cough up—*and* arrested for theft . . .'

'It wasn't theft, you old fool. He gave me the money. I had the password, remember?'

'*And* attempted murder,' the Major continued, entirely ignoring the interruption. 'Crow-Patcher's spilled the beans.'

'There's nothing to spill'—but the tone had become measurably less assured.

'Not the way Mr Crow-Patcher tells it. We've got his

fifteen thou. So, if you'd like to give me the rest of the fifty. In that case, is it? What they call cabin baggage, I believe. Well, you'd hardly want what's in there to go in the hold, would you?'

'How do I know . . .'

'That we're returning the money? You don't, except I'm giving you my word as an officer and a gentleman.'

'Big deal. So you're whiter than white? So what about the little old kidnap? I could call the cops in now from next door . . .'

'All a misunderstanding. Something ex-President Cruba will straighten out himself quite easily if it comes up. But it won't. Not unless you raise it — and if you raise it, and after it's been straightened out, there'll still be the matter of robbery and assault. And that won't be so easy to straighten out. Permanently bent I'd say, that one.' The Major nodded sagely. 'You see, Crow-Patcher's panicked. Made you out to be the most terrible bounder. Ready to turn Queen's evidence, and all that. Says he saw you . . .'

'OK, Major. Tell you what we'll do. There's five thousand for you, and no hard feelings. Is it a deal?'

'Thirty-five thousand, please, to be returned to Mr Cruba.'

'I'll make it ten. No questions. You never found me. Who's gonna know, for crying out loud?' The Major made no response. 'OK, it's a steal but we split it down the middle. Fifty-fifty. Equal shares.'

The Major stood up and held open the unbuckled briefcase. 'Thirty-five thousand if you please, Mr Spotter.' His face brightened. 'Tell you what. If it helps at all, I'll be glad to give you a receipt.'

Grim-faced, the other man unzipped his case.

As soon as Treasure finished the call from his secretary he telephoned Florence Spotter who apparently needed to talk to him urgently. Miss Gaunt had also reported that François Cruba was out of danger.

'Oh, Mr Treasure. So kind. You must be fearfully busy. I wouldn't have troubled you, but it's about Stephen.'

'Your nephew, Stephen Spotter?'

'He telephoned early this morning.'

'From where?'

'He didn't say, except he reversed the charges, so of course I knew. He didn't have change for the telephone, you see.'

'So where was he?'

'At Gatwick Airport. The operator asked if I'd accept a call from there. It was quite early—about seven-fifteen. I was up, of course.'

'And he didn't realize you knew where he was?'

'That's right, Mr Treasure. He gave me no opportunity to explain . . . about the operator, I mean. He said he had to leave the country straight away as soon as he could get a flight. They've found oil somewhere.'

'Did he say anything about Pierre's father? About the stabbing?'

'Nothing, except I wasn't to worry about anything. I wanted to tell him how displeased I was that he'd been pressing Prudence on the dissolution of the Rudyard Trust . . .'

'And Crow-Patcher.'

'Indeed. Thoroughly uncharitable acts on his part . . . and, dare I say, underhand after what he'd told me. But, you see, there wasn't the opportunity. He said he was in a great rush and really ringing to say he couldn't return my car—because it'd been stolen. Stolen!'

'Where from?'

'Somewhere in North London early last evening. He said Everard would be reporting it to the police. If anyone asked me about it I should say I'd lent it to Everard . . .'

'That's Mr Crow-Patcher?'

'That's right. He said the two of them were together last evening. I wasn't to mention I had ever lent the car to him. He said it would probably turn up. Cars were often stolen for joy-riding, and the best place to look was in the car pounds. I don't know what car pounds . . .'

'They're places where the police take cars that are parked illegally.'

'I see. Well, Everard was kindly going to visit all the car pounds. All the same, it's jolly inconvenient . . .'

Not to say suspicious: 'The car's insured, of course, Miss Stopper?'

'That's what nice Major Copper asked.'

'You've spoken to the Major this morning?'

'Indeed. It was far too early to telephone you at your office, so I rang the Major. I do hope you'll think I did the right thing, Mr Treasure.'

'I'm sure you did. What was the Major's reaction?'

There was a slight pause at the other end. 'I fear he never did trust Stephen. Both the Major and Mr Gold believed he had something to do with that dreadful episode on the steps. Not the stabbing. The robbery. They'd been discussing it. They were both at breakfast at the Major's hotel. And then . . .' This time there was a longer pause.

'Are you there, Miss Spotter?'

'Yes, Mr Treasure. Oh dear. When I think of the family shame . . . You see, the Major telephoned me again a few minutes later. He said they'd decided to take the initiative.'

'I see. What particular form of initiative?'

'Oh, to get the money back. They were quite specific on the point.'

'To get it back from Stephen who they thought must have it?'

'They were sure, Mr Treasure. That is, they put two and two together. They believed Stephen and Everard had the money between them.' There was an audible sigh. 'And they were right. Mission accomplished.'

'I'm sorry?'

'That was the last signal. Mr Gold tackled Everard at his home and the Major went to the airport on the off-chance, as it were. I was Staff HQ—for passing messages . . . signals, I mean. It was very efficient. There were fixed times for signalling and special things to say. I had to write them down to avoid misunderstanding . . . Roger . . . and over and upwards. Also the Major thought the police might have tapped this line, though I hardly think Constable Jones would have allowed . . .'

'What happened, Miss Spotter? About the money?'

'Oh, well, as I said, mission accomplished. They have it all. The Major signalled a few minutes ago from Gatwick.'

'And what are they doing with the money?'

'They're bringing it to you, Mr Treasure, at your bank. They'll be there around eleven. We all thought that best, I was to tell you.

'I see. Well, message received, Miss Spotter. And—er—well done everybody.'

'Oh—oh, thank you very much.' She gave a nervous laugh. 'Over and . . . er . . .'

'Roger and out,' Treasure replied, chuckling.

'Roger who?—oh, of course, yes. Goodbye, Mr Treasure,' said Miss Spotter, reverting to civilian life.

CHAPTER 18

Pausing only to check the number, Treasure dialled the Cruba home. He was glad it was Pierre who answered.

'I've heard about your father. It's good news.'

'Yes, sir. I'm seeing him this afternoon. He's going to

be all right — I mean really all right. The knife pierced his liver but not his lung. It was kind of diverted by a rib at the back.'

Treasure had already heard the details from Miss Gaunt. 'He was lucky.'

'So was I, sir,' the boy answered with feeling. 'I've talked to him on the phone already. He says I'm not to blame myself. He's not going to take it out on me.'

'Then I should accept his word.'

'He's a terrific father, sir. I hadn't realized how terrific.' Treasure felt himself veering to the same view. 'He says I should have been able to talk to him about my mother. And about the charity. He says if I felt I couldn't, then it was his fault.' There was a choke in the voice at this point. 'Can you imagine that, sir? *His* fault.'

'Yes, I can, and I think he probably meant it. Tell me, have you seen your stepmother this morning?' Treasure put the enquiry lightly but he was anxious to hear another emotional broken fence had been mended.

'I went to see her, sir. In her room.' The boy had stumbled over his reply. The earlier contrition had gone from the voice. 'I didn't sleep much. I was up and dressed early. I wanted to say I was sorry. Thought she'd be awake.'

'Oh dear. So you thoughtlessly disturbed her at dawn?'

'At seven, actually. She was awake . . . Gérard was with her.'

'I see.' Ask a stupid question . . . the normally resourceful banker was momentarily at a loss. He knew he had to head off further possible revelations he had no wish to prompt or to hear.

'They weren't in bed together, sir.'

Treasure swallowed on the earthy frankness and chose to ignore the unspoken insinuation. 'Gérard probably dropped by to make sure she was all right,' he said. He supposed he had mouthed worse inanities in his time, but not many.

'He said he was just leaving, sir. Going to see Papa in hospital. He's asked me to play squash at ten,' Pierre added a little sourly.

Treasure hoped Opac had been dressed to make the journey, though he had no intention of clearing the point: later it would have proved useful if he had.

'Give your father my best wishes.' He was conscious someone was moving across the office next door. He stood up and walked as far around the desk as the telephone cord allowed. 'I've got to go now. Goodbye, Pierre.'

Mrs Miff entered the room before he had replaced the receiver. He realized who she was even before he noticed the dangling monocle. Both Jonkins and Benny Gold had remarked on the monocle.

She was wearing a simple cotton dress in a grey and blue check pattern. She carried a grey cardigan and a large black leather handbag that matched her low-heeled shoes.

'Mr Treasure, I presume. I am Clarence Miff's wife.'

She was composed and purposeful, showing no trace of the shock she must have suffered little more than an hour before. For this much Treasure was relieved.

Clearly Mrs Miff had to be treated with the utmost compassion: common decency dictated this. Even so, he wished he could have been spared the meeting. The Miffs appeared to have masterminded a morally indefensible plot to liquidate the Rudyard Trust—something that hardly presaged an enduring warm relationship.

'I'm most dreadfuly sorry about the accident. I'd never met your husband but . . .'

'Please sit down, Mr Treasure,' she interrupted abruptly. 'I didn't come for sympathy. Thank you all the same—and for your prompt action. I know you did all you could.' She nodded in punctuation, indicating that they had come to the end of comment on her husband's demise. 'I wasn't sure whether you'd be here still.' There was no attempt to disguise the enigmatic significance of the comment. Mrs Miff sat: Treasure did the same. 'I am known at the Rudyard Trust as Miss McSlope. Our marriage was not the subject of advertisement.'

'Nor that . . .'

'That I'm a Rudyard by descent? You know as much. I see you have my birth certificate before you.'

'I'm sorry. When I started going through the files in the safe I hadn't appreciated . . .'

'We use it for keeping our own important papers? Our flat has no comparable safe place. It's really of no consequence.'

Treasure began to feel less guarded. Mrs Miff's composure was evidently genuine. He sensed she was not about to plead mitigation in the hour she was most entitled to expect some.

If this woman was given to tears it would be in private and not for effect. In an inexplicable way, too, her Lowland cadence and pedantic use of the language bolstered her credibility as well as her dignity.

'Being the Blessed Marmaduke's great-grand-daughter—that might have affected your chances of getting a job here,' he offered quietly, spurred to say what was on his mind, but feeling the way gently.

'It would almost certainly have enhanced my chances, Mr Treasure.'

She was probably right, he thought. 'I don't know what your motives were, of course.'

'The purest—at the start. I was also curious. Later I became bitter, but never personally avaricious nor dishonest.'

'You're very frank.'

'The occasion is privileged, is it not?'

'To a point,' he said, immediately wishing he had

conceded a broader indulgence. He laid his hands on the spread of documents before him. 'You were trained as an accountant?'

'I never qualified.'

'The best ones often don't. Your husband . . .'

'Has no head for that kind of work.'

'I see. So you've been responsible for the cost and budgetry control systems?'

'Entirely. I put them in four years ago. Things were in a muddle before.'

'I could name several private and public companies that jog along with a lot less financial information than you've been producing. It's all pretty sophisticated.'

'I've never cared for the slipshod, Mr Treasure.'

'I can see that. Monthly, quarterly, annual projections. Target and actual income and expenditure analysis. The cost categories are admirably thorough. The moving data, the weighting of the historical basis you've used for extrapolation—all uncannily accurate. You've even got a workable formula for estimating loss of income through . . . er . . .'

'Deaths in membership, Mr Treasure? Not too difficult, given the use of past records—their only use, as it happens,' she added disparagingly. 'There was nothing more sinister involved.'

Treasure gave an embarrassed cough. 'You used a computer from the start.'

'An hour's time bought regularly on somebody else's computer.' She shrugged. 'We took advice from Grenwood, Phipps'—the first Treasure had heard of it. 'Quite quickly we were able to reduce headquarters staff from four to two.'

'Just you and your husband?'

She nodded. 'There were also savings on administration at the clubs.'

'And you've been projecting losses, knowingly and with

remarkable accuracy for several years,' with Jonkins possibly checking the computer print-outs. On second thoughts he believed the bank would be spared that ignominy: it was doubtful if Jonkins could read a computer print-out.

'That's true.' There had been no hesitancy in her reply. 'The shortfalls of income over expenditure were eminently predictable.

'But avoidable? For instance, if fees had been raised?'

'They were, with a consequent fall in new members.'

'Because they were raised too high—and not at all in the case of existing members?'

'The last contingency being expressly forbidden in Founder's Rules. New member's fees have had to incorporate an element of subsidy for old members. One can't run institutions of this kind with varying standards of service depending on an individual's financial contribution. It would be quite inequitable—and be seen to be so. They must all be treated alike.'

'Costs might have been cut. Maintenance seems high. The food bills . . .'

Mrs Miff was shaking her head. 'Victorian buildings, Mr Treasure. Our surveyors are a firm of the highest repute. My husband accepted their advice as, indeed, he was obliged to do under the Rules. As for the food—you are married of course? Perhaps you also have a London club and dine out at restaurants?'

'I do, yes, and I'm very well aware that at home and everywhere else these days . . .'

'The price of maintaining the culinary standards to which you are used have risen astronomically. The Rudyard Clubs also have standards, Mr Treasure. Not so high, but standards.' She paused. 'However, as an economic unit the whole operation has been doomed to collapse. It's too small, while, paradoxically, being unwieldy. It's an anachronism, better dissolved now than later.'

'And this is what your husband would have argued?'

'My husband would have stood by the account of his stewardship—and the Founder's Rules.'

'Am I to take it you're suggesting the charity should be disbanded in its present form: that it should then be reconstituted?'

'Precisely, Mr Treasure. With the family beneficiaries bought off.'

'You mean for less than their absolute entitlement?'

'A good deal less, wouldn't you say? There'll have to be a deal. You can't foreclose on an old people's charity without concessions, and with two of us sympathetic . . .'

'A deal, as you say, would be better than coping with a righteous public outcry, and conceivably legal wrangling within the family.'

Mrs Miff responded buoyantly. 'After that a true charitable intention can be realized. It will involve financial co-operation from club members, their families and others led, obviously, by myself, supported by Florence Spotter.'

'Miss Spotter knows nothing of your plan?'

'Not as yet, but her attitude is predictable.' She paused. 'The three clubs would need to be combined into one, of course.'

'In new premises?'

'A converted and perhaps extended old mansion. There are plenty of suitable places available—mostly Georgian going cheaply in unfashionable rural areas. I saw one quite recently.'

'Forgive me, Mrs Miff. Your reasoning sounds admirable. Can you tell me why your husband didn't put it forward earlier? Why you kept your own family connection—er—under wraps?'

'Because the shortest route was to liquidate the Trust, settle with the graspers . . .'

'Crow-Patcher? Prudence Rudyard?'

'And Stephen Spotter. I had an idea he'd materialize when it came to sharing out the spoils. It's quite purposeless attempting to stop that family from running to form. The way my mother was treated was abominable.'

For a few moments the knuckles of the hands clasping the bag on her lap showed white. Then she seemed to relax. Without emotion she explained how her putatively penitent mother—too putative in Treasure's unspoken view—had been spurned by contemporary Rudyards, and how she herself had been not so much disowned as never owned at all by the same clan.

Slowly, with the unfolding, the banker came to realize the tortuous plot he had unearthed had to do with retribution for two women scorned.

He waited for her to finish her piece, then he asked, 'So you don't feel your plans were high-handed?'

'Practical, Mr Treasure. The alternative of petitioning Parliament for a special Instrument would take years to prepare and push through—especially with more than half the residual beneficiaries opposed.'

'And the gift from Mr Cruba? Of course, you only heard about it yesterday.'

'In fact, on Saturday. Stephen Spotter told us. It would have made no difference if I'd heard of it last month, or last year. It offers no permanent solution. With the Trust constitution unchanged it would only put off the evil day. I assume it's been withdrawn? Stephen Spotter said it would be and he must have had reason.'

Treasure nodded. It was not clear from the way she spoke if Mrs Miff had heard of the attack on François Cruba. 'The ex-President's been injured. He's in hospital. The gift is . . . er . . . frozen for the moment.'

'He was stabbed on the Duke of York steps. It said on the wireless this morning.' Her tone was matter-of-fact. 'A political act, no doubt. I trust he continues to recover.'

Was her supposition about a political motive based on hope or belief, Treasure wondered. 'He's recovering. Tell me, your husband shared your views . . . ?'

'My husband was a sick man,' she interrupted. 'I regret to say he was also a weak one.'

'You married him . . .'

'Out of pity, Mr Treasure, a not unworthy motive. He worried. Sometimes with reason, sometimes without — about his health, his drinking, his job, the rectitude of my plan for the Clubs. He preferred to ignore facts and to . . . romanticize: to dramatize situations — even to the point of playacting.'

'He was playacting when he interviewed a Major Copper and a Mr Gold? Seems he alerted them to the situation in some detail. Spurred them into doing something to help.'

Mrs Miff looked momentarily surprised. 'I see. I wondered if . . .' She collected herself, resuming her original composure. 'It was an ill-conceived precaution on my husband's part. He had been insisting there should be evidence we had not been disguising the issue. I didn't agree, nor did I know there would be two candidates that day. But we were so close to the financial year end . . .'

'And the two looked such unlikely champions?'

She nodded. 'For the sake of his peace of mind I didn't interfere. There was so little that lessened his anxieties.' She paused. 'On that day, and on others, I was sorry for him — because of his past and the way he saw the future. Did you know he'd been obliged to give up his partnership in a private law practice before taking this job?'

'No, I didn't.' He subdued any show of disquiet.

'He had to make good some losses sustained by a client due to carelessness on his part — not dishonesty, I assure you. He was impoverished as a result. Fortunately it was a time of full employment for professional people. The Trust was glad to accept him. At the salary offered, I understand he was the only applicant.' Knowingly she added, 'I'm sure your people were aware of his background.'

'I know there was a misunderstanding here once— about joining fees.' Treasure was careful to keep the tone dismissive.

'Just before I came.' She nodded. 'He was innocent, of course, but accident prone.' Her face clouded.

There was silence as they both marked the painful appropriateness of the allusion. He thought he saw tears forming in her eyes. She blinked and the impression was dispelled.

'I'd hoped our becoming relatively well-off would give a basis for his building confidence in himself, Mr Treasure. His insecurity was largely to do with money.' She dabbed her nose with a man's size handkerchief. 'So you see, my purposes in all this were not entirely altruistic. Now the money is not material, of course.'

Treasure smiled. 'I'm glad we were able to talk. Your frankness is admirable and, if I may say so, brave—and timely. You've given me a great deal to think about. May we leave it there?' She nodded. He glanced at his watch. 'I must go anyway. I mean to take the Trust files with me. You've no objection?'

'None. There's one thing, Mr Treasure. You did telephone my husband at the flat last night about changing the time of your appointment this morning?'

'No, I didn't. Are you sure . . . ?'

'I'm sure of very little about last evening. Clarence was beside himself with worry—over the Cruba gift.'

'Which didn't bother you?'

'I believed Stephen.' She caught the banker's change of expression. 'Who couldn't have had anything to do with the attack on Mr Cruba.'

'Otherwise he wouldn't have risked being so forthright with you?'

'Precisely.'

'Your husband was at home last night?'

'No, he wasn't. But he didn't attack Mr Cruba either.' She forestalled Treasure's tactful protest, continuing 'He went out after supper, at about nine. He came back very late—I'd gone to bed. We sleep in separate rooms. I heard him come in. It was after twelve-thirty. Some time later the telephone rang. It woke me. I'm not sure at what time.'

'You mean you've no idea where he was between nine and twelve-thirty?'

'None. He probably spent the time walking and thinking. He had no money with him. None at all—to prevent his buying drink. A regular, self-imposed discipline.' She sighed. 'He did try, you see.'

'Did Spotter tell you Cruba would be at the Duke of York steps around ten-thirty?'

She looked puzzled. 'No. Did he know that himself?'

Treasure hesitated. 'I can't say,' he replied with semantic accuracy. 'Did he mention anything about Pierre Cruba, the ex-President's son?'

'Nothing.'

He would have sworn her bewilderment was genuine. 'You said you thought the late phone call was from me.'

She nodded. 'Clarence woke me early this morning. He was on the point of leaving. He normally brings me tea first thing. We drink a cup together in my room. Today he said he'd already taken breakfast; that the appointment was changed to eight. Then he was gone. I was half asleep still. We had no other conversation. I naturally assumed . . .'

CHAPTER 19

'Excuse me. I'm Happy Brown. That's my office. Are you the police? They're after me. Left a note.'

'I don't blame them.' Treasure smiled at the confident brunette. He walked from the stairs towards where she was standing in the ground-floor corridor. 'No, I'm not a policeman. I'm a banker. They want to ask if you were here before eight this morning.'

He introduced himself properly and then explained about Miff's sudden death.

Miss Brown was genuinely shocked. 'Poor Mr Miff. I hardly knew him but he was here last night. We were working late. Offered him coffee as he was leaving. He'd seen the light under our door and knocked to make sure we weren't being burgled.'

'What time did he leave?'

'When we did—that's Soo, one of my partners, and me. Let's see. Between ten and ten-fifteen, I'd guess. Soo will know for sure. She keeps our time sheets for charging clients.'

'Is she here?'

'Afraid not. It was raining still. We were lucky. Found a cab just up the street. We offered Mr Miff a lift. He wanted to walk.' She sighed.

He made a mental note to check times and distances. 'You weren't early this morning?'

'Yes, I was. Seven-thirty. Left again about eight. I had to pick up a huge box of sales manuals—for a client meeting in North London. Had the car outside. I did see someone. Not Mr Miff. Whoever it was he fell over the box. Something I'm always doing.'

'What?'

'Leaving things out here in the hall. It's our door. Slams as soon as you turn your back. I'd forgotten something. Shoved the box down the hall and let myself back in the office. I came out just as this man took an awful flyer at the bottom of the stairs.' She made a guilty face. 'That's where the box was. He hurt himself, too.'

'You spoke to him? Know who he was?'

'No to both questions.'

'Anything distinctive about him?'

'The blood on his leg.' She winced. 'He had his back to me all the time. As he was getting up he bared his leg to look at the damage.'

'Bad cut?'

'Nasty, I could see that. I shouted sorry. I was going to help him but he just made for the door. He didn't look round or anything. He was limping quite a bit.'

'Which leg was it?'

'Er . . . the right. You sure you're not a policeman?' She smiled. 'Oh, he did say one word when he fell.'

'What was it?'

'I'm not sure I know you well enough. Actually it was "bugger"—but quite softly.'

'Mmm. Was he tall, short, medium . . . ?'

'Sort of crouched when I saw him. Probably tallish.'

'Remember how he was dressed?'

'Badly, in a long plastic mac with a hood.'

'Colour of the mac?'

She shrugged. 'Dark—black or brown. It was against the light from the door.'

'You weren't suspicious when he ran off?'

'No. Of course I should have been. But he wasn't carrying anything. I mean, he obviously wasn't pinching typewriters.' She clapped a hand to her cheek. 'He was wearing gloves. That's suspicious, isn't it, this time of year? Oh Lord, I'm so trusting.'

'My wife's the same.'

She looked even more despairing. 'I thought he was a messenger.'

'He probably was.'

'We do get a lot here, and they're always in a hurry. I was only concerned about his being hurt. You don't think he had anything to do with Mr Miff?'

'I shouldn't think so. Still . . . I'd let the police know you're back. By the way, Mrs Miff's upstairs . . . if you want to . . .' She nodded. 'Good to have met you. Forgive me. I must dash.'

They parted — he considering, among other things, the coincidence of dark, hooded mackintoshes; she, more singularly, the dearth of unmarried, good-looking bankers.

'Major Copper and Mr Gold are waiting downstairs. They saw the counting of the money as you instructed.'

He glanced up at her quizzically.

'Forty-nine thousand, seven hundred and forty,' she said. 'It's been receipted. Miss McSlope, that is, Mrs Miff, has rung twice. She sounded disturbed.'

'Get her back straight away.'

'I moved your ten-thirty meeting to eleven. It's nearly that now.'

'Ask Rigg to take the chair for me.'

'And your lunch with Mr Crib-Cranton?'

'I've rung him already. It's cancelled. Moved to Monday. Ritz, one o'clock.'

Miss Gaunt scribbled another note in her book, then flipped back a page. 'Mr Jonkins confirms the Cruba transfer to the Rudyard Trust is frozen.' She made a tick with her pencil. 'Mr Hinterton is not in his office today. You can call him at home up to midday. I'll get Mrs Miff. Coffee?' She noted his affirming nod and retreated to her own office outside.

Miss Gaunt was fifty-two years of age, medium height,

thin rather than slim, sober in dress and unobtrusive in appearance except for her teeth, which did rather dominate things. Her untinted, greying hair was worn in a bun. She went to Mass every Sunday and Holy Day, had a regular seat at the opera, a brother in Canada, a cat called Aquinas, and her own small flat in Islington: she also embodied the only reason Treasure could ever find for opposing the retirement of female employees at fifty-eight instead of sixty. Her first name was Emily but her boss had never addressed her by it.

'Mrs Miff. You wanted me?' He went on scanning the mail while he spoke into the telephone.

'Mr Treasure. Something serious came to light after you left. I suppose I should have told the authorities but . . .'

'Please go on.' There was certainly anguish in the tone. He stopped fingering the letters in front of him.

'When I took the cover from my typewriter there was a note underneath . . . in the machine.'

'I see.' On the instant he had a premonition of what was coming.

'It reads, "I stabbed Cruba. Forgive me. Clarence Miff." '

'I'm so sorry. What a terrible thing for you to find. I wonder . . .' He blamed himself for not thinking to uncover the typewriter—then wondered why the police hadn't done it. 'I'm afraid the police ought to be told. Would you like me . . .'

'Thank you, no. I can see to it. There's something I wanted to make clear to you first, Mr Treasure.' She paused. 'This is not a suicide note.'

'I'm sorry. You said . . .'

'You may find this difficult to credit, but my husband couldn't type.'

'You mean he . . .'

'I mean he was never able to master the basic elements

of how to operate a typewriter—even a manual one. The machine here is electric. I unplugged it last night because of the storm. Clarence could no more have made it work than fly. It actually frightened him—like most other mechanical contrivances. Do you understand what I'm saying, Mr Treasure?'

'Indeed I do, Mrs Miff.'

Thanks to the resourceful Miss Gaunt, Pierre Cruba was located at the Lansdowne Club where he was playing squash. Treasure was able to talk to him on the telephone a few minutes after finishing his conversation with Edna Miff.

Pierre affirmed he was alone. No, he wasn't playing with Gérard Opac who had been held up. No, he hadn't actually seen Opac since early morning.

'He cancelled our game by phone, sir. Fixed me up with another partner here.'

'He didn't mention he couldn't play because he'd hurt himself?'

'No, sir. It was a business meeting—for Papa, I think. Is Gérard hurt?'

'I don't think so. There's been a misunderstanding—on my part. Sorry to interrupt your game. Oh, and Pierre?'

'Sir?'

'Just forget I rang; there's a good chap.'

Treasure had taken the call in Miss Gaunt's office. Like Pierre, she wondered why he had gone to so much trouble to check on Opac's physical well-being. She was equally interested to know why he had tried and failed to make her typewriter work. Time would tell, perhaps: Miss Gaunt was, as always, content with anticipation.

'If I need a car meantime, I'll take the Chairman's and drive it myself. Will you fix it?' Treasure replied rather absently to his secretary's only spoken enquiry before returning to his own office. The Rolls was still at

Heathrow, and so was Henry Pink. The venerable Lord Grenwood's hardly used, owner-driven and totally unsuitable Jaguar XJ-S Coupé needed exercising while his lordship was abroad.

Alone, Treasure stared at the mahogany coaching clock on the wall opposite his desk. He needed time, though there was little enough to spare—an hour, perhaps, before the police were round asking relevant questions.

If he was right the scandal he saw erupting would be more than a nine days' wonder—like the consequent trial. He could soften the impact perhaps if he could do some immediate ferreting of his own—but it had to be now. Also he needed collaborators he could trust implicitly, and most of all he needed to talk with Freddy, safe from interruption.

'Freddy, I can't go into detail on the telephone. I've told you it's serious. The Director of—er—that Trust . . .'

'The Rudyard?'

'Yes.' He had been hoping to avoid mentioning names—conscious of the irony that now it was he who was pressing circumspection. 'He came to a violent end this morning . . . Not an accident and I don't believe it was suicide.' He left Freddy to work through the other possibilities. 'Listen, I think I have the answer to what was bugging us last night . . . No, not as simple as that . . . Please try to understand. I know exactly what's been happening and I've got to see you.'

Freddy was exasperatingly unmoved by the drama in Treasure's statement. True he had been 'standing by', as he put it, but knowing that Cruba was out of danger, the police sure the assailant was a common thief, the kidnap over without publicity and any serious drain on the Cruba finances, he had made up his mind to snatch two days on his boat which Treasure knew was called *Refuge*—also why it was called *Refuge*, he had added pointedly.

With three weeks' leave long overdue and a ten-day conference in Nigeria beginning Thursday, Freddy pleaded his intention was not nearly so irresponsible as it might sound. He was tired, overworked and his Range-Rover had broken down which meant he had to take a train to Essex in an hour. The Director of the Rudyard was hardly his responsibility . . .

Treasure interrupted the diatribe. 'Freddy, I'll pick you up outside Moorgate tube in Finsbury Circus in forty minutes. That's on the Northern Line, isn't it?'

'Yes, Mark, but . . .'

'You can get on at Hampstead, then I'll drive you to your bloody boat. How's that? And where in Essex d'you keep it?—I'll need to work out when I'll be back.'

That was fine: Freddy was overwhelmed, reeled off essential directions, and promised to be waiting at twelve-fifteen.

Treasure knew the route to Southend. The stretch beyond through Rochford and up to the River Crouch would have to be checked. It sounded like ninety miles there and back—mostly on trunk roads less crowded over lunch-time: praise be, the rain had stopped.

Whatever the outcome, he knew he had to make the effort. He had telephoned François Cruba before asking his secretary to have Copper and Gold brought up. 'Oh, and I'll need that car in half an hour,' he told her. 'I'm out now till after lunch to everyone—including the police. Especially the police. All right?'

Miss Gaunt added another anticipation to her store.

Benny had never walked on carpet that felt so thick except at the Gaumont State Cinema in Kilburn years ago and that was probably mostly rubber underlay. This was the real thing. Rachel had liked patterned carpet: for himself he always thought self-coloured had more class.

You could see Mr Treasure had taste. Roderick was

admiring the pictures: no prints—they were all hand-painted. It was the quiet you noticed most. Even with the doors open noise didn't seem to carry from room to room: like they saw people talking in the offices along the corridor from the lift—also carpeted—but they didn't hear them.

Every door along that corridor seemed to have a name and 'Managing Director' on it—except Mr Treasure's. How many Managing Directors could you have? Mr Treasure explained they had three. Merchant Banks had three Managing Directors: so you learned something every day.

Benny wished he had left his raincoat with the secretary like she'd asked: such a lady too. Roderick left his coat, so when they got up to leave Roderick didn't shower coins about like heavy confetti because he was holding a coat upside down that had a pocket full of coppers. And Mr Treasure had helped fish out the coins from where they seemed buried in the deep green pile which Benny, on his knees, had wished would sprout and swallow him up. He should be so embarrassed: at least it could have been silver coins.

Treasure kept his over-awed visitors less than ten minutes. He did not tell them that but for their bungled intervention he believed the Rudyard Trust would ultimately have been rescued by Edna Miff's tortuous but legal, inspired and coolly executed plan.

Simply, the banker congratulated the two on retrieving the money, dismissed their concern at the £260 short-fall, reassured them about ex-President Cruba's attitude to the whole affair, and solemnly promised their first good intentions would not be ignored—nor neglected any more. He added glibly to this little speech that while the intentions would be pursued by more orthodox methods the fine principle involved would be the same.

The Major explained to Benny later that all this had

meant they were being let off.

The news of Miff's death shook both the older men, though Treasure had not allowed them to dwell on it for long. He had been anxious to broach the favour he wanted of them, emphasizing that it was highly confidential, that it concerned the Rudyard Trust, and that the fewer people involved the better, at least for the time being. They had promptly agreed to help and carefully listened to their instructions. Naturally, they would set off right away: as usual, Benny's cab was just around the corner.

As Treasure was preparing to leave himself Miss Gaunt reported the message from Happy Brown. Mr Miff had left the office last evening at exactly ten past ten.

CHAPTER 20

'It's much too powerful a toy for Grenwood,' said Treasure, as the Jaguar surged passed the lorry that had lumbered out of their way in the fast lane. 'Hell of a thrust. Unnerving till you're used to it'—which is probably how poor Miff had felt about throbbing electric typewriters.

'I still think Miff's murder eliminates most of the suspects for the Cruba stabbing.' The banker returned to the subject.

They had passed Romford and were already well on towards Basildon. Freddy had been on time, overdressed for sailing, and dragging an inordinate amount of luggage. He had explained he intended travelling direct from his boat to Heathrow on Thursday. Then he had recounted the complicated linking of taxis and British Rail and London Underground trains which he confidently believed would transport him efficiently to the

airport. He seemed equally assured about the availability
of planes by then.

In a way Treasure had been content for his passenger
to prattle on about irrelevancies while they made the
tortuous drive through the City and the East End. After
that it was easier to concentrate.

'You're so sure it was murder?' Freddy sounded
doubtful.

'I'm sure it wasn't suicide. If it was murder the post-
mortem should show something. It seemed to me his neck
was very badly broken.'

'More than by a deliberate fall?'

Treasure shrugged. 'You'd have to be an expert. I
imagine a pathologist could tell the different effects of a
fall and a damned great shove.'

'You don't think he could have thrown himself? I mean
dived backwards,' Freddy persisted. 'That would be the
same as being pushed, surely?'

'Not if he was hit with something first — by whoever
typed the note; the same maniac who got Miff to the
office at eight — who stabbed Cruba when he thought the
kidnappers would be blamed.'

'Meaning it had to be someone who knew about the
kidnap in the first place.'

'And who found out later it was a put-up affair by
Pierre and two harmless old gents . . .'

'Who couldn't be blamed for anything.'

Treasure nodded. 'Then he had a problem. If he had a
motive for killing Cruba and no alibi he needed to shift
the blame quickly and permanently to someone else.
Death is pretty permanent.'

'But Miff himself did have a motive, and you said just
now all we know about him, his movements last night,
what happened this morning, it's all circumstantial. He
was at large last night.'

'But he didn't know Cruba's movements.'

'We don't think he knew.'

'Well, even if he did, he left his office at ten past ten. Cruba was stabbed half a mile away three minutes later—and that's half a mile as the crow flies.'

'It's a fairly straight run through St James's Park.'

'I don't think Miff was Olympic standard . . .'

'I mean by car.'

'The Miffs don't have one, and even if he'd found a taxi he didn't have any money.'

'So his wife says. She's also the one who says he can't work a typewriter.'

Treasure shook his head. 'I admit I wouldn't have credited that one till I tried my secretary's. Have you ever . . .'

Freddy interrupted, unimpressed with Treasure's clerical experiments. 'If he did do the note himself, she could be claiming he couldn't so his death is blamed on someone else. Someone who'd then be blamed for the stabbing.'

'Bit devious.' Treasure frowned, aware that someone had to be devious, that his feelings about Mrs Miff were merely intuitive. 'There must be others who know he was actually afraid of typewriters. Even if there aren't, the man was a lawyer. If he'd typed a suicide note surely he'd have signed it? Known the importance. I mean, why *type* it anyway?'

'If his fingerprints are on the paper . . .'

'Good point, Freddy. But they could have been put there after he died, of course. Or the paper could have been a bit he'd handled already—something off his desk.'

'That's it,' said Freddy triumphantly. 'His wife typed it after you'd left the office.'

'Why?'

'If she knew his death was an accident but that he *had* stabbed Cruba, an obviously faked note would be the best way of shifting suspicion on someone else.'

'That's not just devious. It's positively Machiavellian.'

'It explains why the note wasn't left in the typewriter with the cover off in the first place—where you could have seen it.'

'I have a different theory about that. I think whoever typed that note wanted it found by the police, not me. And I don't believe it was Miff or his wife. Whoever it was didn't trust me to turn it over to the police. He assumed I wouldn't take that cover off and that the police would. He was wrong—about the police, at least. They weren't as thorough as they might have been.'

'Why should he have doubted your . . . your probity?' Freddy asked after a moment's thought. 'Why should you conceal evidence?'

'Just a precaution. I'd have given it to the cops if I'd seen it.' He paused. 'At least, I think I would. Eventually, at least.'

'You *would* have concealed evidence?' said Freddy, but without reproof.

'Let's say I might have put the cover on the typewriter and played for time. The time we're using now. Ah, that's better.' They had been crawling for several miles due to some road repairs. Now they were on a resurfaced dual carriageway. Treasure glanced at his passenger. 'Don't you want to know if that's what I did?'

'I was just about to ask.'

'No, I didn't. It happened the way I told you. But I think I'm right about the phantom typer. He—or she—credited me with a feel for the public relations involved in all this. Faced with a client stabbed apparently by the Director of a Trust the bank's supposed to oversee? I'd need to play for time anyway. Destroying that note would have saved face for Grenwood, Phipps. It wouldn't have suited the murderer, of course,' Treasure added grimly. 'Perhaps he knows me well enough to believe I'd have been faced with a dilemma, at least.'

'You said he or she just now. But you don't think it could have been Miff's wife who stabbed Cruba? Same motive as her husband and then his accidental death . . .'

'Same motive but no more idea of Cruba's movements last night than he had.'

'We guessed Stephen Spotter could have told both of them.'

'And we guessed wrong.' Treasure answered firmly, hoping his assessment of Mrs Miff's character was accurate. 'Spotter didn't want anyone going after the fifty thousand. Even Crow-Patcher had to get the kidnap story out of Florence Spotter, not Stephen, remember?'

'So what about Spotter?' Freddy grudgingly abandoned the Miffs as prime suspects.

'As our double murderer?' The banker switched the air-conditioning to a cooler setting: outside the car summer was a-coming in. 'The Major's sure he didn't do the stabbing. He's certain now he saw Spotter take the case before the chap coming up passed him.'

'He wasn't so sure last night. Don't believe we can trust his judgement. Also, this morning Spotter . . .'

'Was checked in at Gatwick before Miff even left his flat.' He cleared his throat before adding firmly. 'The Major confirmed that when he was there.'

'And Crow-Patcher? Last night we said it might have been a two-man team.'

'The bleary Crow-Patcher was roused by Gold around eight-forty-five in Bloomsbury this morning. It's just possible he could have been to Strutton Ground and back before then, but only just. He'd also have to be a hell of a good actor. And foresighted. There was no reason he'd be expecting a visit from Gold or anyone else then. As for last night, Miss Spotter summed him up as a bit player. Gold feels the same. They don't think he'd have the guts to assault anyone. He wasn't the plastic mac man. Small fry.'

'And we're looking for bigger fish.' Freddy paused. 'Like Opac?'

'Like Opac. My money's been on him. Yours too last night.' He slowed the car as they approached a road sign.

'Sorry. Left here,' Freddy put in hastily. 'It's marked Southend Airport and Rochford.'

Treasure checked the time on the dashboard clock as they changed direction. They had made the journey faster than he had anticipated. 'Accepting Opac knew about the original kidnap plans . . .' he resumed.

'He was on the spot to stab Cruba, with a marvellous excuse,' Freddy broke in. 'He could easily have ordered the taxi, left the Reform, put the mac on over what he was wearing, waited for Cruba, attacked him, dumped the coat in his car and turned up again looking as if he'd just arrived.'

Treasure smiled. 'Some shock, of course, when I rolled up with Pierre at The Boltons to say our tame kidnappers couldn't be blamed for any mayhem.' He glanced at his companion. 'But he had the advantage of knowing I was seeing Miff at eight-thirty and that Miff, for some reason, was working against the Trust. There was a fall-guy waiting to be felled, as it were.'

'Absolutely,' Freddy agreed. 'He only had to make one phone call last night, then lie in wait for that poor devil this morning. You say anyone could have forced the door?'

'With a credit card or something like it. Yes. Very worn lock. He could have typed the note, done for Miff, and gone on his way rejoicing to the hospital. He was in luck with the street door. It's not normally open that early, but he wasn't to know.'

Freddy leant forward shaking his head. 'Mark, I think we should turn back. It all fits. If Opac's our man I can't go off sailing, I see that now.' He leant back again in his seat. 'What you've just said sounds pretty conclusive.'

'Except none of it holds up.'

'In what way?'

'Most, I'm afraid. The taxi was ordered at nine-thirty-four. Mr Gold did some checking. Opac was still at dinner then.'

'Somebody else could've ordered it for him. Yvonne Cruba, for instance. His lover.' Freddy emitted the last phrase in a definitely outraged tone.

'Man's voice, the taxi people say. I don't think he'd have involved anyone else. As for the call to Miff, Mrs Miff is sure it was after twelve-thirty. I left The Boltons before midnight. I don't think he'd delay. Much too decisive.'

'That's supposition, of course.'

'Opac's movements this morning aren't. I didn't tell you. I rang François Cruba himself just before leaving the office. Opac was allowed in to see him at eight, and said he'd been waiting. Even if he'd just arrived, he wouldn't have had time to do in Miff on the way.'

'How did François sound?'

'As good as reported. Better. Among other things, he said if Opac fell over something he'd curse it in French, not basic English. Incidentally, Cruba doesn't believe the chap has a cat in hell's chance of taking over from him as Ngongan President in Waiting. Opac takes the same view.'

'You asked him?'

'No, Opac volunteered it. Cruba doesn't know who attacked him, but he's certain it wasn't Opac on the political make. Opac went to the hospital this morning to tell him just that. He thinks he may be suspected.'

'I should think he does.' Freddy was outraged again.

'He has no political ambitions any more. They don't fit in with his love-life. A month ago he accepted a job with an American university. He'd been waiting to break the news to Cruba . . .'

'Who doesn't know about Opac and his wife, of course.'

'On the contrary. It's the reason he waited but he told Cruba today. Yvonne's going with him. Asking her husband to divorce her, or get the marriage annulled.'

Freddy gave an irritated sigh. 'So *you* think our front runner's a . . . a non-starter. I can tell you I don't . . .'

'Except I changed horses this morning.'

'In favour of?'

'Someone with the same opportunities as Opac for getting up-to-date information. Someone who's been running his own show while everybody's been thinking he's an Establishment man. He's our murderer all right.' Treasure scrutinized another road sign. 'We turn right here, I think?'

'The Stambridge road, yes. So who is it, Mark?'

'Who is it? Oh, come, Freddy. It's you, of course.'

'There never was any deal with the French and British Governments about Cruba living here. He applied for temporary domicile and got it. You handled it, though, plus embellishments, on a strictly private enterprise basis. Arranging to have his money controlled by Grenwood, Phipps was very daring, but really quite simple. And all to protect your friends running Ngonga.

'Yes. Simple but clever. No formal documentation. Nothing proving there'd been a deal. No meetings between us that anyone knows about. Just that letter from Cruba to me giving us power of attorney. He believed his stay here depended on that. I believed it. Very hush-hush, of course. So much so the only person in the FO who knew about it was Freddy Hinterton.' Treasure snorted.

Freddy continued to stare at the road ahead. He had not spoken since Treasure had begun accusing him.

'So since last year Cruba finances have been virtually controlled by the Ngongan Government,' the banker

continued. 'They know exactly how his funds are
disposed. Copies of the confidential reports I've been
sending you no doubt go straight to the Ngongan
Embassy. No chance of funding insurgent activities let
alone an army. And if they ever wanted to sequester his
assets — always possible, especially if he died — how very
convenient to know where they are. Helps enormously
with that kind of brigandry.

'It was lucky François never took up your offer of
protection. No doubt you discouraged him. The
arguments against are very sound. Used them myself on
Saturday. Anyway, that saved his status being specially
scrutinized by the powers that be. Just a rich foreigner on
an extended stay. No special privileges requested. None
provided. Nothing to account for.

'So it was a nice indefinite hold situation. Except just
recently the boys in Ngonga have been getting jumpy.
Opinion has it the people wouldn't mind having their old
chief back. What to do about it? Liquidation of old chief
the ideal solution. Dynamite, though, if his murder were
traced to the new Government.

'So it's Freddy to the rescue — or rather, Copper and
Gold with a kidnap set-up just crying out to be used. You
used it, Freddy.

'You had no special agents laid on last night. You never
involved M16, the Diplomatic Protection Corps, or anybody else. You nearly had a fit later when you thought I
was asking to see your security chief. You'd already had a
nasty turn when you found out the kidnap was a non-
event.

'The stabbing tied in with the kidnap was perfect. With
no kidnap the attempt on Cruba's life would look just
what it was — a cold, political assassination that went
wrong. And only a matter of time till someone figured
who was responsible.

'No doubt you intended tipping off the newspapers

about the kidnap last night, but not after you knew the story was useless. So you were lumbered with a dead or alive Cruba, a pending political scandal, and no thanks due to Hinterton.

'What a Godsend poor, dispensable Miff must have looked. What a fool I was for practically pushing him at you. The ready-made scapegoat. Except he couldn't type. Botching that up as well's going to cost you, my friend. Life instead of the six or seven years you'd have got for Cruba. That's assuming they'd nailed you.

'Were you more afraid of your Afro-Communist friends than you were of getting nabbed? Do they liquidate failures? They can use all the credibility they can muster at the moment—at home and abroad. Is it likely they'd have sacrificed you, exposed you as a psychopathic crank and nothing to do with them? Or maybe it was the power behind them that bothered you.'

Freddy shifted in his seat. He frowned but still said nothing.

'How's the leg, Freddy? Miss Brown said whoever fell over the box would be a sticking-plaster case for a while. You looked pretty stiff-legged when I picked you up. Incidentally, she saw your leg. The light was bad but not that bad. If it had been a black leg she'd have told me. You and Opac really were the only ones who knew about my meeting with Miff.

'Are you thinking some of the evidence is er . . . circumstantial still? Not really. It's all there for the devilling. I'd hoped we could prove the opposite. We haven't. The police are good at devilling. Given the same facts, they're going to reach the same conclusion. I just wish I knew why the hell you got into this.' There was still no response.

'Look, I think we've had enough joy-riding, Freddy. I'm going to turn round and drive you back. If you want to call a lawyer on the way I'll . . .'

'Just keep driving, Mark. It's left at the next fork. A farm track. You'll manage.' The voice was taut; the words expressionless.

Treasure turned to Freddy and found himself staring across the barrel of a small automatic pistol.

CHAPTER 21

Treasure swallowed, then looking ahead again, raised his eyebrows. 'Fat lot of good that'll do you. Shoot me and they won't need the devilling. My secretary knows I'm with you. Unless she hears from me by three she'll transcribe a tape I gave her. It's got the whole story. So come on, Freddy, don't . . .'

'That won't matter,' the other broke in. 'We're still going to my boat. It's less than half a mile. I don't want to harm you. I . . . I wouldn't need to kill you, just . . .'

'Just a nasty injury? All right. Please yourself. You won't . . .'

'We're going to sea. Both of us. You'll be bringing the boat back later. It'll be easier if you co-operate. Yes, my leg's hurting. I couldn't drive with it. Managing the boat I might have done on my own—still could.'

The lane was little more than a wide path flanked by scrub and muddied by the recent rain. They were deep into Essex salt-marsh country. The last and isolated habitation had been a mile back. The landscape was nearly level and almost treeless save for some sentinel osier willows. There were no hedges to block the view; the only features the sparsely vegetated flat mounds of red clay—the residue of salt-making a thousand years ago and more.

A solitary barn stood some way off to the left. In the middle distance there were clusters of sailing-boat masts on either side with a pair directly ahead.

Freddy watched Treasure's undisguised examination of the surroundings. 'Past the point of hailing the locals,' came the blunt comment. 'Two of us share a mooring down here. The other man's in America.'

'You've arranged to be picked up?'

'In certain circumstances, yes. You see, I was giving you the benefit of the doubt . . .'

'That was mutual.' Treasure interrupted tersely.

'It's an East German trawler. Twelve miles out. She'll wait. Flying would have been easier.'

'But you picked the wrong day.'

'This way you'll be occupied till I'm safe home.'

'Home being?'

'Wherever my friend and I choose. We've been separated a long time.'

'Someone waiting for you on the other side? Reward for services rendered. Blonde is she, Freddy?'

The other man paused. 'He's with the Soviet Foreign Service. The British made him leave London some years ago.'

'When we chucked out all those KGB people in the Embassy? I remember. My word, you have been faithful. But what'll you do?'

'Whatever's useful.'

'Mmm. After today I imagine your range of uses'll be a bit limited. Still, you're a very committed traitor. I expect . . .'

'My commitment to socialism has endured since university.' Freddy spoke flatly, ignoring the insult.

'Where it was predictably covert. Well, well, I always thought of you as High Tory. And currently you're devoting yourself to Afro-Communism? Inducing the chaos that precedes Third World membership of the Soviet Empire.' The banker affected concern. 'The Cruba bungle will set things back a bit for Ngonga, won't it? I'm surprised they're letting you break cover. Your real masters, I mean. Wouldn't it be better if you took the rap yourself? After all, you don't have to implicate . . .'

'I offered. It's up to me.'

'Is it? You surprise me.'

'Better to explain what's been happening where my words won't be censored. The world should know . . .'

'And outside clink too.' Treasure interrupted. 'I think you're very wise,' he continued with the maximum contempt in his voice. 'Where you're going they won't lock you up for knifing Cruba or murdering the innocent Miff.'

'I'm sorry . . .'

'About Miff? Sacrificed to a greater cause? Your sincerity is touching.'

The other's voice hardened too. 'I deny having anything to do with Miff.'

'Stout fellow! And Cruba?'

'The whole truth if necessary. I took it on myself to cut down that bastard. An impulse I don't regret.' The delivery quickened. 'He's so plausible, of course. If they had him back. The oil. He'd steal it . . . as before. He doesn't care about the people. He'd do a deal with the Americans. That's what he and Opac have been fixing. I know what's been happening, don't you see? Even *they* don't understand the danger.' Now he was practically pleading.

'You mean your Ngongan friends?'

'That's right. He had to be stopped. The chance was there. I acted on my own. There wasn't time. Something like it might not have come up again. We didn't want a martyr. We wanted a close-fisted swine trying to hold on to the asking price for his own son. Risking his son's life and losing his own for greed.'

'Great scenario, Freddy. Pity you blew it. So you did it on impulse? No orders? Now that could have been embarrassing.' Treasure brought the car to a halt on a patch of scrub.

The track had opened out to finish near the head of a small creek running in south from the river. There was a path leading to a short wooden jetty: the boats on either side floated on the rising tide. Both vessels were cruising yachts: the bigger one, a Westerly Longbow, had *Refuge* stencilled on the bow.

'You sure about that trawler, I suppose? Seems awfully short notice. Rotten if we're left milling about in the North Sea.'

'My . . . my friends have gone to a lot of trouble . . . quickly.' But the assurance had gone from his voice. 'Now, if you don't mind.' He motioned with the gun for the banker to get out.

Major Copper stood up as they were making for the boat. He had been lying behind a mound about fifty yards from the car. Treasure, carrying the luggage, had just stepped on to the jetty. Freddy was limping some distance behind him with the pistol levelled at his back.

'Put the gun on the ground, Hinterton,' the Major snapped loudly. He was standing firm, chin up, feet slightly apart, hands grasped behind his back. The bowler added authority. For a moment all three men stood motionless. 'Perhaps you didn't hear me. I said . . .'

'Come any closer and I'll shoot you.' Freddy's gaze darted between the others. 'It's Copper, isn't it?'

'And Gold,' came a thin voice behind him. 'We made it Mr Treasure. Some drive. Cab's behind the barn.'

Freddy swung around. Benny was about the same distance away as Copper, but on the other side. He had come from behind a stunted willow.

The man with the gun stepped backwards until he was leaning against the car. He had widened the gap between himself and Treasure but he had all three men in view, 'I don't want to hurt anyone but . . . You! Stop!'

But the Major continued to move forward purposefully. 'Hard to hit a barn door with that thing even close to. Thirty-two, isn't it?' he called.

'Hold it, Major. He'll shoot all right.' This was Treasure. 'Look, I think you'd be better going for help. He can't get far . . .'

'If either of you run off I'll . . . I'll kill Treasure.' The others sensed panic in the voice.

The Major had stopped on the banker's words. Now he was moving again towards Freddy. His pace was easy and determined. Curiously he felt no urge to hurry—to get it over: no need to shorten the savouring.

From the moment the two had stepped out of the Jaguar—when he knew Treasure had guessed right in sending them ahead as witnesses—Roderick Copper had accepted the danger. But after he stood up the sense of fear left him.

He was a professional soldier doing what he had been paid to do—all those years ago. What did it matter he'd been passed over? Who cared now if both his medals had been given to everyone in uniform in 1939? There was no one here who'd scoff about his spending D-Day on Lake Windermere—under orders.

'Stop, man. He's a murderer.'

He ignored the entreaty: he was the senior officer present, after all. So Hinterton was proved a traitor to the West—just the role to stiffen a soldier's resolve. The Major measured the ground ahead: another twenty-five yards yet—twenty before that pistol got dangerous in the amateur way it was being held. Head high, now: look the enemy in the eye.

Pity he wasn't leading the regiment, that there wasn't even a company of infantrymen deployed behind him . . . a platoon . . . just one thin file of soldiers. Was he imagining the wail of the bagpipes at Alamein?—they sounded real enough. Little Benjamin Gold had heard those pipes—Benny who he could see now starting over the uneven ground towards the man with the gun.

'All right, Freddy. You'll need to be a bloody good shot to get three of us.' Resigned, Treasure had dropped the cases and was making for Hinterton. 'Put the gun down. You haven't got a chance.'

'Leave him to me, Mr Treasure. Stay where you are, Benjamin.' He, Copper, was the most expendable after all. There was no one to mourn over him, and once you'd made up your mind—as his old mother might have said: except he hardly remembered his mother, and certainly not when she was old. She had abandoned him and his father when little Roderick was five—run off with a commercial traveller. It had been temporary homes with relatives after that, then the cheapest of boarding-schools.

In a way the army should have been the making of him, given him an identity—a transferred provenance, some-thing to build on. No bricks had been supplied. It might have been different if his mother had stayed: funny thing to be thinking about still when someone's about to take a pot shot at you.

He was very close now—six or seven paces. 'Give me the gun, please.' No point in trying to rush him: anyway the Major was too old to take running jumps at people.

Fatalistically, he watched Hinterton lift his other hand to the pistol grip. The Major kept coming. The steadied gun seemed now to be pointing directly between his eyes: two more paces.

Treasure was running forward. 'Freddy, not more innocent people. For God's sake don't.'

Hinterton put the gun barrel into his mouth and pulled the trigger.

No scandal attached to the death of Freddy Hinterton— an overworked member of the Foreign Office who took his own life while under great stress.

Many eminent persons — including the Foreign Secretary and Mr Cruba — were engaged in the conspiracy of silence over the real facts. Some less eminent but equally wise and patriotic mortals were also involved. Major Copper and Mr Gold signed Official Secrets Undertakings with pride and solemnity. Treasure alone knew it was Mrs Miff who made the cover-up possible.

The post-mortem on Clarence Miff indicated death by injuries sustained in a fall — a reasonable deduction in the unsuspicious circumstances. The report also revealed irreversible cirrhosis of the liver.

When Mrs Miff had learned all this she had still not reported the fake suicide note to anyone except Treasure. She destroyed the note shortly afterwards in his presence.

When the banker had told her, in confidence, a full investigation might prove Hinterton had murdered her husband, stabbed Cruba, and more besides, she judged such revelations would only provide satisfaction for sensation-seekers. The muck-raking would not bring her husband back, nor, in any event, could his life have endured much longer. The evidently deranged and fixated Hinterton she deemed had already paid the supreme penalty: things should be left as they were.

Treasure had concurred with this irregular but practical decision.

In view of the post-mortem report on Miff, the police lost interest in Happy Brown's injured messenger, much to her own relief. The coroner's verdict later confirmed that death had been accidental. There were no loose ends.

Six months after the officially rumoured Communist attack on ex-President Cruba in London, he and his Party were overwhelmingly victorious in the Ngonga elections. By then Mr Cruba's third marriage had been annulled, and he had re-married his second wife,

Beatrice. The initial reconciliation had been brought about by their son Pierre who was given time off from Eton to attend the wedding.

Earlier, renewed interest by the CID in reports that Pierre Cruba had been kidnapped was finally quashed by Bishop Clarence Wringle, retired. The aged prelate had volunteered corroborating testimony that on the day in question, the engaging young man, while twice propelling him across Walton Place, had introduced himself, obtained the bishop's name and address, provided a gift for the poor, offered transport in a waiting cab to wherever he was going (except the bishop was going for a walk), and the information that the boy was off to visit Miss Florence Spotter at Rudwold Park, Surrey.

The Rudyard Trust was saved through conscientious application by a chastened Mr Edwards, guidance from the Charity Commissioners, co-operation from the Official Custodian for Charities, and help from Mr Cruba.

The Trust was re-formed shorn of Marmaduke's restrictions and after ex-gratia payments had been made to all Rudyard descendants in full and final discharge of their entitlements. Instead of the millions some had expected, each was offered £10,000.

After first registering outrage, the Crow-Patchers had later meekly accepted the money. This was sensible. Mr Cruba had contracted to underwrite the losses of the unaltered Trust for fifty years, if necessary. Edward and Dina decided not to wait. The undeserving Stephen Spotter made the same decision, asking for cash in settlement to be sent to him *Poste Restante*, Khartoum.

Prudence Rudyard had expired peacefully before the offer was made. At the time she had been watching part of the fifth repeat television showing of *The Forsyte Saga*, a story about a family she had lately been insisting was closely related to her own—by marriage.

Mrs Miff and Florence Spotter virtuously refused any money but still renounced their rights as residual beneficiaries.

As arranged, Mr Cruba was then free to cancel his underwriting commitment. In exchange, he provided a substantial interest-free bridging loan for the Trust while it was being re-formed.

The sale of the old Rudyard Club properties, their phased closure, the re-modelling of the mid-eighteenth-century mansion near Oxford bought to replace them, and the transfer of members was all accomplished with exemplary speed and efficiency. This was in great part due to the dedication and capacities of the new resident Director, Edna Rudyard Miff.

Major Copper and Mr Gold did not enrol as new members, although places will always be available for them. Neither was completely certain about institutional life, and together they had accepted a more attractive option.

Miss Spotter, left alone at Rudwold Park, had the building converted into flats. The one next to her own she let at a nominal rent to her two gentlemen friends. She enjoyed preparing the main meal they came to share daily. It was no more than she had done for Prudence—who she missed—and Roderick and Benjamin were much more agreeable company.

The Major renewed early interests in bee-keeping and bird-watching, and found a church in the district entirely to his tastes. Benny enrolled as a biology student through the Open University, visiting the family—and the new baby—as often as he chose: it was only twenty minutes on the train to Putney.

At the bank, it was just before Christmas that Lord Grenwood remarked to Treasure, 'Heard about the new deal for the Rudyard Clubs. Met young Jonkins in the lift.' No drollery had been intended: the Chairman of Grenwood, Phipps was quite old enough to consider Jonkins a stripling. 'Done marvellously well.'

'Who?'

'Jonkins.'

'He's retiring next week, I believe,' Treasure commented with enthusiasm.

It was true: the Jonkins were moving to the sea—a bungalow at Bognor Regis. Mrs Jonkins had always set her heart on Bognor Regis.

Grenwood looked surprised. 'Private income, I suppose? I can't afford to retire'—everything being relative.

Treasure smiled an indulgence. 'It was touch and go whether we'd have to get Parliament to alter the Rudyard Deed.'

'Ironclad job, was it? Built 'em to last in those days. Remember Marmaduke Rudyard? No, 'course you wouldn't. Failed social climber and a fool about women. Very thick with my father.' He stopped, thought about correcting the last implication, then didn't bother. 'He relied on the bank. Made him a rich man.' No doubt the bank benefited too—reason enough why the First Viscount suffered an upstart womanizer.'

'The way he had a trust deed drafted, he must have believed profoundly the dead know what's best for the living.'

'Ah, he had his reasons. Convinced the socialists would pinch everything that wasn't nailed down. They mostly fooled him, though. The Off-Gents is the only one of his charity shows not taken over by the state.'

'Reds under the bed complex?'

'*In* the bed, my dear chap. That's what Marmaduke thought. Still, with the Off-Gents he stopped 'em even getting upstairs.'

Treasure thought of Miff. 'Not quite,' he ended ruefully.

Bestselling Crime

☐ No One Rides Free	Larry Beinhart	£2.95
☐ Alice in La La Land	Robert Campbell	£2.99
☐ In La La Land We Trust	Robert Campbell	£2.99
☐ Suspects	William J Caunitz	£2.95
☐ So Small a Carnival	John William Corrington	
	Joyce H Corrington	£2.99
☐ Saratoga Longshot	Stephen Dobyns	£2.99
☐ Blood on the Moon	James Ellroy	£2.99
☐ Roses Are Dead	Loren D. Estleman	£2.50
☐ The Body in the Billiard Room	HRF Keating	£2.50
☐ Bertie and the Tin Man	Peter Lovesey	£2.50
☐ Rough Cider	Peter Lovesey	£2.50
☐ Shake Hands For Ever	Ruth Rendell	£2.99
☐ Talking to Strange Men	Ruth Rendell	£2.99
☐ The Tree of Hands	Ruth Rendell	£2.99
☐ Wexford: An Omnibus	Ruth Rendell	£6.99
☐ Speak for the Dead	Margaret Yorke	£2.99

Prices and other details are liable to change

ARROW BOOKS, BOOKSERVICE BY POST, PO BOX 29, DOUGLAS, ISLE
OF MAN, BRITISH ISLES

NAME...

ADDRESS ....

....

....

Please enclose a cheque or postal order made out to Arrow Books Ltd. for the amount
due and allow the following for postage and packing.

U.K. CUSTOMERS: Please allow 22p per book to a maximum of £3.00.

B.F.P.O. & EIRE: Please allow 22p per book to a maximum of £3.00.

OVERSEAS CUSTOMERS: Please allow 22p per book.

Whilst every effort is made to keep prices low it is sometimes necessary to increase cover
prices at short notice. Arrow Books reserve the right to show new retail prices on covers
which may differ from those previously advertised in the text or elsewhere.

Bestselling Thriller/Suspense

☐ Skydancer	Geoffrey Archer	£3.50
☐ Hooligan	Colin Dunne	£2.99
☐ See Charlie Run	Brian Freemantle	£2.99
☐ Hell is Always Today	Jack Higgins	£2.50
☐ The Proteus Operation	James P Hogan	£3.50
☐ Winter Palace	Dennis Jones	£3.50
☐ Dragonfire	Andrew Kaplan	£2.99
☐ The Hour of the Lily	John Kruse	£3.50
☐ Fletch, Too	Geoffrey McDonald	£2.50
☐ Brought in Dead	Harry Patterson	£2.50
☐ The Albatross Run	Douglas Scott	£2.99

Prices and other details are liable to change

Bestselling Fiction

☐ No Enemy But Time	Evelyn Anthony	£2.95
☐ The Lilac Bus	Maeve Binchy	£2.99
☐ Prime Time	Joan Collins	£3.50
☐ A World Apart	Marie Joseph	£3.50
☐ Erin's Child	Sheelagh Kelly	£3.99
☐ Colours Aloft	Alexander Kent	£2.99
☐ Gondar	Nicholas Luard	£4.50
☐ The Ladies of Missalonghi	Colleen McCullough	£2.50
☐ Lily Golightly	Pamela Oldfield	£3.50
☐ Talking to Strange Men	Ruth Rendell	£2.99
☐ The Veiled One	Ruth Rendell	£3.50
☐ Sarum	Edward Rutherfurd	£4.99
☐ The Heart of the Country	Fay Weldon	£2.50

Prices and other details are liable to change

ARROW BOOKS, BOOKSERVICE BY POST, PO BOX 29, DOUGLAS, ISLE OF MAN, BRITISH ISLES

NAME..

ADDRESS ....

....

....

Please enclose a cheque or postal order made out to Arrow Books Ltd. for the amount due and allow the following for postage and packing.

U.K. CUSTOMERS: Please allow 22p per book to a maximum of £3.00.

B.F.P.O. & EIRE: Please allow 22p per book to a maximum of £3.00.

OVERSEAS CUSTOMERS: Please allow 22p per book.

Whilst every effort is made to keep prices low it is sometimes necessary to increase cover prices at short notice. Arrow Books reserve the right to show new retail prices on covers which may differ from those previously advertised in the text or elsewhere.

Bestselling SF/Horror

☐	Forge of God	Greg Bear	£3.99
☐	Eon	Greg Bear	£3.50
☐	The Hungry Moon	Ramsey Campbell	£3.50
☐	The Influence	Ramsey Campbell	£3.50
☐	Seventh Son	Orson Scott Card	£3.50
☐	Bones of the Moon	Jonathan Carroll	£2.50
☐	Nighthunter: The Hexing & The Labyrinth	Robert Faulcon	£3.50
☐	Pin	Andrew Neiderman	£1.50
☐	The Island	Guy N. Smith	£2.50
☐	Malleus Maleficarum	Montague Summers	£4.50

Prices and other details are liable to change

ARROW BOOKS, BOOKSERVICE BY POST, PO BOX 29, DOUGLAS, ISLE OF MAN, BRITISH ISLES

NAME...

ADDRESS..

....

....

Please enclose a cheque or postal order made out to Arrow Books Ltd. for the amount due and allow the following for postage and packing.

U.K. CUSTOMERS: Please allow 22p per book to a maximum of £3.00.

B.F.P.O. & EIRE: Please allow 22p per book to a maximum of £3.00.

OVERSEAS CUSTOMERS: Please allow 22p per book.

Whilst every effort is made to keep prices low it is sometimes necessary to increase cover prices at short notice. Arrow Books reserve the right to show new retail prices on covers which may differ from those previously advertised in the text or elsewhere.

A Selection of Legend Titles

☐	Eon	Greg Bear	£3.50
☐	Forge of God	Greg Bear	£3.99
☐	Falcons of Narabedla	Marion Zimmer Bradley	£2.50
☐	The Influence	Ramsey Campbell	£3.50
☐	Wyrms	Orson Scott Card	£3.50
☐	Speaker for the Dead	Orson Scott Card	£2.95
☐	Seventh Son	Orson Scott Card	£3.50
☐	Wolf in Shadow	David Gemmell	£3.50
☐	Last Sword of Power	David Gemmell	£3.50
☐	This is the Way the World Ends	James Morrow	£4.99
☐	Unquenchable Fire	Rachel Pollack	£3.99
☐	Golden Sunlands	Christopher Rowley	£3.50
☐	The Misplaced Legion	Harry Turtledove	£2.99
☐	An Emperor for the Legion	Harry Turtledove	£2.99

Prices and other details are liable to change

ARROW BOOKS, BOOKSERVICE BY POST, PO BOX 29, DOUGLAS, ISLE OF MAN, BRITISH ISLES

NAME...

ADDRESS..

....

....

Please enclose a cheque or postal order made out to Arrow Books Ltd. for the amount due and allow the following for postage and packing.

U.K. CUSTOMERS: Please allow 22p per book to a maximum of £3.00.

B.F.P.O. & EIRE: Please allow 22p per book to a maximum of £3.00.

OVERSEAS CUSTOMERS: Please allow 22p per book.

Whilst every effort is made to keep prices low it is sometimes necessary to increase cover prices at short notice. Arrow Books reserve the right to show new retail prices on covers which may differ from those previously advertised in the text or elsewhere.

Bestselling General Fiction

☐	No Enemy But Time	Evelyn Anthony	£2.95
☐	Skydancer	Geoffrey Archer	£3.50
☐	The Sisters	Pat Booth	£3.50
☐	Captives of Time	Malcolm Bosse	£2.99
☐	Saudi	Laurie Devine	£2.95
☐	Duncton Wood	William Horwood	£4.50
☐	Aztec	Gary Jennings	£3.95
☐	A World Apart	Marie Joseph	£3.50
☐	The Ladies of Missalonghi	Colleen McCullough	£2.50
☐	Lily Golightly	Pamela Oldfield	£3.50
☐	Sarum	Edward Rutherfurd	£4.99
☐	Communion	Whitley Strieber	£3.99

Prices and other details are liable to change

ARROW BOOKS, BOOKSERVICE BY POST, PO BOX 29, DOUGLAS, ISLE OF MAN, BRITISH ISLES

NAME..

ADDRESS...

....

....

Please enclose a cheque or postal order made out to Arrow Books Ltd. for the amount due and allow the following for postage and packing.

U.K. CUSTOMERS: Please allow 22p per book to a maximum of £3.00.

B.F.P.O. & EIRE: Please allow 22p per book to a maximum of £3.00.

OVERSEAS CUSTOMERS: Please allow 22p per book.

Whilst every effort is made to keep prices low it is sometimes necessary to increase cover prices at short notice. Arrow Books reserve the right to show new retail prices on covers which may differ from those previously advertised in the text or elsewhere.

Bestselling Romantic Fiction

☐	The Lilac Bus	Maeve Binchy	£2.99
☐	The Sisters	Pat Booth	£3.50
☐	The Princess	Jude Deveraux	£3.50
☐	A World Apart	Marie Joseph	£3.50
☐	Erin's Child	Sheelagh Kelly	£3.99
☐	Satisfaction	Rae Lawrence	£3.50
☐	The Ladies of Missalonghi	Colleen McCullough	£2.50
☐	Lily Golightly	Pamela Oldfield	£3.50
☐	Women & War	Janet Tanner	£3.50

Prices and other details are liable to change

ARROW BOOKS, BOOKSERVICE BY POST, PO BOX 29, DOUGLAS, ISLE
OF MAN, BRITISH ISLES

NAME...

ADDRESS ....

....

....

Please enclose a cheque or postal order made out to Arrow Books Ltd. for the amount
due and allow the following for postage and packing.

U.K. CUSTOMERS: Please allow 22p per book to a maximum of £3.00.

B.F.P.O. & EIRE: Please allow 22p per book to a maximum of £3.00.

OVERSEAS CUSTOMERS: Please allow 22p per book.

Whilst every effort is made to keep prices low it is sometimes necessary to increase cover
prices at short notice. Arrow Books reserve the right to show new retail prices on covers
which may differ from those previously advertised in the text or elsewhere.

A Selection of Arrow Books

☐ No Enemy But Time	Evelyn Anthony	£2.95
☐ The Lilac Bus	Maeve Binchy	£2.99
☐ Rates of Exchange	Malcolm Bradbury	£3.50
☐ Prime Time	Joan Collins	£3.50
☐ Rosemary Conley's Complete Hip and Thigh Diet	Rosemary Conley	£2.99
☐ Staying Off the Beaten Track	Elizabeth Gundrey	£6.99
☐ Duncton Wood	William Horwood	£4.50
☐ Duncton Quest	William Horwood	£4.50
☐ A World Apart	Marie Joseph	£3.50
☐ Erin's Child	Sheelagh Kelly	£3.99
☐ Colours Aloft	Alexander Kent	£2.99
☐ Gondar	Nicholas Luard	£4.50
☐ The Ladies of Missalonghi	Colleen McCullough	£2.50
☐ The Veiled One	Ruth Rendell	£3.50
☐ Sarum	Edward Rutherfurd	£4.99
☐ Communion	Whitley Strieber	£3.99

Prices and other details are liable to change

ARROW BOOKS, BOOKSERVICE BY POST, PO BOX 29, DOUGLAS, ISLE OF MAN, BRITISH ISLES

NAME...

ADDRESS ....

....

....

Please enclose a cheque or postal order made out to Arrow Books Ltd. for the amount due and allow the following for postage and packing.

U.K. CUSTOMERS: Please allow 22p per book to a maximum of £3.00.

B.F.P.O. & EIRE: Please allow 22p per book to a maximum of £3.00.

OVERSEAS CUSTOMERS: Please allow 22p per book.

Whilst every effort is made to keep prices low it is sometimes necessary to increase cover prices at short notice. Arrow Books reserve the right to show new retail prices on covers which may differ from those previously advertised in the text or elsewhere.